WES COOK

THE RUINER

A CASEY SPARKS NOVEL

The Ruiner: A Casey Sparks Novel

wescookwrites.com
ISBN: 979-8-9851991-0-9
Cover designed by MiblArt.

For Joe and Becky

1

Casey Sparks knew things he should not. Sometimes when he touched an object, a memory of its owner or a vision of its past would transfer to him. It didn't always work when he wanted it to, and sometimes it happened out of the blue. But whenever it happened, he knew he could trust the information. And standing on the sandy bank of Murder Creek, a distributary of the Alabama River, he knew for certain the boat fire had not been caused by engine trouble, and the three fishermen who had been on board would never be found alive. All of this was a certainty. The little charred piece of wood in his hand told him so.

Dwayne Beniot slapped a mosquito on his thin chest, leaving a tiny bloody smear. He washed off his hand in the creek and said, "You got stage fright or something? Let's get a move on. I'm getting eaten alive over here."

Casey shook his head and dropped the burnt wood. "Sorry. I found a chunk of that boat that went missing a few weeks ago on the big river. I guess when it blew up, bits of it that didn't sink floated downstream, and some of it ended up here."

"Blew up? How do you know? Oh, right. See anything else?"

Casey had. He had seen bursts of disjointed moments.

Something ramming the fishing boat, men in the water, screams, fire, and ultimately the explosion. But the fire and explosion had come later than the rest after the men were already dead. "Probably nothing the sheriff hasn't already pieced together." Casey relieved himself in the woods and then walked back into the creek. When he was calf-deep, Dwayne pushed an innertube towards him. Dwayne had attached it with a bright-yellow nylon rope to his own and to a floating cooler they shared.

"Engine fires break out more than folks realize," Dwayne said.

Casey caught the innertube. "Yeah. But I don't think that's what happened." He sat down and paddled until they reached deeper water, where the current took over. It pulled them to the middle and down the creek.

"Either way. That's why I prefer to float."

Dwayne reeled himself even with the cooler and plucked out a Budweiser. Taking a sip, he let his head fall back and closed his eyes. Casey plucked a beer too. The sky was cloudless, and the light breeze and warm creek water brought little relief from the already too-hot south Alabama July afternoon. The beer brought a little more.

Casey kept his eyes open. The banks of both sides of the river alternated between thick bushes, pine forest, and thin patches of sandy beach. He found himself scanning the water as they floated along. The fisherman had disappeared at night, not in the light of day, and it had happened in the big river rather than the little creek, but it hadn't been far away from where they were, not really, and it had only happened three weeks before. Casey felt strange worrying about something in the river. He knew it so well and had always before associated it with fun and relaxation.

A few of the sandy patches of riverbank were large enough to accommodate five or six tents and a firepit, and so the creek had been a favorite camping destination for their local boy scout troop. They would put in on a Saturday morning, canoe or kayak until dark, camp on a beach, and row out on Sunday morning. Casey and Dwayne had both made it to Life rank in scouts, but neither quite had the ambition to make Eagle. By the time they were in their late teens, Dwayne's focus had shifted almost completely to girls and guns and Casey's to anything that would help him cope with and hide the fact he was gay. Cherry Hill, Alabama was as good a place as any for Dwayne's preoccupations but didn't offer much for Casey.

Floating around a bend, he saw Amy Gale holding court with a handful of other older teenagers who worked with Casey and Dwayne at the Catfish Shack. Two of the young men were lobbing M-80 firecrackers into the forest and giggling with each explosion.

Dwayne opened an eye at one of the booms and laughed. "Amateurs." He started paddling. "We are making another pit stop."

Casey sighed. "You want to hang out with the waitstaff babies?"

"Amy's with them. And you need to socialize. I could barely get you out of the house today.

"I'm throwing the damn party tonight, aren't I? I even have most everything set up."

"I know, but this is part of it too. The Fourth of July tradition is all day, not just your party. And you are going on, what, three weeks since your breakup? You've got to get out of the trailer, lighten up, and snap out of it. And as your best friend, it's my duty to confiscate that bottle of tequila Amy's holding and get you drunk."

Casey joined in the paddling, and they dragged their tubes onto the beach.

Approaching Amy, Dwayne said, "Going to need to see some ID, miss."

Amy brushed her dark hair back with a single extended middle finger and smiled as she held it in place.

"That's not government issue."

"Do all old dishwashers work part-time for the cops now?" The other servers laughed.

Dwayne looked at Casey and shook his head. "I'm 25. That's not old."

"Whatever."

Dwayne started to respond but was cut off by one of the servers at the edge of the water, pointing and shouting, "water moccasin." Dwayne darted towards him and leaped into the creek after the snake. He splashed through the shallows and then swam freestyle after the quick S shape in the water. Most of the others moved toward the action, but Casey stayed back with Amy. He'd seen this before more times than he could remember, and Amy simply didn't care.

They looked at each other and shared a smile. She handed him the bottle.

"You going to rat me out too, officer?"

Casey took a long pull and winced it down. "You're safe. The cops already have enough fry cooks on staff."

Amy watched Dwayne from a distance for a moment, and then she looked at Casey and frowned. "Are you OK? You've been really quiet at work and not acting like yourself lately."

Casey feigned a smile. "I'll be fine. It's just dating trouble. I promise to be more upbeat at the party tonight."

"You better. I expect you to read my fortune or something. You are really getting good at those magic tricks. Are you sure you don't really have some dark powers?"

Casey snickered, and a real smile grew across his face. "A magician never reveals his secrets." He took another gulp of tequila and handed the bottle back. She received it in one hand and hugged him with the other. "If you need me to kick somebody's ass, you just let me know."

Casey hugged her back, his hands squeezing bony shoulders. What she lacked in size, she made up in fire. "Thank you."

"Of course. You would do it for me."

She was right that he would defend her. He had done it before. When she came on at the Catfish Shack as a waitress a couple of years prior, he had been there four years already and was one of the senior kitchen staff. At first, the other girls disliked her because she was popular with the boys and made better tips than most of them. For revenge or simple meanness, many of the girls mixed up her orders, stole side dishes, swapped salad dressings, and generally tried to run her out. A former server went so far as call her to the parking lot after work one night to brawl. Casey stepped in that night and had kept an eye out for her ever since. She could hold her own, but he still tried to protect her from as much of the restaurant hazing as he could.

She was different than the other girls there. She was a lot like him. The daughter of the reverend of the largest church in Cherry Hill, she was raised mostly without a TV, books, computers, or a cell phone. Her mother had passed away when she was little, and her father never remarried. He had kept her under this thumb as best as a man unqualified to raise a child and married to his job could, but around age thirteen, she had found ways to get around his rules. Upon realizing all the things she had been missing out on, she was equal parts bitter at her father and eager to experience everything life had to offer; the more exciting, the better. And she had dedicated herself to both causes with a zeal her old man could only dream of inspiring in his congregation.

The crowd watching Dwayne gasped when he caught up with the snake on the opposite bank. He hooted and held it aloft in one hand, supporting the snake in the middle with an open palm. Each side reached down almost to his shoulder. He called to the waiters. "It's not venomous. It's not a cottonmouth. Check it out." He crossed the creek, one-arm swimming some of the way, still holding the snake, and the crowd scattered. Even Amy took a few steps back from her already distanced position when he stepped onto the beach, handling the brown water snake with both hands.

Casey turned to her and said, "It's OK. He's kept snakes practically his whole life. He knows what he's doing."

She mouthed the word "nope" and took a few more steps back.

Casey walked over to Dwayne and took a closer look. "If it's not a moccasin, what is it?"

"It's a brown water snake."

"Yes. I can plainly see that."

"That's the common name, smart ass. Not too creative, I guess. Anyone want to hold it?"

The crowd shrunk back further with the suggestion. Dwayne knelt by the water and let the snake glide from his hands into the stream. "Wish I could keep it, but water snakes need special enclosures. And I don't have room for anything like that. Plus, I don't like keeping wild-caught animals. Seems cruel."

"Let's get going. You've terrified the waitstaff enough for one day, and I need to finish getting the trailer ready."

"Not before you get a shot of tequila."

"I worked that out with Amy already. I didn't even have to tase her."

"Good work. I guess you are right."

Casey and Dwayne plopped back in their innertubes and floated away. Casey waved at Amy as they set off, and Dwayne held up a middle finger as he closed his eyes and hung his head back. Casey was feeling less apprehensive about the party after talking to Amy. But there was something about the vision that he couldn't get out of his mind. Although Dwayne was right that accidents happen on the water all the time, nothing large enough to ram and flip a fishing boat should be in the river. But that is what Casey saw, and when he saw it, it was always true.

2

By 6:30 that night, a dozen or more people had arrived at Casey's party, and by 7:30, the headcount was pushing thirty-five. The first pops and crackles of fireworks from the few other houses and trailers along Rabbit Run Road sounded in the distance among the waking cicadas and crickets. Most of the party was going on in the backyard of Casey's trailer, but he was inside doing magic tricks for Amy and three of her friends. All of the friends had at least once "picked a card, any card" and had answered in the affirmative when asked, "Is this your card?".

"OK. Let's do something more interesting." Casey pulled a small notepad out of a junk drawer and tore off a piece of paper. He carefully ripped it to make it as close to square as he could, then drew a circle in the middle. He handed the paper and pen to Amy. "Write a word. Any word you want in that circle."

Casey turned his back to her.

"Done," she said.

Back still turned, he said, "Now fold it in half once, then again."

"Done."

Casey turned around and held out his hand. She dropped the paper in his palm.

He squeezed the scrap of paper and pretended to be working out the word. At this point in the trick, most magicians would tear the paper into four pieces and hand back the scraps for the person to burn or otherwise destroy. That would give the magician the opportunity to peek at the fourth piece, which they had conveniently palmed. And they knew which one to keep because of how the paper was folded. One piece would always conveniently contain the circle and the word. Casey sometimes performed the trick that way too. But only when the paper didn't tell him its secret. When he squeezed the paper that night, he knew two things at once. The first was that Amy had given a handy to a cashier behind the Piggly Wiggly for a dime bag of weed before coming to his party. And the second was that the word "butterfly" was written in pink ink and soaring cursive on the little paper square in his hand.

Casey wondered later why he had missed the third vision. The two others had been like recent memories. As if he had been there watching Amy as she giggled and urged the cashier to finish. Had been there on the blacktop in the July Alabama heat with beads of sweat forming on his forehead while the cashier moaned, eyes cycling between closed ecstasy and scanning, wide-open paranoia. The second vision had been just as clear. Casey was confident he could have forged the word "butterfly" on a fresh sheet of paper and fooled any handwriting expert. After the first two visions, his mouth went dry, and for an instant, his stomach fluttered as if he was falling. The moment of panic left him as quickly as it had come, and he dismissed the feeling. But Casey pondered many times later why he did not pick up more, why he did not know Amy Gale was about to die.

"So, what is it?" she said. Her folded arms and accusing eyes were given away by the start of a smile and deepening dimples. Her friends closed in beside her.

He squinted his hazel eyes and looked at her sideways. "I am sensing two, no, three syllables," he said, chopping the air with one hand pretending to sound out the full word. "And some sort of creature." The sensation of falling struck again. It lasted a fraction of a second but was far more intense than the previous episode-less roller coaster and more free fall. Before Casey could think to stop himself, he said, "The Ruiner."

Amy raised a confused eyebrow at him.

His stomach dropped again, but this time from embarrassment. Casey brushed back a patch of unruly light-brown hair from his eyes, and he let out a quick, nervous laugh. "Not sure where that came from." Amy's eyebrow returned to position, but she sustained her pseudo-stoic pose. "Your word. It's a bug, but not a dragonfly or wasp... And not a cicada either. Focus on the word, Amy. I need you to send it..."

A woman's scream from outside cut him short, and both Casey and Amy turned to the window as something on fire burst through, and with it, louder sounds of pandemonium. Casey dumped the remaining beer from his red solo cup onto the small burning rock, melting a hole in the cheap carpet. Just before rushing out the back door towards the chaos, he looked at Amy and with a wink, said, "Butterfly."

Casey crouched and snuck to the railing of the redwood deck and peered out through the slats. There were screams, yes, but also cursing and a good bit of laughter from the frantic crowd. Most of the guests were running to the front of the trailer or taking cover behind kegs, tables, or friends. But many, including Amy, who burst from the trailer laughing, ran instead to the fireworks table further out in the backyard. Almost a quarter of a football field beyond the table, Dwayne Beniot stood next to a camouflage duffel bag full of fireworks. He held a sparkler in his teeth like a cigar and steadily shelled the partygoers with Roman candles, four in each bony hand, a redneck superhero in the dying light of dusk.

One of Casey's co-workers, a young hostess who had been working at the Catfish Shack for only a few months, scrambled past him in the yard below. When a popping string of firecrackers landed ten feet in front of her, she yelled and hustled to the nearest piece of cover. The cooler she squatted behind, though, offered almost no protection from the fireworks. Casey called to her to reposition. But as she turned to respond, a little yellow comet ricocheted off the top of the cooler. It nicked her in the shoulder and zipped past Casey's head before bouncing off the closed back door. She let out a high-pitched scream and raced around the edge of the trailer, patting her shirt as she ran.

When the group of partygoers made it to the fireworks table, Dwayne tossed aside his Roman candles, scooped up his duffel bag, and retreated further into the vast yard. In the years before, it had alternated between a crop field and a cow pen, but this night, it functioned just as well as the front line of a good ole country fireworks war.

Casey made a run for the abandoned cooler. He snatched two cold beers and spied the fireworks table, wanting to take inventory. He had left the big guns, the large mortar shells, in boxes underneath. A bottle rocket war was one thing, but a bunch of drunken people with mortar shells was something else altogether. It is all fun and games until someone gets an eye blown out or a hand blown off.

Several packages of Roman candles, bottle rockets, and strings of firecrackers remained on top of the table; easy pickings for the liquored up and excited. And the boxes underneath appeared untouched. Casey hoped for the best. He returned to his spot on the deck, drug a cherry tomato plant in a twenty-gallon pot over for the extra cover, and cracked open a beer. After all, some things cannot be stopped once they have been set into motion. Things like hurricanes, floods, and groups of drunk people with fireworks.

For the next ten minutes, Roman candle shots and bottle rockets flew and popped in all directions. Dwayne had started it, but in the chaos, most of the participants set off their weapons indiscriminately instead of aiming at him. Still, there was one group of three guys coordinating to target Dwayne. They worked him further back, almost to the tree line at one point, until he outflanked them and somehow beat them back to the fireworks table.

Casey stood up, leaned on the rail, and shouted, "Save some for later!"

Dwayne looked up and waved. "Nope!"

With one long, skinny arm, Dwayne swept most of the remaining contents of the table over the side into his open duffel bag. He looked out to spot his pursuers and then knelt. Something new went into the bag.

"No, no, no," Casey hollered.

Dwayne looked back, shrugged, and ran back out into the fray.

Casey crouched back to his spot and opened the other beer. Hurricanes, floods, and Dwayne Beniot.

Dwayne resumed the assault. As the others ran low on ammo, they converged on him. He held them at bay for a while, but when he was about to be overrun by the growing crowd of others, Dwayne's voice rose over the pops and cracks.

"I'll do it. I swear, I'll do it," he said.

The crowd halted their advance for a moment and muttered to each other before rushing towards him. When they did, Casey braced for the boom. The sound was thunderous. The yard exploded in color as hundreds of streaks of multicolored sparks raced in every direction, thirty feet high and one hundred feet wide. The combatants instantly retreated to the trailer, checking on the way to see if they were on fire. Many had holes in their shirts or pants from the explosion or the battle before. Dwayne's shirt had caught fire, but he shed it quickly and with a laugh, patted out his smoldering hair before following the group.

He threw his arms up in victory and, with his singed mullet still smoking and his ears undoubtedly still ringing, yelled, "Happy Birthday, America! Take that, fuckers!"

A few muttered obscenities later, the party continued more or less as if it had never happened. If you lose, you are supposed to take your lumps and move on. Such are the rules of a fireworks war. In practice though, people were often less than magnanimous.

To help smooth things over, Casey recruited a few people to set up the folding tables and chairs for an early supper and summoned others to bring out the food. As usual, he had worked out a deal with the Catfish Shack to cater his fourth of July party. They provided fried catfish, of course, along with macaroni and cheese, mustard greens, cornbread, and hushpuppies. In addition, some guests brought homemade peach and blackberry cobblers. The food worked wonders to ease the mood.

Casey and a few others set off the remaining fireworks while the guests ate, but after the war earlier and the food coma so many were in, the planned program was anticlimactic. About half the crowd left after the fireworks. The others sat around the folding tables, drinking beer, nibbling on the leftovers, and playing drinking games.

Casey made a plate and was halfway through a piece of fried catfish when Dwayne walked up and plopped a clear gallon milk jug next to Casey's plate.

"The finest watermelon moonshine east of the Mississippi. Only the best for the host with the most."

Casey took another bite. "Is it finer than the concoction you made last year that nearly poisoned half the Shack?"

Dwayne shook his head and frowned. He sat and pulled a bag of homegrown brown swag weed from his pocket and plucked out a pre-rolled joint. "Some people just can't hold their liquor."

They both laughed.

A big guy with black powder burns on his right cheek and shoulder passed by the table and gave Dwayne the stink-eye. He held a bunched-up t-shirt in one hand and his girlfriend's waist in the other. She stuck out her tongue.

Dwayne pretended not to see the couple but turned a moment later to make sure they had kept walking.

"Good thing you didn't bring the flamethrower again this year," Casey said.

"You know those volunteer firemen still won't serve me chili at the cookoff? I apologized and everything, but two years running and still no love.

Casey shook his head. "And their booth wins every year too. Damn good chili."

Dwayne hit the joint again and held it out to Casey. When Casey reached for it, he saw an angry red spot the size of a half-dollar on Dwayne's chest just below his tattoo of the Atlanta Braves logo.

"Looks like you took some fire too," Casey said, inhaling and pointing to the wound.

"Yeah. One of them tagged me good."

"Karma," said Casey, exhaling a thick cloud of smoke.

"For what, the flamethrowers?"

"No, for that time you hit me with that wild pitch back in high school. What goes around comes around."

"You shoulda got out the damn way." Dwayne stood and spit on the grass. "Alright then. Been fun, but I got ladies to see." Casey extended the joint back to Dwayne, but he waved it off. "Keep it. Might help you with that post-traumatic baseball syndrome you still got after eight damn years."

Casey smiled. "Thanks for the moonshine. See you at the Shack tomorrow?"

Dwayne nodded and tipped a nonexistent cap to Casey before heading into the trailer.

After eating, Casey half-filled a bucket with water and walked out past the fireworks platform towards the woods. He lit a cigarette and looked for any grass fires still burning from the fireworks. Everything was out, but in the first minute, he had gathered three abandoned t-shirts. He poured out the water and began gathering the discarded clothes in the bucket instead. The bangs and pops of the neighbors' firework displays were coming with less frequency. Still, when they did, he stopped and watched the colorful crowns of the larger ones above the trees before continuing his search for clothes. In one spot near the tree line were two t-shirts on top of a single shoe. He deemed the yard clothes-free after the bundle went into the bucket, along with a couple more t-shirts and a pair of shorts. He wondered who had lost their pants, but touching them revealed no vision.

Another round of fireworks blasted in the distance as Casey was walking back to the trailer. He turned to watch. The last of the pops was a bright-white burst which fell and faded slowly away in the black sky. Casey followed it down to something else which drew his attention; dim strings of colored lights hanging in the woods.

At first, he thought they were fireflies, but some of them were not blinking off. And drawing closer, he could see there were reds and blues mixed in with the green. Some of these lights moved straight up from the ground in tight lines six feet long before arcing back down briefly and disappearing. A set of eight of these hung together in the air. The top arcs of each pointed in towards the others, marking the circumference of some dark central point.

Something in him, maybe the same something that let him know things, urged him to stop. And when he did stop, he found himself within ten yards of the tree line. He shuttered when he realized he had been drawn in. True, he had drunk north of six beers already and smoked part of a joint, but neither would cause hallucinations. Yet there he stood, staring at these things which seemed to be actively working to hypnotize him. And were they growing brighter now?

With some effort, he took two steps back, and when he did, the lights in the woods drifted back a little way too. He took a few more steps, and the lights floated further still. And when Casey took yet another step back, what had appeared to be subtle lights darted back into the woods. But instead of slipping silently into the darkness, they crashed through the brush. Branches snapped, and the surrounding trees shook as if the unseen part of whatever those lights were attached to had been huge and powerful.

The violence of the movement jolted Casey from the trance, and he ran as fast as he could, bucket swinging, back to the fireworks platform. Catching his breath there, he scanned the dark tree line and then the remaining late-stayers. No one seemed to have seen him running. Casey steadied himself and tried to ignore the feeling of being watched, even as he kept his own two eagle eyes on the tree line. After another cigarette and several minutes of stillness, he returned to the party. But he did not turn his back to the woods for the rest of the night.

3

A quarter-mile north of Casey's trailer, Chuck Spivey frowned at the darkening woods of the Mitcham Breech Hunting Camp. He sat at the patio table on the back porch of his house and sipped coffee from a mug with "1992 National Champions. Roll Tide" printed on both sides. In front of him was his laptop and two neat stacks of SD memory cards from the trail cameras he had collected over the past few days. A spiral notepad was open to a worn page with a uniform grid drawn in black ink. For nearly twenty years, he had repeated this wildlife survey every month.

Last year the number of deer and turkey harvested from the hunting camp had been lower than average. It had not been historically terrible, but recent trail cam numbers were trending in the wrong direction. If it kept up, he was in for a rough season. And if there were not enough deer to keep the hunters coming, he would be out of a job and the house that came with it.

Chuck finished his cup of coffee in a long gulp and studied the grid in his notebook. He flipped back to look at pages from the same month from past years. Each page contained a date at the top, the number and location of the trail cams on the left side, and a series of animals listed horizontally along the first line. At the bottom were notes about the previous month. He would add a comment if it had rained more than half the days or if there had been a late or early frost. Likewise, he would report when he captured animals not in the grid, like in May 2005 when he had caught seven separate photos of skunks and one gigantic black bear. No bears had appeared this year. Instead, the first thirteen SD cards featured the usual critters: deer, hogs, turkeys, rabbits, foxes, raccoons, squirrels, bobcats, and opossums. Each earned slashes in their appropriate blocks in his notebook. The variety was right but not the amounts.

He removed the card, placed it in the appropriate pile, and inserted the next one. The picture viewer window appeared on the laptop screen, and he clicked to maximize the view. The first two images showed the same doe, but the third was something else. A long blurry shape was going out of frame near the ground, like a tapered saw blade with the cutting edge pointed up. The image that followed had been taken a few seconds later and showed nothing at all. Chuck made a mental note to go back to the blurry one later.

The next dozen showed the more mundane and expected variety of creatures. Chuck marked each in the notebook. He clicked to advance to the next image and stared, frozen in place. The thing appearing on the screen was not an alligator but a massive olive crocodile with dark stripes along its tail and body. The entire creature was in the frame and illuminated by the white flash of the trail cam. It had been walking towards the camera. The foreground clearly showed a thin vertical pupil inside a silvery right eye and a human leg held in its jaws, knee bent. A muddy white shoe with a series of multi-colored stripes was still attached to the foot being dragged behind.

Chuck willed himself up and into the house. Moving through

the living room into the kitchen, passing the oversized painting of Paul "Bear" Bryant, depicted wearing his trademark houndstooth hat and crimson jacket, on his way. From under a shelf filled with commemorative Alabama football Coke bottles, he plucked a bottle of Jack Daniels Black and splashed two shots into his coffee cup. He topped the whiskey off with Folgers and swallowed half before placing a hand on the receiver of the old wall phone. He didn't pick it up off the cradle. He had to call the sheriff, right? But would the sheriff shut down the camp? Sure, he would.

No gator, much less a croc, had ever been reported in all his time on the property. Sure, there were occasional stories from lease-holding hunters about encounters with bears and big cats. And once, two young men from Birmingham who were on their first real trip to the woods and were almost certainly smoking what Chuck called "wacky tobaccy" told him they saw a Bigfoot on the property. But not once had anyone mentioned seeing giant reptiles. Of course, there were alligators, even large ones in the Alabama River, but the river was a good twenty-five miles away, and the hunting camp only contained small streams not large enough to support such creatures.

Chuck downed the rest of the hot toddy and made another before returning to the computer. He studied the image for a moment but clicked to the next when he heard Marion's approaching humming behind him. An innocent rabbit appeared on the screen, and Chuck turned around, trying to achieve the same look.

"Hey, baby," Chuck said.

She walked to the edge of the porch with a glass of wine and looked at the sky. The light wind blew ruffles in her long sundress, and Chuck felt the first pangs of guilt.

"All the neighbors done with their fireworks tonight?" Marion asked.

"A few pops here and there still, but mostly done."

"The display on TV from Nashville was wonderful." Marion pulled up a chair at the patio table. "We should try to get back up there again. It's been too long, and I miss the mountains."

Chuck chose not to comment about whether Nashville was in the mountains or not. It is not, of course. He had made the mistake of arguing with her about it before, and it ended up being one of those fights all about winning instead of being right. So maybe she was poking him a little to gauge his mood. But he was not about to take the bait. He simply responded, "That would be nice, dear."

She sniffed at the air and picked up his coffee cup. She had been trying to convince him to switch to red wine ever since a heart murmur sent him to the ER a few months back, and the test results had been troubling. Chuck started to respond, but she cut him off with a tender touch on his shoulder.

"Think I might have another glass of wine. Need anything? It's OK if you want a refill."

Chuck needed there to not be an impossibly large crocodile on the property and for the camp to be corpse free, but he was not going to mention those things. She had been through enough, and there was no reason to worry her needlessly-even if she could not tell a damn hill apart from a damn mountain.

"No, thank you," Chuck said.

Marion went to the kitchen, and Chuck ticked a mark next to the rabbit column in the notepad and continued to the next frame. Six images later, Chuck stopped again. "On second thought, bring the Jack Daniels. And bring the whole damn bottle of wine too."

"What on earth is it?"

When Marion returned with the drinks and a perplexed look on her face, Chuck turned the laptop to face her.

Evalyn Vale stood in the frame, wearing a dark robe with a silver rope knotted around her waist. Tufts of her wind-blown, white hair were stuck to her sweaty cheeks. A large worn book was in one hand, and a large canvas bag was in the other.

"Your old friend is back."

Marion thrust the bottle of whiskey at Chuck and sat down in a huff. "Friend? That's a mighty strong word, wouldn't you say? Last I checked, friends don't try to ruin your life."

"Would trespassing bitch be better?"

Marion topped off her large wine glass. She stared at the image.

"Can you make that bigger? I want to see the book. It looks familiar."

He enhanced the size, but it blurred the image. Marion sat back and shook her head.

"So what now?" she said.

"I don't want to have to call the sheriff down here, ya know. I really don't..."

"Why not? If anyone deserves it, she does."

"We can't have the whole town talking about us having a witch doing God-knows-what out in our camp. Summoning the devil, human sacrifices..."

"Human sacrifices? After what she did to me, that's what you have to say? Have you blocked everything out?"

Chuck blushed and placed a hand on Marion's arm. She pulled away but relented when he tried the second time. "I'm sorry. What I meant was, you know what they'll say...after last time. You know better than anyone how people talk around here. How they make up stories and spread 'em around like the plague. But we need hunters booking cabins, and we need the ones already booked not to cancel. Something like this could scare them all away. It could get me fired. And put us out of the house."

"The sheriff would run her off."

"Yes. He surely would. But we have to let her know we saw her."

Marion raised both hands. "The sheriff taking her in would tell her that."

"I don't want to make it worse. We should try to talk to her first."

"I haven't darkened that woman's door in, what? Fifteen years at least? There's no telling what she'll say."

"Nothing pleasant, but she'll quit coming out here if she knows we're on to her. That's all you have to do. I'll go with you."

"She'd see it as a threat. This is something I need to do alone."

"OK. It really is better for everyone. No cops to exacerbate the situation, and she'll stay away. I don't trust her being out there. And what if she got hurt and tried to sue? Those woods can be dangerous."

Marion took a drink of wine. "You're right. Wouldn't want her to get mauled by a rabbit."

"I'm serious," Chuck said. Eaten whole by a crocodile would be more like it, he thought.

"Death awaits you all with big pointy teeth," Marion said, dangling two fingers over her mouth in her best John Cleese impression.

"I really am," Chuck said, but with a smile he could not quite stop from coming through.

"I am too. Stop mansplaining. I'll handle it."

When Marion finished her wine and retired to bed, Chuck

clicked back to the picture of the crocodile and examined it more closely. Based on the location, he judged the distance between the trees on each side of the trail meant this thing had to be at least sixteen feet long. He opened the file explorer window. The timestamp was 3:37 A.M., June 13th. Three weeks ago. It occurred to him then the date would have been around the time he saw the story of the missing boaters on the news out of Mobile. Folks in town talked about it partially because there wasn't much else to gossip about but also because none of the men had been found.

The urge to call the sheriff struck him again. It felt even more like the right thing to do. Not so much for the croc but because of the body. Chuck dismissed it. A sizeable animal with serious food demands would have figured out how to get back to the river by now. Successful animals don't get big by being dumb. The leg is croc turds, and the croc is long gone. Nothing to see here. What they don't know won't hurt 'em. He took a final look at the image and shut down the laptop before joining Marion in bed.

4

Marion parked three houses down and sat in her truck looking at the A-frame house where she and her old coven had spent dozens of nights. It was the first time in nearly fifteen years she had laid eyes on it. The memories flowed back. Most of them were good. Just like most of the girls in the coven had been good. She missed the comradery, sense of community, shared values, an appreciation of the mystery of nature, and practicing new techniques. It was a supportive place, a happy place. It was only at the end when things had turned bad. And when it had gone sideways, it had happened fast.

Though not exactly eager, Marion had wanted to deliver the message in person. Partially because she wanted to see the old place again and partially because she was curious if she could sort out why Evalyn had been on the hunting camp property. She had seen the book in the picture before, but she had been unable to place it. Most of all, she wanted to protect herself because she knew what Evalyn was capable of.

Three other trucks were parked on the street directly in front of Evalyn's, but the beat-up Toyota Camry was not in the driveway. Not that it should have been. She knew it would be unlikely for the car to still be running, much less still owned by Evalyn after all this time. But the presence of the car would have meant Evalyn was home. It was only through the grapevine that she knew Evalyn still lived in the house at all. The gossip from old friends and members of the coven would have reached her had Evalyn moved. Small towns hold long grudges, and few in the coven had forgiven Evalyn.

Marion took a deep breath to prepare herself to walk to the house, and just before she opened her door, she looked in the side mirror and saw a faded red Toyota Camry. She sat back and looked forward. The car passed, slowed, and pulled into the driveway. Marion took another breath to slow her heart, and she made her move.

She walked quickly and used the parked trucks as cover before closing in. Evalyn was standing at the open trunk of her car when Marion, from ten feet away, said, "Long time, no see."

Evalyn froze for a moment, then shut the trunk and turned around with a smile. "I'm surprised you still remember your way out here. You look well. For an old lady, I mean."

"You look like shit." The words slipped out on their own. Marion had planned to stay calm and not let her emotions take over. The moment Evalyn flashed her sly smile, though, the plan was out the window.

Evalyn laughed. "It sure was nice catching up. Go away."

She started for the front door, and Marion caught up with her halfway there and stepped in front of her, cutting off her path. "We need to talk."

After her attempts to walk around Marion had failed, Evalyn whistled loudly and waved at her front windows.

There was movement through the window, and a moment later, a man wearing a hooded, orange robe and a face covering that resembled a cloth fencing mask stepped out the door and began walking toward the women. Evalyn took advantage of the distraction and made a quick move to the right and scurried behind the man and in through the door. The man blocked Marion from following.

Marion stepped back, and in a loud voice, she said, "I'm calling the sheriff now. We have pictures of you trespassing at the hunting camp. It's not our land, remember? It belongs to a very rich man. If he finds out about this, he will press charges. Do you want to talk this out like adults, or do I need to make the call?" Marion dug around her purse and pulled out her phone. The man took a step forward. Marion dropped the phone and pulled out a small bottle of pepper spray instead and pointed it at the man's face. "I don't know what that mask is made of, but at the very least, you'll have a hell of a time taking it off without your eyes catching fire if you take one step closer."

The man halted.

In her loud voice again, she said, "Last chance."

Evalyn appeared in the doorway. She tapped the man on the shoulder. He walked into the house but stood behind Evalyn. Two more men in matching hoods and masks joined him. "Fine. Say your peace."

"When did you get thugs?"

"You can never be too careful. What do you want?"

"I remember the day you finally worked up the courage to buy a book at my store. It was a copy of Buckland's *Complete Book of Witchcraft.* You were looking over your shoulder like God himself was going to snatch you up and give you a whipping. And now you have your very own followers. That's quite the accomplishment."

"What do you want?"

"What are you doing out there?"

"It doesn't concern you. Just like the direction of the coven didn't concern you. But yet you had to try to control everything back then. And you destroyed everything. All because you were afraid to get your hands dirty. Not this time. I'm not going to let you destroy this.

"It's your fault what happened. You saw how uncomfortable your practice was making the other girls. They were new. They needed positive guidance, not to be blindly led down the left-hand path."

"You sound just like those church folk. My girls were perfectly happy learning to hex their cheating ex-boyfriends. It was barely even magic at all on their level. We were all finding our own ways."

"Not like that. It's supposed to be about balance."

"Bullshit. It's about power. Your power to have your way. Don't pretend you gave anything back when you were doing spellwork trying to heal people. There was no balance in that. No. That is you harnessing energy and using it for a selfish end. It's no different than what I do. But you call your way right and my way wrong."

Marion threw up her hands. "We'll never agree about the past. Let's focus on the present. Stay off hunting camp property. You've been told." She turned and started for her car.

"I can't do that yet."

Marion stopped and turned back to Evalyn. "Why the hell not?"

Evalyn walked into the yard. Four men in matching robes and face coverings followed. "What I am working on is too important. It's going to change everything when it's complete."

Marion walked backwards. "Great. Do it somewhere else."

Evalyn continued to advance on Marion. "It won't matter who owns the property when this is done."

Marion nearly fell when her foot stepped off the curb. She had not realized her proximity to the road. Evalyn and the men were too close. If they had wanted to rush her, there was little she could have done to stop them. The pepper spray would not keep all five of them at bay. She used the only other weapon she had. Fully in the road now, she stopped and spoke. "You were holding a book in the pictures. I know what it is."

Evalyn put up an arm. She and the men ceased their advance.

Marion watched Evalyn's stare and could tell she was trying to work out her next move. Marion felt like a treed animal being watched by a circling pack of wolves below.

The men stayed put, but Evalyn walked to Marion and stopped only when the two were nose to nose. "No. You don't. If you did, you wouldn't have come trip-trapping over here all by yourself. Forget what you saw and leave it alone. And tell that husband of yours to do the same. This is your only warning." Evalyn reached the men, and they stood watching as Marion pulled away.

Marion could see the group in her rear-view window. Evalyn had the same predatory look in her eye.

5

Casey took his usual route to Chuck and Marion's house through the grass, weeds, and exposed red dirt fronting Rabbit Run Road between the properties. The tree line was off the road about twenty feet, and Casey had worn a path right next to it over the years visiting the couple. On this visit, though, he walked a little closer to the highway than the trees.

The wood line behind Chuck and Marion's house was perpendicular to the road. Like all seven other properties spaced out along the two-mile stretch, the land had been prepared in the 1930s for bunk houses for the men working the oil wells. The oil had long since dried up, but Chuck still rode around the property with orange flags to mark and re-mark abandoned wells when he found them. They had not been decommissioned properly and posed a danger to hunters. The houses had been torn down in the 50s, and the forest had taken over the wells. But from the sky, the lots along the winding Rabbit Run Road still looked like a child's drawing of some crazed cartoon character's uneven-toothed smile. Casey's backyard was larger, but Chuck and Marion had plenty of space. A detached two-car garage, Morgan shed, and a good-sized herb and vegetable garden fit easily in the area. Two long rows of raised beds, several arched trellises, and dozens of pots made up the garden, which seemed to expand with each passing year.

Casey rounded the corner as Marion cut sprigs from one of her large rosemary plants and placed them in a brown wicker basket. He had seen her do this before, had even helped her a few times when her arthritis had been flaring up, and he always thought it was funny the way she thanked the plants for their leaves and flowers. She sold most of the herbs online and could have hacked them all off the bushes unceremoniously but instead chose to harvest them with respect. He appreciated her realness. Even so, and despite his "gift," Casey was still more interested in the type of magic done with cards over the herb and candle variety.

He approached the entrance to the garden and said, "Special delivery for a special lady."

Marion dropped the basket and whirled around wide-eyed, brandishing the garden sheers in a shaky hand. When she got a good look at him, her eyes closed, and her hand dropped, but it had taken longer than it should have. When she opened her eyes, she flashed an embarrassed smile and waved him into the garden.

"I'm so sorry. I thought you must have heard me coming."

"It's fine, sweetheart. It's just been a mornin'." She pulled off her gloves and started to kneel to pick up the spilled sprigs.

"I'll get them. Here. I'll trade you," Casey said, handing her a grocery bag with four large Tupperware containers inside. "A bunch of good stuff from my party last night. I got the Shack to pitch in. Lots of catfish and those hushpuppies with the jalapeño peppers inside Chuck likes so much."

"You are too good to us. I'll stick this right in the fridge and won't worry about cooking for the next two days. What a nice surprise."

Casey gathered the rosemary and followed Marion inside.

Chuck was lounging on the old leather couch, Budweiser tallboy in hand, and baseball was on the TV. He glanced at the noise and back at the TV. "She's puttin' you to work, I see."

"Just a little. Early game, huh? How are the Braves doing?"

"Up a run in the 2nd, but the damn Mets have two on and no outs. You want a beer?"

"Nah. Gotta run to work soon, and I'm still recovering from last night, but thanks."

"Suit yourself. It's the hair of the dog for me." Chuck groaned at the TV. "I swear, these umps are blind in one eye and can't see out the other."

Marion called for Casey from the kitchen. "I'm being summoned. Nice to see you, Chuck."

Chuck put up a hand, and Casey slipped into the kitchen. Marion had placed two mugs next to a pot and was packing herbs into metal infuser balls. Her hands were still shaking.

"Are you OK? I'm really sorry."

Marion smiled at the work her hands were doing. "It's not you, dear. Honestly. I just have a lot on my mind today."

"You tellin' him about our little intruder?" Chuck said, rounding the turn into the kitchen.

"I am not. And don't you bring it up."

"OK, OK." Chuck snatched a beer from the fridge and inspected the Tupperware, slipping out two hushpuppies into a napkin. He gave Casey a thumbs up and, on his way out of the kitchen, pointed to Marion's phone. "Look like you have messages."

Marion snapped again, "In my day, you weren't expected to be available all the time. I think it's just plain rude to expect that of a person. People think they are so damn important these days."

Chuck gave Casey a look that said, "You are on your own," popped a hushpuppy in his mouth, and disappeared back to the living room.

Marion took a deep breath, and the second the pitcher whistled, snatched it from the stove and poured water into the mugs. "Let's go to my office. I need to sit down."

What she called her office could just as easily have been called a library. Apart from two antique armoires and a small wooden desk under the lone window where she packaged herbs, every inch of remaining wall space contained floor-to-ceiling oak bookshelves. They were full. A few stacks of extra books stood in piles in the corners.

Two Vietnamese chairs with arms and feet intricately hand-carved into the heads and feet of dragons sat in the middle of the room. Each was upholstered with deep-red fabric with small, stitched golden symbols Casey did not recognize.

Marion lit a sandalwood incense cone on the small table between the chairs and sat down with her tea. "This is better."

"It's all the books, I think. Something is comforting about them."

"Absolutely. So much knowledge on those pages. It makes you feel like you can find the answer to anything. And plus, I love the smell." She blew steam from her mug. "I miss the store, but at least Chuck built these shelves for me. I got to keep most of the books I wanted right here. How's that for romance?"

"Chuck is a good man."

"And you'll find a good one too one day. Though you may need to venture out of Cherry Hill."

"Leave this progressive metropolis behind? But where would I find a good taxidermist or bait shop in some big city?"

"Life demands sacrifices sometimes, sweetie," Marion said. She took a sip of her tea. "Whatever happened with that last one? Kyle, was it? The way you talked about him, I thought you had found a keeper."

Casey shifted in his chair unconsciously. "Yes. I thought things were going great. We had been out a bunch of times, and I thought he liked me as much as I liked him, but I guess I was wrong."

"You didn't talk to him about it? Communication is key, you know."

"My roommate walked in on us, and that freaked him out. He left right after, and I haven't spoken to him since. I tried to get in touch, but he's not responding. I understand if he's mad, but I thought we had a real connection going. Really the first time I've felt that."

Marion patted his arm. "I'm sorry."

Casey shook his head and smiled. He was surprised to feel a tear slide down one cheek. He wiped it away, hoping she had not seen it. "Enough about me. What's with the intruder? Did someone break in?"

"That's nothing you need to worry about. Chuck's just being an old fool. No one broke in."

They drank their tea in silence for a long time. Casey looked at the bookcases and read the titles he could make out. She had organized the shelves roughly by topic. Runes, tarot, and other divination techniques shared one area. Books on Wicca were on another alongside Golden Dawn and other Gardnerian and Crowley-related practices. One shelf was dedicated to gardening and herbalism. The books there represented a staggering variety of regions and techniques. On the opposite side of the room were shelves filled with works on ritual magic and mythology from various parts of the world. The common Greek, Roman, and Norse varieties were represented, along with several containing myths and stories of Native Americans. Those and a handful of South American, Chinese, and Indian books had enthralled him in earlier years.

There were books on psychic phenomena too. Casey had read about psychometry, the power he seemed to possess, where a person would get impressions by touching or handling an object. But other than descriptions and anecdotes, the books offered little about how one would strengthen such talents. He knew he had the power, but the utility seemed limited to card tricks or being one of those TV psychic cold-readers. The illusionary aspect of cold-reading was appealing, but he couldn't and wouldn't get past the moral problem of using it to tell grieving parents lies about their dead children.

One lone bookshelf contained rare books. Many of these were skillfully hand-bound traditionally or unskillfully held together with yarn. A few were simply pages in manilla folders. In most cases, Marion had either ordered these for people who never picked them up or could not pay for them when they had eventually arrived. Some of these were original handwritten volumes. Some of those were purportedly personal books of shadows from witches and warlocks that had made their way into the open market after the authors had died. Casey had looked at some of them before, but the impressions he would get from handling them were often unsettling. He was usually left with the impression that no one should own them. Maybe Marion felt the same way, and this room she had made was a sort of safe house for them. He had never seen her read those.

Marion broke the silence. "Did you have fun at your party?"

Casey recounted the bottle rocket war, the food, and the card tricks.

"Did you have any impressions?"

"Yes. I was doing some mentalism; the trick I showed you once where I guess the word written on a piece of paper, and I saw the word. It was clear as day. And I also saw something she had done earlier in the day."

"What was it?"

Prickles of heat redden his face. "Just a few minutes of her at the Piggly Wiggly." He shifted position to face Marion. "There is nothing useful about these visions. I know from experience that they don't seem to mean anything. Nothing is actionable."

"The fact you can do it is meaningful in and of itself. You have a gift."

Casey slumped back in his chair. "Being a piano virtuoso would be a useful gift. At least I could tell people about that. I'm grateful you and Dwayne don't think I'm crazy, but anyone else would."

Marion waved her hands. "I've been telling you for years you should look into magic. Real magic, not just the tricks you can do. There are things you can do to make it stronger and people who would appreciate your talents. I don't know why you won't let me teach you."

Casey's phone made a loud alarm sound, and Marion flinched.

"Those confounded gadgets. I swear," Marion said.

Casey looked at the pop-up on his phone and sat upright. "My God. It's an alert from the Sheriff's Department. Amy Gale is missing."

"The reverend's daughter?"

"Yes. She's the one I was just talking about. The mentalism. The impressions...and I forgot. When I was doing it, I had a moment, a couple actually, of panic. And when I came out of it, I said something; I don't know what it means. Something like 'The Ruiner.'"

Marion glanced at her feet and stood up without making eye contact. "I'm getting more tea. Would you like another?"

Casey instinctively stood with her, but Marion motioned him down.

"I'll get it."

When she returned, Casey was looking at his phone.

"A bunch of people at work are texting me about Amy. The sheriff is interviewing people."

Marion handed him a mug. "Are you going to tell the sheriff about your vision?"

"I don't know."

"Did you see her leave?"

"I don't remember her leaving. There were a lot of people there."

"Did you see anything suspicious there?"

"No. It was just a party." Casey put a hand over his mouth. "No. Wait, I did see something, but it's hard to explain." Casey's stomach dropped again, and when he looked at Marion, her face was stern.

"Try," she said.

"I saw something in the woods. Some kind of light being."

He described it to Marion while she sat silently.

"I think if you told the police that, they would rip your trailer apart piece by piece looking for her and whatever drugs you were on. And how is this not the first thing you told me about?"

"I honestly don't know. It was captivating when it happened, and

I hadn't thought about it all day until now. It's like it doesn't want to be remembered."

"You should leave it out." Marion took a sip of tea and absently added, "It won't do us any good for you to get locked up right now."

He looked at her, and she opened her eyes a little wider, urging him to respond, so he did.

"Right. I mean, it's only been overnight. She's probably just off with friends or something. The whole town knows she's a wild child, and her dad is kind of an asshole. She probably just ran off for a while."

"Most likely," Marion said, standing up. "And you are going to be late for work if you don't get going."

Marion walked him to the back door, and a few feet out, he turned to wave. Marion was still standing there with a look of dread on her face.

6

Casey walked through the staff entrance of the Catfish Shack into a hot fog of greasy steam. He half-expected the sheriff's deputies would still be there and intercept him for questioning at the door, but they were long gone. A few co-workers were in the kitchen doing their pre-work, but no one seemed to be talking about the police. And aside from the music on the radio, Lynard Skynard's "Simple Man," the kitchen was quiet. Casey peeked out one of the tiny diamond-shaped windows of the doors leading into the dining area. The busboy motioned with a pitcher of cut lemons at the new hostess. She checked her watch and pointed at the closest wait station, and he moped away, head down. No customers were inside yet, and no fuzz to be seen.

Casey took a deep breath, turned, and snatched a hairnet from a box by the salad station. He had not realized how scared he had been of talking to the police until that moment. He had no reason to be worried, he thought. Some strange things happened, but they had nothing to do with Amy. Still, he felt lighter as he put on the hairnet and tied a red bandanna over it.

At the door of the walk-in fridge, he checked the board to find his prep-work assignments. He completed each task with mindless efficiency and then rechecked the dining area. Finding it still empty, he headed out the back door for a cigarette.

Dwayne leaned against the wooden fence surrounding the dumpster behind the Catfish Shack. He looked like an unfinished scarecrow with his hair-netted dome aimed down at his phone, baggy pants, and stained apron. Dwayne looked up briefly and flashed a middle finger at Casey as he approached.

"Nice to see you too," Casey said, lighting his cigarette.

"Talk to the po-po yet?"

"Nope. I guess they'll come around if she doesn't show up soon."

"Twenty bucks says she ran off with Tommy."

"Who?"

"Her boyfriend. He works over at the Piggly Wiggly. Decent dude."

"Why didn't she tell me she had a boyfriend?"

"I don't know, but you haven't been the easiest to talk to lately."

Casey thought back to the vision. It had been her boyfriend, not some random cashier. The impression was right, but his interpretation was off. He could not read minds, not exactly anyway, so why would he think the worst of Amy? It was just a tryst between two lovebirds, not payment for the weed. "Does Tommy have a shaved head, kind of a rat face?"

"You don't have to be a dick about it. But yeah, reckon if you're an asshole, you'd call the guy rat-faced. It's not like he can help it." Dwayne waved a finger at Casey like a cartoon teacher lecturing a class. "Of all the people who'd you think wouldn't be judgmental."

"OK, OK. I'm sorry," Casey said.

Dwayne laughed and leaned back against the fence. "Dude does have beady little eyes a little too close together. But the heart wants what the heart wants, I guess."

"Was he at the party?"

"I didn't see him. Don't mean much, though. I'd bet she left with him or met up after and shacked up at his place and just didn't feel like callin' Daddy."

Casey nodded and flicked the cherry off his cigarette. "Probably right."

The lunch shift was slow, but the time passed quickly for Casey as his thoughts kept returning to Marion. She had seemed bothered by something. And when she had heard about Amy, she had gotten even more uptight. He realized then the conversation with her had worked him up about talking to the police. He decided to drop by later with some wine to see if she'd be more inclined to talk.

Reservations were light for the evening, and Casey was cut around 3:00. He took off quick. The thick air hadn't helped his slight hangover, and he was eager to get some rest somewhere easier to breathe.

Returning home, Casey kicked off his black work shoes and stripped. The air was cold on his body where the sweat-soaked shirt and pants had been sticking to him all afternoon. He walked naked to the bathroom and took a long shower. Afterward, he took the dirty clothes to the laundry room and tossed them into the washer. As he was about to head back to his room, he noticed the bucket of clothes he had gathered after the fireworks war.

He retrieved each item, shook it out, and placed it in the washer. They were all singed, but he figured someone might want some of these clothes back. At the bottom of the bucket was a single small woman's shoe. Apart from some stray leaves stuck to the side, it looked close to brand new. Casey grasped it, intending to brush the leaves off, and was immediately transported back to the night before.

He found himself looking through the eyes of someone else, riding along as this person ran past others in his backyard. He recognized some of the people and could see tracers of bottle rockets and Roman candles flying past. The sulfur smell of gunpowder mixed with the sweet pine and grass was strong with each inhale. *Her breath*, he thought, *My God, I can feel her breathing.* And it was a she. He knew it for certain even before he realized he could feel her breasts moving up and down as she ran. And she was happy, thrilled even, to be running free in the heat, laughing giddily with a slight beer buzz.

He watched from her vantage point as she looked down to light a Roman candle and then shook it in no particular direction. She cheered as each of the colorful shots arched into the sky.

Casey had always been a detached observer in his visions; never before had he experienced these in first person. He tried to drop the shoe, but his hand would not budge. It was as if an electrical shock or magnetic attraction was holding him in place. A bond had been made, and he was powerless to control anything.

She ran closer to the tree line. Casey could feel another Roman candle in her hand and guessed she would light it next, but instead, she stuck it in her back pocket, pulled a joint out of her bra, and lit it. Casey tasted the peppery smoke and felt the warm buzz begin to take hold. The top of his head (or was it her head?) started to tingle. She turned towards the yard and trailer and watched the fireworks war from the exact opposite position Casey had seen it the night before. Most of the crowd was drifting to the other side of the yard. She took two more hits off the joint before putting it out on the bottom of her shoe and pinching the end. It burned Casey's thumb and forefinger for a brief moment. She placed it in her bra and was turning towards the treeline when she saw the lights.

Casey screamed. He screamed from inside her head to run and struggled again to drop the shoe, but his body back in the trailer was no longer his to control. She was getting closer to the lights, closer than he had gotten himself. And her eyes locked on them. There was no apprehension in her at all. His instincts had told him to run, but her instincts were absent. He screamed again, but nothing he did registered with her. She moved closer still.

Through her eyes, he could now see the strings of lights he previously thought must have been connected actually were. She saw it too but assigned no meaning to the large translucent bell and how the colorful paths flowed down from it. The horror set in for Casey, but she was transfixed.

The thing in the woods was a colossal jellyfish impossibly suspended in the air. The strings were the bio-luminescent tentacles hanging beneath. Dumbfounded but still enthralled, she did not scream, not even when it began to float towards her. The last things she saw were tentacles, first brushing against the arm she had subconsciously raised to protect herself, then sweeping over her face. Her final thought was that those were the most beautiful colors she had ever seen. Casey watched as the creature centered itself over her, and then the stinging cells in the tentacles fired in unison. Intense stinging pain coursed through Casey, and he burst out of her body to the ground. He made it to his feet as the monster carried Amy Gale's rigid body into the thick woods. Her shocked eyes were wide open and looking slightly up. One of her arms reached above her like an outfielder waiting to catch a fly ball. Casey took steps back and realized he was holding her discarded shoe. He dropped it with no resistance and found himself standing in front of the washing machine staring at Amy's shoe on the floor of the trailer.

Casey stood in place for a moment, trying to collect himself. He might have stayed there for several minutes, but he heard his roommate Jake's truck pull up outside. The sound snapped him out of the trance. He pulled a burnt t-shirt out of the washing machine and used it to grab the shoe, careful not to make direct contact, then rushed to his room and locked the door.

Casey laid down by his bed and pushed the shoe under. Still wrapped in a t-shirt, it lay among the flotsam of books, old magic trick items, and other personal effects he couldn't bring himself to throw out. Jake came in through the front door, and Casey closed his eyes to focus on the sounds. The thin front door slamming, keys thrown hard on a table and sliding off, and Jake yelling into his phone. That was good, Casey thought. Distracted Jake is good. Casey looked under the bed one last time before getting up and spotted something he hadn't used in years. It was a better hiding place for the shoe.

Once the shoe was secure, Casey grabbed his keys, stepped out of his room, and found Jake, as he had hoped he would, pacing the living room, red-faced and barking into his cell phone. "No. No. She's a liar... I never... You know how much of a bitch she is! No! I haven't seen her in months."

Jake's crazed eyes locked with Casey's for only a second and conveyed nothing short of contempt, his regular expression over the past few weeks.

The two had never been close. It would even be a stretch to call their past relationship friendly. Still, when Casey's parents had died seven years before and he had needed a roommate to help make ends meet, Casey went with the devil he knew. And it worked out for a long time, mainly because Jake spent most of his time away in the woods or with girlfriends. But things changed after Jake walked in on Casey and his friend in bed. Casey was still processing what had happened. Jake barely needed a full second to form his opinion, and he made it a personal mission to out Casey to everyone they both knew and harass him mercilessly at every opportunity.

Casey had tried to avoid Jake since then, and when Jake glared at him on his way to the door, Casey simply lowered his eyes and slipped outside. He quickly started the car and pulled out onto Rabbit Run Road. He drove aimlessly and found himself turning on Highway 12. He had avoided a confrontation with Jake, but knowing Amy was gone, really gone, had rendered him numb. But as he replayed the sight of her carried away into the woods over and over in his mind, he couldn't stop the tears. His friend, practically a little sister to him, had been murdered. Casey knew that somehow. Wolves and sharks kill people, but they don't murder. But the jellyfish creature had an intelligence far beyond animal instinct. It knew what it was doing. It had been a murder, and it wasn't going to stop.

Ahead, Casey saw the turnoff to the Red Lion. He did not want to be around people, but he did want a drink. He took the turn.

7

The Red Lion Lounge sat in the shade of a thick stand of pine and oak trees a hundred feet off a small two-lane road seven miles south of Rabbit Run Road and five miles east of the Cherry Hill town square. And it roughly marked the halfway point between Cherry Hill and Interstate 65. Situated less than a mile inside the Maubila county line, it was the closest legal bar to thousands of rural people living in many surrounding so-called "dry" counties. The potholed blacktop parking lot extended from the building to the street, where a ten-foot by ten-foot brick wall stood in a strip of grass between the entrance and exit. Two dusty, red-painted concrete lion statues were perched at the top on either side, their front paws suspended in the air as if pouncing.

The building itself would have looked more at home in 1700s England than in present-day south central Alabama, but there it had stood for almost 100 years with crossed thatched tutor sides, hung sash windows, and a huge wooden front door. Some of the locals reckoned it was meant to be a tourist destination. Others figured whoever built the place simply had too much time and money on their hands. But no one knew for sure. And that was the most peculiar thing. It was like one day it sprung up from the ground like some strange weed with an interesting flower that everybody noticed, but nobody ever got around to pulling.

Casey made straight for the far end of the bar and had a double Jack and Coke in front of him in no time. Two men in their 60s sat at the other end, chatting between pulls of beer and munching free peanuts. He could make out bits of their conversation and gathered they knew one of the missing fishermen. The place was dim, and only a few tables were occupied in the open lounge area. Casey was glad it was dark. It would give him some cover if he started crying. He thought he might.

Casey finished the drink and had just ordered another when the front door opened. The late afternoon light blazed in, making a shadow of the woman who entered. When the door closed and she was halfway to the bar, Casey saw it was Marion. Surprised to see her in a bar, he stood to meet her, but a woman Casey had never seen before intercepted her. Marion hugged her, and after the embrace, she wiped tears from her eyes. Both women headed back towards the front door. The one Casey did not know looked around the bar first.

Casey watched as they disappeared into a corner near the front door. He followed and found there were small alcoves on either side of the hallway but no doors apart from the main entrance. A smile stretched across his face. A secret door, he thought. He started to tap at the wall but remembered Marion had looked upset. He didn't want to intrude, but he did need to talk to her. She was the only one who would or could believe what he had seen. So instead of trying to find the door, he walked back to the bar and out the side exit to the fenced-in outdoor area.

There was no one outside, and Casey went to the fence and looked at the building. There were no windows. Casey looked up then. The building was tall enough for a second story, and the ceiling over the lounge area was very high, but the rest of the building's ceilings were standard height. It was conceivable there were rooms, secret rooms.

"May I be of assistance?" a man's voice said a few feet from Casey.

Casey jumped, and a nervous laugh escaped him. The man had a full black beard and was wearing dark sunglasses. Casey could not see his eyes. "No. Just checking out the building."

"I saw you inspecting the main entryway as well."

"Yes. I did…"

"What are you looking for?"

"I thought I saw a friend come in. My neighbor, actually. I was trying to see where she went."

"Why did you withhold that?"

"Are you a security guard or something?"

"Something. So why did you lie?"

"It wasn't a lie. I was literally checking out the building because I saw my friend come in, and I saw her go up front with another woman, but there didn't seem to be anywhere to go. So, I figured there may be some room I didn't notice, upstairs maybe, and I came here to see what I could find out, and now I'm talking to you."

"What's your friend's name, and what is yours?"

"Her name is Marion. And I'm Casey."

The man with the beard smiled for the first time, revealing clean, straight teeth. "OK then. When they come down, I'll let her know you are here. Please wait at the bar in the meantime."

Casey nodded, returned to his previous spot, and ordered another drink. Casey wondered if the man had acknowledged the existence of the upstairs room on purpose and concluded he had. It was reciprocity for trusting him with his name. Still, something was strange about the man. His accent came from north of the Mason-Dixon line. And the language pattern was strange; far too proper. Casey put it out of his mind and focused on the door. It kept him from thinking about Amy. He desperately wanted to see the secret door open again and made a mental note to ask Marion about it.

He had switched to beer because he had a good buzz going that he wanted to keep manageable. A light came in through the front entrance again, and this time the figure was a skinny man with a hat and a gun belt. When he made it to the bar, Casey saw the secret door open and Marion walk out with the other woman.

And almost immediately after, the bearded man, who Casey had not seen reenter the building, was behind the bar and said, loud enough for everyone to hear, "Deputy, let me buy you a round. What are you having?"

Marion changed direction and walked out the front door. Just before the light came through the entryway, the man with the beard dropped a glass and made a loud sound of surprise. Casey was impressed. The misdirection worked on the deputy, and as soon as the door closed, the other woman made her way to the bar area. Casey looked up and saw the man with the beard signaling him with eyes to follow Marion.

Casey waited until the deputy was engaged with the woman, and he slipped from his seat, quiet and unassuming as a church mouse. Another glass shattered right before he opened the door.

Once outside, Casey ran to Marion's truck, which was reversing out of a space close to the main road. He waved his arms, and she slowed and rolled down the window but didn't stop.

"I have to go. I'll call you later."

Casey kept pace with the car. "Amy is dead. I had an impression. It was that light thing."

Marion shook her head. "I'm so sorry. But I really have to go."

"That thing was a jellyfish. I know it sounds crazy, but..."

"I need to reason some things out. In the meantime, lay low and keep an eye out for any strangers you see coming or going from the woods. And don't go out there yourself. I'll call you soon."

She rolled up the window and took off. Casey found himself standing alone in the parking lot, filled with more questions than before. All he knew for certain was he had to do something to make sure what happened to Amy did not happen to anyone else.

He was heading back inside to talk to Marion's friend when the deputy threw open the door and jogged to his cruiser before peeling out and disappearing down the road. Right after, the fence gate on the side of the building rolled open, and a shiny new Chevy truck emerged. Marion's friend sat in the passenger seat, and the bearded man was behind the wheel. Casey took a step towards the truck and saw the man wave, but he didn't slow down. The truck pulled onto the street going the opposite direction as the deputy and sped away with similar speed. There was no way for Casey to catch up with them in his clunker.

Instead, he drove to Murder Creek, where he searched the internet on his phone for anything he could find to shed light on jellyfish, shapeshifters, and anything called the Ruiner. There wasn't much on the name or evil jellyfish, but plenty about shapeshifting. Practically every culture in the world seemed to have some legend or another about things in the woods that could turn into bats, wolves, tigers, deer, coyotes, or any number of other species. He searched until the sun went down, finding more and more examples. All boogieman stories told to children to keep them in line and out of the woods. Or so Casey would have thought before his own encounter. What he had seen was real, and Marion and those people at the Red Lion knew more than they were telling. He would have to convince her to talk.

8

A pair of two-toned blue cop cars idled in Casey's driveway close to the street. Above them hung a busted streetlight. And had it not been for the porch light being on, the cars would have been hard for Casey to see on the white shell driveway. But he did see them. And he also saw Jake's truck was gone.

Casey found it ironic Jake had left on the porch lights. After all, it had been Jake who had three times shot out the streetlight in the front yard with his .22 rifle. He had told Casey the county had no right to keep the light shining "on my property." The property, which of course, was not his. And further, it was OK to shoot it out because "the damn thing is brighter than the fucking sun at noontime." That had been closer to the mark. The county had sent workers out to fix it the first two times but stopped coming after it mysteriously blew out again. Casey held out a sliver of hope the deputies were there because of the light, but he knew the idea was bullshit. Still, it gave him enough courage to turn right into the driveway instead of right on past. It would only delay the inevitable after all.

As Casey pulled in, each patrol car's driver's side door opened. The men who emerged were very different. The first one out,

Sheriff Larry Johnson, stood at least six-foot-five. Despite a hint of a beer belly and the fact he was pushing fifty-five, he looked like he could have suited up at defensive end for the New Orleans Saints and held his own. His uniform was military-pressed and crisp. And after making his way up the steps to the front door, he stood still as a soldier facing Casey's car. The other officer Casey had recognized from the Red Lion a few hours before was Deputy Mark Wallace. He was a squirrelly man of average height whose thin shoulders seemed to slump too far down, making his narrow neck look too long and his Adam's apple and head look too big. It was possible too, Casey thought, that the man didn't own an iron. By the time Casey made it to the door, Deputy Wallace was pulling a crumpled notepad out of his back pocket.

"Casey Sparks?" Sheriff Johnson said.

"Yes, sir," Casey said, coming to a stop in front of the pine stairs leading to the door and looking up at the two men.

"I'm Sheriff Johnson. This is Deputy Wallace. Know why we are here?"

"I'm guessing it's about Amy?"

"Bingo. Mind if we come inside and have a little chat?"

"No problem," Casey said, making his way up the steps and thankfully managing to put the key in the lock the first time with shaky, numb hands.

The trio entered the trailer, and Deputy Wallace immediately started taking notes. Sheriff Johnson motioned to the couch, and Casey sat down. The sheriff remained standing.

"Do you know where Amy is, son?"

"No, sir," Casey said. He was impressed by the couch move by the sheriff. There was no natural way to sit. Lean back and cross a leg; you come off too casual. Slouch, and you look guilty. So, Casey leaned forward and placed his elbows on his knees, even though it meant stretching his neck to look the sheriff in the eye.

"Seems she was last seen here. Did you see her here?"

Casey nodded. "There were a lot of people. I throw a fourth of July party every year. It keeps getting bigger."

"But did you see her?"

"Sorry. Yes. She was hanging out with some other girls. I didn't recognize them."

"Other eighteen-year-old girls?"

"I'm not sure. Could be."

"At a party where alcohol was being served, right?"

It hadn't occurred to Casey until then that he might have to worry about underage drinking. In his experience, rural sheriff's departments nearly always turned a blind eye to such things unless driving was involved, but the law is the law. And the last thing on his mind was getting up to any shenanigans with Amy or her friends. And as the implications washed over him, his feet, like his hands before, felt stuck in an icebox. And invisible pens and needles poked his cheeks. "I didn't serve any of them. And I didn't invite them either. Like I said, it gets bigger every year. Word of mouth, I guess."

"Did you see them drinking?"

"I don't remember."

"Could have been? It was a party, right? A lot of people."

"It's possible," Casey said. Nearly certain was more like it, he thought. That bottle of tequila she had at Murder Creek didn't drink itself.

"Did you talk to her?"

"I did a couple magic tricks for her. I mean, I was doing them for a lot of the people."

"What kind?"

"Card tricks, mainly, and some mentalism."

Sheriff Johnson walked into the kitchen area, separated from the living room by a short set of cabinets and a bar. Casey could only see his midsection and watched him stand in front of the refrigerator for a moment before opening various drawers. Casey heard him jostling the contents. Soy Sauce packets crinkled, and loose change jingled. A drawer closed. Another opened, and forks and knives clanged together. Now inspecting the pots and pans cabinet, Sheriff Johnson said, "How do you know Amy?"

Casey took the opportunity to rest his neck by looking down. "We work together. She's a server at the Catfish Shack. And I cook. But you already know all that, I'd guess. Plus, she's practically small town famous because of her dad. And she's got a bit of a reputation. Preacher's kids, you know the stereotype."

The jostling noise stopped, and the sheriff rounded the bar. "You mean she was a hell-raiser?"

Casey looked up again to answer. "I mean, that was her reputation, but I can't speak to whether or not it's deserved." Casey was concentrating hard on referring to Amy in the present tense. He was worried both about slipping up and talking too slowly.

"What happened here?" Sheriff Johnson pointed to the hole in the speaker next to the TV."

Some of Casey's previous answers had been misleading, but this was the first outright lie Casey told. "It's been torn up a while now. My roommate Jake did it. I think he tripped and kicked it or something." Jake had done it, but not because he tripped. He had come home about three weeks before while Casey had been on the couch watching TV. Jake had never said a word. Simply walked up to the couch, took the remote control, and flung it point-blank into the speaker. The remote tore through the screen and the cone, destroying both.

The sheriff inspected the hole further before starting another line of questioning. "Were you romantically linked to Amy in any way? Have a crush or anything?"

Casey shook his head. The pins and needles had spread to his whole face, and his frozen hands and feet were no longer cold; they were nonexistent. "No. Never."

Sheriff Johnson waved Deputy Wallace over and whispered something in his ear. The deputy's face didn't betray the message, but he asked his first question when looking back at Casey. "See anything suspicious that night? You already told the sheriff some folks came you didn't know, but were there any strange characters? Any fights?"

"There was a fireworks battle of sorts," Casey said, looking back and forth between the two men," but no punches thrown or anything like that."

"Was Amy involved?" said Sheriff Johnson.

"Yes," Casey said before he could stop himself.

"There were a lot of people. How do you know she was out there too?" Deputy Wallace said, once again scribbling in his infernal notepad.

"Not a lot of the girls ran out there, but I think she was one of the few who did."

"Hell-raising and all," Deputy Wallace added.

"Is it possible she got hurt out there?" the sheriff said.

Casey knew then he was about to have to lie to the police a second time, but he tried his best to do so by omission, hoping it would feel less like deception and more like misdirection. "Anything is possible, I guess, but as far as I know, no one was seriously hurt by any of the fireworks."

"And you saw her after?"

"No. Watching her go out there is the last time I remember seeing her." Casey was sure they would see through his answers and slap the cuffs on him then and there, so when Sheriff Johnson responded with "OK then. Mind if we look around?" Casey could barely hold back an exhausted yet triumphant laugh when he responded with a maybe too informal, "Fine by me."

This was followed by what Casey figured were routine questions about whether or not he had weapons in the house or if some vicious dog was hiding in a room somewhere. Casey let them know there were no animals, but there probably were weapons in the house, but only in Jake's room since he spent most of his time when he wasn't out womanizing, stalking in the woods trying to blast every living creature he could find to kingdom come. That seemed to be an acceptable answer, and Sheriff Johnson went outside. Deputy Wallace walked down the hall into Jake's room.

The feeling was starting to come back to Casey's hands and feet, and the pricks in his face started to fade. He sat back, let out a deep breath, and remembered the shoe. But they wouldn't find it, he thought. No way. Still, his hands and feet stayed cool even as his face started to feel normal again.

Deputy Wallace finished in Jake's room and asked if all the guns were registered. Casey shrugged, and the deputy shook his head and walked down to Casey's room and closed the door. A minute later, Sheriff Johnson, too, came back inside and joined the deputy. Casey checked his phone over and over and watched as two minutes turned to five and five turned to ten. His confidence in the hiding place was strong, but when the two men emerged from his room holding a pair of handcuffs, Casey thought for a split second about running.

"What are these for?"

When Casey looked again and realized they were his, he couldn't help but chuckle. "They are trick cuffs."

"They are the same model we have, son."

"True. The cuffs themselves are real, but they have been modified so you can break right out of them. You can buy them online. Put them on. You'll see."

"How about you show us instead," Deputy Wallace said.

Casey turned his back to the sheriff and held both hands behind him. "Go ahead. Nice and tight."

The sheriff obliged, and Casey turned back to face him, "Here goes." Casey made two quick motions behind his back and held out the open handcuffs in his right hand. "Ta-da."

The sheriff examined them more closely and smiled. "The teeth."

"That's it. It doesn't take any force at all to open them. Give it a try."

Sheriff Johnson closed one of the cuffs. "What about the double lock?"

"Clear epoxy."

"Smart," Sheriff Johnson said. He picked at the double lock hole with a fingernail and found it filled, and he twisted the cuff, and it fell open with little effort. "Well, what do you know? You learn something new every day."

He handed the cuffs back to Casey. "We're going to be on our way, but we may have more questions, and we may need to come back out. I'd appreciate it if you didn't stray too far from Cherry Hill. If you remember anything at all, call the office any time."

"Yes, sir. I'm not going anywhere."

As soon as Casey heard their cars making satisfying crunching sounds on the shell driveway, he ran to his room to check the hiding place and found they had looked, but as intended, had not seen.

9

Chuck rolled out of bed early and slow-walked out of the bedroom to keep from waking Marion. His treacherous knees and ankles cracked as he went, and when a loud pop escaped from his right knee, Marion shifted position and smacked her lips. Chuck halted, still as a rabbit, as she settled back to deeper sleep. He made coffee and drank the first cup at the patio table while he made a mental list of things to take with him. A rifle, of course, maybe a handgun too. Lots of ammo. An ax. His cell phone to take pictures and a spare trail cam and memory card in case Evalyn or her group had come back and disabled or destroyed the camera that had given her away the first time. He collected these things into a camouflage backpack, which by then matched his outfit, and poured a second cup of coffee into a thermos. Just before leaving, he walked lightly back into the bedroom. He leaned over and kissed Marion on the forehead before drawing back upright and whispering, "I love you." The four-wheeler might wake her, he thought, but by then, he would be down the trail, and she wouldn't worry. If she had woken before and had seen him taking the 7-millimeter rifle and the Desert Eagle hand cannon, she would have asked questions and not liked the answers. She didn't know guns like he did, but she knew the ones that meant business.

And this was business for him. He wanted to forget about the crocodile and the God-forsaken foot, but unless he checked out the location for himself, he couldn't be sure about his logic. Then there was the call the night before from a sheriff's deputy. The deputy asked questions about a missing girl, the reverend's daughter no less, and the party at Casey's house. Of course, he had no information to provide, but something was not right. Marion had been out with Casey when the call came in, and she had seemed unsettled when she returned. He had decided to spare her the extra stress and not mention the call. But the most important reason to go out and take a look was Marion. If she were attacked in the garden or stumbled on a body while out on a hike, he could never forgive himself.

The muddy, green four-wheeler was parked in a small, unlocked Morgan shed behind the house and past the garden next to the larger, locked garage. Marion went on sometimes about how he should lock the shed up at night, but Chuck never would. It was a conscious decision on his part. It didn't feel right to give in to fear. He'd lock the garage with her car and his truck, but only because it was a fight he couldn't win. But there was something about opening the little unlocked shed and seeing everything in place that put Chuck at ease. It was like the free, easy feeling of pissing outdoors. It was a reliable, albeit fleeting, bit of Zen. It was the way things should be.

He loaded the backpack behind the seat and drove further into the yard before meeting the dirt road and slipping into the forest. Dew sparkled and reflected the first rays of orange sun on the needles of the pine trees lining the dirt road. Decades of hunters and their four-wheel-drive trucks had worn deep ruts in much of the road, and Chuck had to drive far to one side to stay on level ground. It was slower than taking the truck, but if he came across a downed tree, he'd be able to drive around with the four-wheeler. And he didn't want to be delayed. Not this morning. A mile or so down the road, approaching Cabin 1, three does dashed from the clearing behind the cabin and ran towards the tree line. Their white tails pointed to the sky as they bounced into the woods in a hurry. Chuck slowed as he drove past the cabin to check for any signs of human activity. Seeing none, he continued on.

Another mile or so past the first cabin and down a hill sat another. Cabin 3. Not Cabin 2, because why number them in a non-confusing way every damn year, Chuck always thought. He never did ask his boss if he could change the numbers, though. Cabin 3 sat at the crest of another large hill, and the sinkhole and trail cam, which photographed Evalyn and the crocodile, sat 500 yards or so down the gentle slope. Chuck slowed on approach and examined the outside before parking the four-wheeler in front. He sat there for a while, letting the silence retake hold, and watched bumblebees and dragonflies working the pink and yellow wildflowers in the brush. A single red-tail hawk circled two wide rotations above Cabin 3 before dipping a wing and sailing into the distance. When he proceeded, he went on foot. In case anyone or anything was down there, he wanted the element of surprise to be on his side.

The game trail was a couple hundred yards down the hill from the cabin through a thick patch of pine, oak, and sassafras trees. He moved through the woods, stepping toe to heel like the old-timers claimed the Cherokee and Creek had done when they lived in this area. However, he still managed to snap the occasional stick underfoot. He stopped every fifty feet or so to listen and used the scope on his rifle to spy the area around him. Each time it was quiet except for one gray squirrel scampering in the distance and a few Judas crows betraying his position to the other animals with their loud caws. When he reached the game trail, he stopped again at the edge of the woods to listen and look. He saw nothing but could smell the heavy, sweet fragrance of an expansive honeysuckle bush overpowering the pines. Its floppy yellow and white flowers moved with the light breeze and with the efficient work of the many honeybees and few plump bumblebees passing from flower to flower, gathering pollen.

Stepping into the narrow game trail and turning right, Chuck continued his routine of stop-look-listen. A few minutes after starting down the path, he spotted fresh deer tracks, and further down, there were newer coyote tracks and scat. All was quiet as he approached the trail cam. It was concealed by a dark case and a tuft of artificial leaves and was attached to an oak tree just inside the wood line. Most of the game trail was about three feet wide, with a telltale worn patch in the middle (humans aren't the only creatures of habit). Still, Chuck had selected this spot because the trail cut through a relatively clear area where the line of brush and trees was about twenty feet apart. It was also where two game trails converged. He found more worn deer and turkey tracks but nothing else. Chuck scanned the surrounding area with the scope before using the end of his rifle to scatter small branches and clumps of leaves around, searching for any evidence of human or crocodile movement.

A limb cracked behind him, and he spun around, rifle to his shoulder, to see a raccoon staring at him, standing motionless. Chuck let out a deep breath and lowered his weapon. His chest tightened, and he noticed the cold of sweat spots on his back and shoulders under the backpack for the first time. *That's my reaction? When my real target is a 2,000-pound armored ambush predator with massive, crushing jaws and a tail that could break me in half. And the only way to kill it would be a perfectly placed shot in its tiny brain, which, if the croc sees you first, would be all the more impossible to pull off since you would almost certainly be running backward, shitting your pants at the same time as you try to aim and fire. Jesus, I might as well be hunting a dinosaur with a slingshot and a blindfold.*

Chuck collected himself and scouted the area for another few minutes. Finding the trail cam untouched and nothing out of the ordinary, he used his scope to look at the top of the next hill over, the ridge ringing the sinkhole, and noticed a tiny wisp of smoke. He snapped back into stealth mode and moved closer.

Marion called the sinkhole a cenote. When he asked her what the difference was, she told him a cenote was a type of sinkhole, so they were both right, but technically a cenote has exposed groundwater at the bottom. They had seen huge ones on a trip to Mexico years back. Some were hundreds of feet deep, and they saw people swimming and diving into them. Chuck thought those people were off their rockers and said so, but Marion reminded him he had been young once, too and would have done the same thing. He couldn't argue.

The sinkhole at the Mitcham Breech Hunting Camp was tiny compared to the ones south of the border. Chuck reasoned it resulted from an ancient meteor strike because it sat precisely in the middle of a 200-foot circular depression at the top of a short hill. Together the features resembled a stumpy volcano. The opening of the sinkhole was a rough circle about twenty feet across. Around the rim was exposed white stone with thin lines of thick green moss growing in irregular patterns in the cracks like living veins of gold in quartz. When the sun was high and directly overhead, you could see down to the bottom of the clear bluish water. Chuck had once looked down with his scope and spotted a few small trout-like fish schooling in the middle depths and pale crayfish in clusters picking at the rock. He had seen good-sized bones settled at the bottom too.

Chuck halved the 100-yard distance to the sinkhole and again scanned the area with the scope. Someone was standing on the ridgeline with a pair of binoculars. Chuck crept from his position to take better cover behind a nearby tree and looked again. It was a man and not Evalyn, and he was still there looking in his general direction, though not directly at Chuck. He wore a dark orange robe with a grey rope-like belt, and his face was covered by a hood. The man lowered the binoculars and walked down the hill towards the sinkhole and out of Chuck's view. Chuck scanned the ridge a while longer and was about to move forward when he felt something poke his lower back just under the backpack and heard a voice say, "Lower the rifle."

Chuck was still, and in a voice somehow conveying the opposite of the panic he felt, said, "It's OK. I'm the caretaker of this property. I'm not trespassing."

"Lower the gun and drop it," the voice answered.

Chuck lowered the rifle and let it fall to the ground in front of him.

"Put your hands behind your back."

Chuck said, "I will not." And spun around, pulling the desert eagle from his chest holster and raising it.

The man behind was knocked off balance and took a step back. His rifle was still pointed at Chuck but aimed at his feet now. The man wore the same robe as the man on the ridge. His face was partially covered by a hood. The part Chuck could see was vaguely familiar.

"Who are you?"

"I am a follower of Mother Evalyn."

"Mother? Good lord. What is your name?"

"There are no names."

"For fuck's sake. I ought to shoot you down, holding a gun on me at my own place. Get the other fella in the robe and whoever else you came here with, and get the fuck off my property."

"But it's not yours anymore. It belongs to her now."

"The hell you say. Evalyn is a nut job. This isn't her place, no matter what she told you."

"You should turn back now. It would be better if you did."

"This here is a Desert Eagle. It fires .50 caliber rounds, and if you don't drop your gun right now, you're gonna have a hole in your gut big enough to pass a watermelon through. If your weapon moves up even a hair, I'm pulling the trigger."

The man in the robe stared at Chuck for a long time, but the expression on his face wasn't one of anger. Instead, it was contemplative, even serene, Chuck thought. The cold sweat from under the backpack continued to spread further over Chuck's shoulders and back, and he shuddered.

"What's it gonna be?" Chuck asked, extending the gun an inch closer to the man and lowering it to point directly into his belly.

The man sighed and lowered his rifle, then put it on the ground and shrugged. He started towards the sinkhole and, over his shoulder, said, "Have it your way. We'll go talk to her."

Chuck hollered at the man to stop, but the man in the robe continued to walk. Chuck followed him up the ridge, and at the crest, Chuck stopped. Another man in a robe, probably the same man Chuck had seen, or at least he hoped, was placing wood into a small fire at the edge of the sinkhole. He looked up at the pair and continued his work. The fire was surrounded by intricate, multi-colored patterns drawn around it with what looked like chalk or colored sand. Some of the geometric patterns had circles at the intersections filled with candles or piles of coins. There were two circles much larger than the rest. Inside one was a single copper-colored coin twice the size of a half-dollar. Inside the other was some kind of statue about a foot tall made of stone, wood, and feathers. As Chuck moved closer, he thought it was supposed to be a woman and noticed sparkling green jewels where the eyes should be.

"Who else is out here? Cause all of you have to collect your things and go. You can do your spells or whatever on your own land..."

"I already told you. It's not yours anymore. It's hers," said one of the men in the robes, and he pointed into the sinkhole.

A rope ladder hung in the hole near where the man had been. Chuck said, "Who else is here?"

Both men shrugged. Chuck raised the gun at the man by the fire and motioned him away. When both men stood back, Chuck rounded the sinkhole so he could watch them and take a look down without being bum-rushed. The sun wasn't high enough to light up the chamber all the way to the bottom, but what Chuck could see baffled him. A giant ivory snake clung to the far wall of the sinkhole. Chuck could only see what he judged to be the top half, and it was at least ten feet long and as big around as his thigh. As he watched, the men in robes fell to their knees and began chanting. The snake was making fast progress to the top, undulating in long curls, when Chuck saw something extra forming at the front of the creature. Chuck looked away and then back and saw not only what looked to be salamander-like legs but also a head growing more angular. He began to raise the gun when he heard a whistle and saw both men in robes holding him at gunpoint.

"I tried to tell ya," one of them said. "It's your turn to drop the gun again. But don't worry, we'll make it fair. We'll give you a head start."

Chuck looked back at the shifting thing in the hole. Its length had shortened, but the legs at the front were almost fully formed, and the head was unmistakable. It was becoming a crocodile. And then it lifted its head towards Chuck and winked.

"Drop the gun, man," the other said. "You are making it too easy."

A shot was fired, and Chuck heard it whiz past his head. He looked at the men, and though the gunshot had deafened him temporarily, he could tell they were both shouting the word, "Run."

And so he did. Chuck dropped the gun and ran as fast as he could up the hill. Looking back at the sinkhole as he dropped over the ridge to the other side, he saw both men watching him with guns at their sides. Then, almost entirely transformed, the creature made a final push out of the hole and dashed in his direction at a speed that made Chuck's stomach drop to his balls. Chuck ran out of control, nearly tripping several times down the hill, but managed by some miracle to stay right-side-up. He wanted to look back when he reached the game trail but could hear, or thought he could, something behind him. And he didn't want to risk losing even a second of a lead. Sweat poured into his eyes, and an invisible rope tightened around his ribs, but pushing through the pain, he hit the game trail at full speed. He kept the pace until the honeysuckle bush, where he cut hard left into the dense woods. He continued for another twenty yards, slowed, and lost his footing on an exposed root of a large live oak. Exhausted and out of breath, with his heart beating alarmingly fast, Chuck was sure he was going to have a heart attack. He felt every second of his sixty-nine years; helpless and face down on the ground as the adrenaline rush was wearing off. Finally, with the last bit of energy he could muster, he freed himself from the backpack and rolled over onto his back. Looking up through the branches of the live oak, he could see the baby-blue sky above and a tiny puff of cloud trying to grow, drifting slowly from east to west.

As his heart rate slowed, his fear refocused back from internal to external threats. He imagined when he sat up, he would be face to face with the crocodile, mouth open with bits of flesh skewered by its teeth like bloody rags resting on its hideous gums. Or the snake would be wound up like an oversized rattler waiting to strike. It would wink at him again just before biting him in the face and crushing him into goo. But neither happened. All he saw when he could sit was the honeysuckle bush still filled with bees at the edge of the game trail and a gray squirrel leaping into the brush behind it. He could see thirty yards through the trees from where he sat, and the woods were quiet. He took his phone from his pocket and managed to find Marion at the top of his contacts list and hit the call button. With each ring, his hope fell further until he heard her voice. For a split second, he thought he had reached her in person, but it was only her voice message notice. He spoke immediately after the beep, describing what he had seen, and then he heard something behind him. He turned and dropped the phone.

A tall naked woman was standing there and moving closer to him. Her jade skin glowed faintly and reflected the sunlight light where it shone on her through the windblown leaves above. Her goldish-green eyes were locked on his, but her face was in constant motion. At first, her features seemed Asian, but as her nose, cheekbones, and forehead shifted, she appeared African. The transitions continued, and all of her faces were beautiful and captivating. For a moment, her beauty distracted him both from the horror of the shifting and from noticing she was not walking but floating towards him as if she were being pushed by a current in the water. The woman smiled at Chuck as she got closer. Her inhumanity, the painted false smile of a geisha paired with the emotionless reptile eyes broke his stillness. But not before she had him in her grip.

10

Marion woke to the sound of her cell phone ringing in the kitchen and rolled over with an annoyed grunt. She closed her eyes again and tried to fall back to sleep but knew she wouldn't be able to. Marion envied people who could go to sleep the minute their head hit the pillow and stay or return to dreamland while hitting snooze after snooze on their clock radio or phone. Those were the same people, she thought, who could take a nap without it leaving them feeling disoriented and half-drunk. She had never been one of those people. Her brain was like a frantic puppy. The second it sensed consciousness, it leaped to work and demanded attention. She put out an arm and felt for Chuck but found flat sheets and a bunched-up banket instead. She thought he'd be on the patio, probably reading news on the computer, but he wasn't there either. She poured herself a cup from the still-warm coffee maker, put her phone in the pocket of her nightgown, and walked outside into the garden. Like any other morning, she sat at a wrought-iron table, sipped coffee, and woke up while taking stock of her plants. That morning she enjoyed the colors of the blooming marigolds and zinnias. The Goliath sunflowers were pretty too, but their huge heads had already fallen over like moping children. Also, like children, they grew up too fast. The sweet aroma of rosemary and basil came to her in waves as the shifting breeze alternated direction. The sky overhead was robin-egg blue with few clouds, but she could see dark ones in the east and decided to wait a while before grabbing the water can. Mother nature might help her with the chores today, she thought. After a while, she remembered the phone call and saw it had been from Chuck, and the messaging app was blinking and showed a "1."

Marion heard a computer voice say, "You have one new message," and she hit "7" before the robot could continue. It was Chuck's voice, but he sounded panicked and out of breath. "Marion. There are people here doing some kind of witchcraft. They have idols and strange drawings on the ground. I didn't see Evalyn, but they are with her group or cult or whatever. They have guns, baby. I'm going to call the sheriff now, but I had to warn you first. And there is something else. Some kind of monster...and..." And then there was a clunk and silence. Marion held the phone to her ear while she ran into the house and locked the door behind her before looking out the kitchen window. No one coming yet. She hit the speaker button on the phone and put it on the counter while rummaging through a junk drawer for a scrap of paper and a pen. Listening to the silence on the voice-mail message, she wrote one of her own. When she was done, she took the note and phone with her to the hallway and pulled the attic string with her free hand. The folded stairs came down with a springy clang, and little puffs of ancient pink insulation floated down from the empty hole. She sprinted up the creaky wooden stairs one-handed and in the dark but found what she was looking for. She had stashed it under some old magazines close to the entrance just in case she had to do what she was doing now.

Just after coming down the ladder, she heard something else from the phone. It was far off and slight, but it was, without a doubt, Chuck. And it was a scream. She hung up on voice mail, sent a quick text before pocketing the phone, and ran back to the kitchen window to scan the yard again. Seeing no movement, she risked the outside and took the object she had retrieved from the attic to the garage. Running back to the house, she heard the four-wheeler.

She bolted to her bedroom and grabbed a ceremonial knife from her bedroom drawer. After catching her breath, she ran to the kitchen and looked out the same window as before. Two men in orange robes pulled into the backyard. She texted once more and looked again. They would be at the door in a matter of seconds. She spun around and tripped over a kitchen chair and went to the floor. She dropped the knife when she went down. It came to rest between the refrigerator and cabinets. She got to her feet and nearly bent down to grab it, but when she heard the men yelling just outside, she bolted.

The kitchen door crashed open as she ran down the hallway. She slid sideways past the attic stairs and into the bedroom. The window there was unlocked, and if she could reach it before they got to her, there was a chance she could outrun them to the garage, and she could escape. She pulled back the curtains and started to raise the window when she saw one of them in the yard staring at her. He pulled a gun and ran towards the window.

She could hear the other one stomping up the attic steps. She took a deep breath and busted out of the bedroom. She slid past the attic stairs and, in one fluid motion, folded them flat and pushed up. The stairs slammed shut, and she ran to the front door and opened it. She saw the man in the robe at the same time as she heard the gunshot. He moved from the side of the house to the front in a flash, flanking the front door, and she had no choice but to run back in for cover. She went for the bedroom first. But as she started down the hall, the other man fell from the attic opening along with shards of broken steps and cotton candy-sized chunks of insulation. Shifting course, she ran to the kitchen instead. The gunman outside fired again. The bullet punched through a side window a foot in front of her and into the refrigerator's freezer section.

"The sheriff is on his way! You're going to get caught," Marion yelled, standing in place, corralled in the kitchen. *I was just in the bedroom and could have taken the 9mm from Chuck's nightstand. Why didn't I think of that?* Marion admonished herself with wrenching regret. But she had opted for flight over fight and had been laser-focused on escape. Besides, she hadn't fired a gun in at least ten years and was a terrible shot even then. If the man had been on the other side of the house when she got to the window, it would not have mattered. But he had been there, and now she was surrounded. Then Marion remembered the knife.

She was kneeling to pick it up when the man who had been in the attic rounded the corner.

"Stand up and show me your hands," he said.

She tossed the phone under the fridge in a subtle motion but otherwise stayed where she was for a moment, crouched down with her back facing him and one arm in the space between the refrigerator and cabinets.

"Stand up and show me your hands right now," he said louder.

Marion stood up and turned around with both hands raised. She looked at the hand closest to the refrigerator, opening and closing it as if it were a nervous tick.

"Turn around and put your hands behind your back," he said.

She was shocked. She didn't think there was a chance in hell it would work, but it had. It had worked on him just like it had worked on her. When Casey was a boy learning magic, one of his first tricks was a simple routine with a coin and a pen he made disappear and reappear. She had been so impressed she asked him to tell her how it was done. At first, he stuck with the old "a magician never reveals his secrets" line, but he had been so excited it had worked so well, that he eventually relented and agreed that just once, he'd let her in on the secret. The hard part of the trick, which took some practiced dexterity, was the sleight of hand bit; certain grips and moves hide the coin and make it reappear. But the misdirection is what sold the trick. Casey told her if he looked at something, she would too. People are drawn to movement. When he did the trick for her again, she didn't catch all his moves, but she caught enough. And she was amazed at how easy it had been to trick people. But just like Casey's trick, the misdirection was the easy part. The hard part would be the execution of the sleight of hand.

The man in the robe had asked for her to stand up and show her hands. Marion complied with both requests but not in the order the man had commanded. When her hands went behind her back, the knife slid down her right sleeve, and she caught it by the hilt and pulled it all the way free with her left hand. The man moved closer to her, and as she turned around, she spun fast and slashed at him with the knife. It struck him in the arm just above the elbow, and he let out a high-pitched yawl and dropped the gun. If the knife had been sharp, it would have cut him to the bone and severed tendons, but it wasn't made to be a real weapon. Still, it was heavy, and the attack had been swift and effective. She ran past him and down the hallway to the bedroom. She threw the window open and leaped out into the yard. Her ankle twisted when she landed on the grass, but she continued on, limping to the garage. Each step sent a new and slightly different sensation of pain to her. On the way to the garage side door, she had time to think she'd need to ask for some ice at the sheriff's office. But when she reached the door, the reflection of the man in the robe was growing fast. She didn't have time to form another thought before a white-hot blast of agony to the back of her head sent her into darkness.

11

Casey parked in the middle of the empty lot of the Red Lion. It was 10:30 in the morning, well before the bar opened for business. Even now, he had not yet made up his mind about breaking in. He knew he could. There was hardly a standard lock he could not compromise. But getting in was one thing; not getting caught was another. And he could disguise his hand movements well enough, but the place had cameras covering every angle on the outside. Marion had not called like she said she would, and she had ignored his texts that morning too. Instead of pushing it with her, he decided to try his luck with the folks at the Red Lion.

As he sat there weighing his options, an aging Toyota Tundra pickup pulled into the lot and parked in the closest space to the door. A skinny woman about forty years old hopped out wearing jean shorts and a red tank top. She started for the door before looking up and returning to the truck to put up the windows. Casey leaned forward and looked up through his windshield. Clouds were gathering. Good call, he thought. He watched her go to the imposing wooden doors at the bar entrance and fish a large key ring from her green canvas bag. The thick wooden doors were fifteen feet tall with rounded tops and planks arranged vertically to mimic what you might see on a castle. With a grunt, she unlocked and swung the doors open, latching each to the face of the building using hooks and chains. A standard glass and metal door stood behind. She opened it with little effort and slipped inside.

Casey scrambled out of his car and to the door. He slipped through, and the woman, who was by the bar, walked fast towards him. "We ain't open yet. Shit, I forgot to lock it behind me."

As she drew closer, Casey recognized her. She was the woman with Marion. "I'm not here to drink. I'm worried about my friend…"

"Get on out. Come back at noon."

"You know her. Her name is Marion."

"I don't know anyone by that name. You need to leave."

Casey squinted at her. And moved to the alcove where he'd seen her disappear with Marion the day before. "I saw you with her yesterday. Right here. She ran when the deputy came.

The woman darted to the alcove and positioned herself between Casey and the hidden door. "I'm sorry, but you are mistaken. I'm going to need you to go."

"I know how Amy died, but I don't understand it. I think you and Marion know what's going on, and I'm not leaving until you tell me something. Marion isn't returning my calls or texts. And I identified myself to ole ZZ Top yesterday before you two zoomed out of here like a bat out of hell. You know who I am."

The woman released a long breath. "You must be Casey."

He nodded.

She stepped past him and locked the door. "Alright then. I'm Nina. Follow me."

The interior of the Red Lion was modeled after a medieval hunting lodge. Suits of armor inset into the walls flanked the central seating area. And an elevated section with booths separated by plush red velvet fabric lined the far and near walls. An ornate wooden railing divided those sections from the rest of the seating. A small stage was against the other wall opposite the large, dark wooden wrap-around bar. Four pool tables and two lanes for darts were in an alcove near the entrance. Several deer and boar heads hung near the top of the high walls alongside neon Schlitz, Budweiser, and Miller Lite signage. A large chandelier made from antlers and metal hung from the ceiling in the center of the room. Three dozen half-burned-down candles looked to be stuck in place with wax and decades-old dust. Casey hadn't noticed the detail on his first visit. That night the lights had been low. With all the interior lights on, it felt like a different place altogether. She motioned him to the bar where he took a seat on one of the plush red stools, and she rounded behind.

Nina pulled two short glasses down from a rack above her and poured a generous shot of Wild Turkey in each. She pushed one in front of Casey and said, "You might need this." Nina threw back her drink before reaching into her bag and drawing out a small, folded piece of paper. She placed it on the bar.

"First off, I don't know who Amy even is, but me and-what did you call him? 'ole ZZ Top,' do know why Marion isn't calling you back. Did you hear any gunshots this mornin'?"

"Gunshots? No. But I live next to a hunting camp. My brain doesn't register distant gunshots anymore."

Nina filled her glass again and sighed. "This ain't easy, you know," she said, taking the shot and grimacing. "Shit. We talked about how a day might come when our little conspiracy could matter, but I never thought it would really happen. But it has. And congratulations, Mr. Sparks, you've drawn the shittiest hand of the bunch."

Casey looked at her and waited for her to come out with some revelation, but she just looked at him, shook her head, and poured another shot. Casey grabbed her glass and slid it away. "Can we back up, please? I'm pretty good with cards, so maybe everything isn't lost."

"Marion and Chuck are," she said. "I can't say they are dead, but then again, I can't say they ain't either."

Casey stared at her. She started to speak but handed him her phone instead. The text message app was open to the screen with the history of texts between her and Marion. She pointed at the conversation from earlier in the morning.

Marion: They've taken Chuck and are coming.

Marion: They are here. If I don't respond or contact you soon, you know what to do.

Nina: Are you there?

Nina: Please tell me it's a joke.

Nina: If I don't hear back, I'll do it.

Casey flicked the messaging app away and went to her contacts and found Marion. The number was right.

He put the phone on the bar and picked up the whiskey. He examined the color and put it down. *I've had too much of this shit already this week*, he thought.

Nina said, "She told me I could trust you. Is that true? Can I trust you with what I have to say, Casey Sparks?"

Casey felt a cold sweat break out on his face and chest. It was all too surreal. Yet deep down, he had known the stakes. Amy was dead, and he knew it for certain. And now Chuck and Marion were gone, maybe even dead too. He pushed away from the bar. Standing up and bracing himself with both hands, he said, "You can trust me with anything. I've known them both for most of my life. They've been like parents to me ever since my real ones died. I owe it to them."

Nina gave him a sad and sympathetic smile. The smile one gave to someone impossible to console or who soon will be once they understand how far into the shit they really were.

"Do you know who Evalyn is?"

"No."

"Wow. She really didn't tell you anything?"

"Who is she?"

"About fifteen years ago, Evalyn was a member of a coven with Marion and me. There were a couple dozen other people too. Mostly women. We met regularly for a couple years until one night she and Marion got into an argument. Evalyn wanted to try some things the others found unsettling, like blood magic, inviting spirits into their bodies, and working with negative thought forms. Heavy stuff that was way too advanced for the group and dangerous. Most of the rest of us were happy with basic healing spells and chanting. Hell, it was little more than a social club for a lot of the girls. When the split happened, most everyone sided with Marion. Only a small handful stayed with Evalyn."

"Fifteen years ago. What does that have to do with now?"

"Evalyn has been laying low ever since, but recently the trail cams caught an image of her on the hunting camp property."

The intruder, Casey thought.

"Marion told her to stay off the property, but Evalyn refused. And whatever she told her after that scared Marion enough to come talk to me about it. She was worried that whatever they were doing out there might be dangerous."

"And you think Evalyn is responsible?"

"Yes. Marion and I talked about what we would do in case they came after her."

"What do they want with Marion and Chuck?"

"I don't know about Chuck, but Marion is probably the only one as powerful as Evalyn. It could be that Evalyn simply wanted to get her out of the way. Marion must have found out what they were doing. She had some hunches and was researching."

"Have you called the sheriff?"

Nina frowned. "They are in on it. At least some of them are."

"I saw Marion bolt when she saw that deputy yesterday."

"He was asking me a lot of questions about her. My guess is he was trying to see if she was talking and if I knew anything. There is a small group of us in this area. We all know each other...at least the ones who go back a ways. If they suspected I was aware of anything, they'd probably disappear me too."

"My friend Amy died. Was killed actually by something unnatural...paranormal."

"How do you know that?"

Casey recounted his story to Nina.

They sat staring at each other for a long time.

Nina broke the silence. "Marion told me she suspected they were trying to summon an entity, though she didn't know which one. And they were doing it in the woods at the hunting camp because of some unique feature on the property. I don't know what that could be. Lay lines, maybe. At any rate, it was something dark. What happened to your friend could certainly be related somehow."

"If we can't go to the sheriff, what do we do?

"We gotta fight fire with fire, as the sayin' goes. Marion was supposed to be gathering some things to bring to me tonight for safekeeping, but they got to her first. If she had found out what Evalyn was doing and had time, she would have hidden the information at her house. That was part of our plan. If we can find that, we can try to counteract their magic with ours."

"Then what?"

"I'm still working it out. There are others Marion and I know who might have the answers, but we don't know for sure who we can trust. "Nina picked up the folded piece of paper and held it in front of her. "Speaking of trust, Marion left this for you. She told me you could tell me what it says without looking. She said all you had to do was touch it. If anyone else told me that, I would call them crazy. But she believes you are the real thing. Will you tell me what's on the paper?"

Casey plucked the paper from Nina's hands, hoping to see the word, but had a vision instead. He was sitting in one of the red chairs in Marion's office. Two men in orange robes pulled books off the shelves one by one, inspected the spines, and tossed them on the floor. Another man kicked over the desk and the chair next to the one Casey was sitting in. When the two men had worked through nearly half of the books, a light glare swept across the room, and one of the men ran to the window, and then both of them left the room.

"I don't think they have it yet," Casey said, dropping the page. "Evalyn's followers left in a hurry."

"What did the paper say."

"It said, 'Go Braves.'"

"How?"

Casey shrugged. "No telling. It happens at random. I saw a kind of scene this time," he said. Casey felt a rush of energy. "Let's go see."

"Hold your horses. We can't go right now."

"Why the hell not? You know I'm who Marion said I am, and they have our friends," Casey said. Nina kept shaking her head.

"If we go rushing in, I'm certain they'd take us. Evalyn is dangerously crazy, but she isn't stupid."

"We could take guns. My roommate has an arsenal at the trailer..."

"We can't risk it. We are the only ones who can do the ritual."

"I don't even know anything about spells or rituals."

"Maybe not, but Marion said you might have a big part to play in all this. She said you might be the only one who could end it."

"I can't play a part if we sit around and do nothing. Amy Gale was last seen at my trailer, and you and I both know they aren't going to find her, not alive anyway. And with every passing day, they'll be under more pressure to solve it. If I'm not already suspect *numero uno*, I will be soon. Plus, they'll find out about Chuck and Marion being gone before too long, and if they are as corrupt as you say, I'll take the fall for that too. Unless, of course, we can get them back. You said Marion might have hidden some things?"

"Marion told me if she had to get out in a hurry, she'd stash some things in the garage. Things we'd need for the spell. And also, I think she would have hidden her phone somewhere. She would have wanted to protect both of us from those psychos. They have all the advantages right now. If you can find the phone, we can have some confidence they don't know we're working to stop them. She and I kept our recent communications a secret, knowing something like this might happen, but if my name comes up, they'll know where to find me. And they will."

"I'll wait until it's full dark but not a minute later. And you should stay here. It would be suspicious if you took off."

"Agreed. It's better to stay separated. Good luck."

"Thanks. I better get out of here before the crowd shows up. I'll let you know how it goes."

12

Casey was ten yards into the woods, walking horizontally to Rabbit Run Road in a deluge of rain. The storm system, which earlier in the day caused light rain, had grown in the west and become a moderate rainmaker by the afternoon. By evening the storm was producing hail and dropping tornadoes two counties over. And the whole thing was supposed to continue strengthening and get to Cherry Hill within an hour. He was halfway to Marion's house when he thought he noticed lights and prepared himself to dash towards the road if the lights seemed to organize into strings. They could have been reflections of a moon peeking between clouds, shimmering in bursts off the raindrops and collected puddles, or they may be imaginary. Every few steps, he wiped his face with the inside of his t-shirt and rescanned the area.

Casey felt the hair on his arms stand up, and he dove to the ground. An instant later, a bolt of lightning slammed into a pine tree and lit up the woods in stark white. Bits of charred wood and chunks of the tree rained down around him as he lay on the wet ground, his whole body tingling from the close strike. Before he pushed himself up, he saw headlights from the road and stayed put as two trucks passed his position. He waited to see if the taillights brightened, but neither did. So he quickened his pace the rest of the way to the house; jellyfish be damned.

From the edge of the woods, Casey briefly watched the property for movement. He saw none and, eager to be out of the woods, made his move. He took a deep breath and darted from the woods, mud splattering everywhere, making the twenty feet to the back of the garage in a flash. He pressed his back to the structure like a man standing on the ledge of a tall building and tried to listen. His ears, still ringing from the lightning, heard nothing but the rain flooding down from the garage and the sounds of the dozens of tiny waterfalls formed in channels from the folds in the metal roof. Each string of water dug its own hole in the dirt and added its own tune to the symphony of noise.

Casey crept to the corner of the shed and peeked again at the house. The side garage door faced the house. Instead of running, Casey snuck there, choosing silence and stealth over speed and viewability. Casey was decked out in the darkest clothes he had: a dark-red backpack, a pair of black dress pants, black Doc Martin boots, and an inside-out Widespread Panic band t-shirt. Casey was surprised to find it was the only black shirt he owned. Casey slipped around the corner to the door. He looked into the garage from an angle through the four-paned glass window and saw it was dark. He tried the knob. It was locked.

Casey looked both ways as if checking traffic and sneaked across the yard to the side of the house. He knelt under the bedroom window and noticed something above him move. He had to hold back a yell and was about to run when he realized it wasn't a hand, just the flapping wet end of a curtain someone had closed outside the window. Casey settled himself, moved to the front of the house, and slipped behind a huge azalea bush. He was moving to the second one when another truck barreled down the road. It came so fast, Casey had time only to freeze in place. A red glow lit his face as the truck tapped the brakes at the curve in the road. Casey had time to think he must look like the world's largest opossum, holding still with eyes wide, caught rooting around a flower bed. If the truck stopped, though, he would not play dead. Best not to stretch the impression quite that far. When it was gone, Casey crept to the third bush and hunted around the flower bed with both hands. He began to worry they had moved it, but just when he was about to try another spot, his hand felt the fake rock half-buried at the base of the unkept azalea bush. He slid the bottom hatch open and plucked out the house key. It was attached to an oval Disney World key chain with a picture of Cinderella's Castle on one side and a green witch holding out an apple on the other.

After backtracking, he opened the garage side door and walked in. Both vehicles were parked in place, and the rest of the space was filled with standard outdoor equipment. Chuck had made shelves for the garage too. Each held items specific to certain activities. It was a degree of organization foreign to Casey, and he had no idea where to start looking. He unzipped his backpack, fished inside a garbage bag, and found his phone. The garbage bag had saved it from being soaked like everything else inside. Casey opened his phone, put a finger over the bulb, and searched one side, letting only the tiniest beam of light escape. He found nothing. On the other side, the light revealed a long brown snake crawling on a tarp in the gardening area. When he jumped, his finger slipped off the bulb, and intense light filled the room. If someone were in the house looking in his direction, Casey would be caught. But he let it shine a moment longer because he was not entirely wrong about the snake. It had been a snake, but not when Casey saw it. It was the shed skin of what was probably a rat snake. But more importantly, it sat atop a box covered with a dusty blue tarp with handprints on top. Casey blocked the light again and reached under the corner of the tarp where the prints were. He imagined grasping the writhing owner of the skin on top and screaming but was relieved when his hand found a small box instead. He retrieved it and looked at it in the light. On top was a yellow post-it note with "For C" written in Marion's handwriting. There was a small lock on the front that Casey knew he could open with just about any bit of thin metal, but instead of wasting time, he put it in the garbage bag in the backpack and moved to the house.

The screen around the back porch had been misted by the rain. Tiny drops of water were trapped in the squares, making it impossible to see through from the outside. Still, Casey opted to approach the house from the back anyway. For one thing, there was more cover there. And for another, it was closer to the woods. *There may be monsters out there, but they don't know the place like I do*, he thought. If he had to make a run for it, the closer to the woods, the better. The patio was abandoned, and the kitchen door was locked. He used the key, but before opening the door, he stood under the relative protection of the awning and took off his boots. He stuffed them in his backpack outside of the garbage bag and slipped inside.

The quiet in the house was unsettling. He could hear the rain, which had grown even heavier, but there was no other sound. Not a single light shone aside from the green glow of the microwave clock. He fingered the bullet hole in the refrigerator and followed the path with his eyes. Small shards of glass glimmered on the breakfast table next to gently moving curtains. The usual earthy scent of fresh herbs was present. He moved to the counter where

Marion kept her phone charging but found only the cord.

He walked without the phone light to the living room but turned it on his phone, careful to keep his finger over the bulb, to search the room for Marion's cell phone. He did the same in the hallway and nearly screamed again when he stepped on a sharp piece of splintered wood and fell forward against the remains of the attic stairs. He limped to the bedroom and looked in the closet and under the bed but found nothing of use. The thought occurred to him he could simply call the phone. After all, if they had taken it, they would already know he and Marion had been in contact. So, he sat on the bed and dialed her number. At first, the call did not seem to go through. He heard only silence on the line. But when the first ring sounded, his stomach lurched. What if someone else answered? What if they were in the house now? He listened to the ringing with one ear and tried to listen around the house with the other but heard only the sound of rain and the *tap, tap, tap* of small hailstones hitting the windows. When her voice mail message played, he disconnected the call, waited thirty seconds, and dialed again. This time, he limped to each room to listen, and in the last room, the kitchen, he heard something. A slight buzzing noise from the refrigerator, or more precisely, under it. He reached down and was just able to pull it free by the ends of his fingers. Then he heard something else.

It was slight but unmistakable. First, one car door closing, then another, then another. Casey crept to the broken window and saw the truck in the driveway. It had pulled in without lights. And three figures were jogging to the kitchen door. Casey scuttled across the floor to the hallway and into Marion's office. His vision of the room had been exact. He knew it would be. It made him angry. It was one thing to hear they were gone. It was another to be in the wrecked house and know for sure.

The room had been tossed. Only one red chair with dragon carvings and the two armoires stood upright. He pulled the skeleton keys from both armoires and took off his backpack. He placed the backpack inside one and stepped in after. Once inside, he turned the latch to lock himself inside and wedged a key against the wood to keep it in place. Less than a minute later, the overhead light in the room switched on and a woman's voice, harsh but quiet, said, "What's wrong with you?" and the light switched off again.

Passing flashlights occasionally brightened the cracks inside the armoire door. And the thuds must have been books being thrown about, Evalyn's crew checking covers and tossing aside those which didn't match what they were looking for. This went on for what felt like half an hour, though Casey knew it had only been a few minutes. When he heard a faint man's voice call Evalyn from another room, the sounds stopped. Casey slowly pressed his ear against the door of the armoire, desperate to hear some sounds to tell him where they were, but there was only silence. Then all at once, something sharp jammed into the space between the doors and started to turn. Casey held the key tightly in place, and the little bar kept the doors together. Inches from him, a man groaned, struggling with whatever tool he was using. He gave up for a moment, and a light shone through the keyhole. Again, the object was thrust through the opening. This time, the wood gave a little more, and the glow of the light revealed the hunting knife. The blade twisted and tore away splinters from the door just above where he held the locking bar in place with the key. Again and again, the man tried to pry open the doors, but Casey held firm. On one attempt, the man thrust the knife in all the way to the hilt, and Casey felt warmth on his stomach. He didn't know how bad the cut was, but after a moment, he felt the pain along with the blood, which was still flowing and starting to warm the top of his left thigh.

Casey made himself as flat as possible against the back of the armoire as the man repeatedly tried to open the door. As suddenly as it had started, it stopped. But right away, he heard the same sound from the other side of the room, then ripping and crashing sounds as the doors of the other armoire were torn open, and the contents were strewn about the room. The man returned to what Casey was now thinking might be his starter coffin, and the knife shot through, not the middle opening, but from one of the sides by the hinges. The man pried, and Casey could see the bottom of the door giving way. He felt the left door sag and saw the knife go in at the top. It was just a matter of seconds before the door would give way. Casey waited for the door to fall and was about to push the other door with everything he had when Evalyn shouted from the other room: "Got it!"

The knife was withdrawn, and Casey felt the armoire being kicked or punched and then lesser noises of people talking in another room. After a while, that sound faded, and all that was left was the sound of rain and the louder *knock, knock, knock* of large hailstones hitting the windows hard. Casey waited there in the dark for a long time. He didn't press his ear against the door again. He thought the bleeding had stopped, but his stomach was throbbing and sore. Between the bleeding and the darkness, Casey was having trouble keeping his balance. When he thought he might pass out, he dropped the key and let himself out into the study. The chair was no longer standing, and nearly every book was on the ground. The smell of burnt paper hung in the air. The pain in his foot had been superseded by the pain in his stomach, and he could no longer sneak effectively. The best he could manage was a sort of controlled stumble, which he performed to the hallway and then to the kitchen. The truck was gone, and he pulled out a chair in the kitchen, but before he could sit, he fell against the refrigerator and slid down into a seating position. He had two thoughts then. The first was it was going to be a hell of a walk back to the trailer, and the second was that the others had found the spell, he thought. *They beat me to it.*

The feeling of lightheadedness slowly subsided, and Casey tried to stand again. He was able to support himself with the refrigerator and worked his way up. Before he left, he had to see what had burned. He found flipped furniture and the couch cushions strewn about the living room. And in the fireplace, a smoke-stained spine and part of the back cover were the only remains of one thick leather-bound book. The rest had burned away to ash. Casey knelt and risked using the flash to take a picture of the back cover. He could discern distinctive markings on that piece. The spine, however, was unrecognizable. He stood and noticed Chuck's laptop on the ground between the patio and living room. The screen had been broken. Casey picked it up and stuck it in the garbage bag. He was no expert, but he knew you could pluck a hard drive out of a computer, broken screen or not.

On his long, wet, and painful hike back to the trailer, the thought he had over and over was, *Please don't let them have the spell.*

13

Sheriff Johnson ordered "the usual" at the counter of Fred's Fine Foods and put $6.50 on the counter. A young woman scooped up the cash and put the two quarters in a tin coffee can with a napkin taped to it with "tips" written in red magic marker. She handed him a large sweet tea and a receipt, and he walked to the front window to look out over the central lawn of the town square. The view had been much the same twenty-five years prior when he first started with the department. Only the names of the stores had changed. As the town had declined and most of the businesses folded, the ones who could stay open moved locations to the front of the square. It was important to keep up appearances. A visitor to town could be excused from mistaking Cherry Hill for a prosperous little hamlet if they only drove on Main Street and never looked down any side roads.

The highlight of the downtown area was the Maubila County government complex, the largest building in the county. The three-story red brick building on the north side of the square filled the entire block. It featured limestone columns and a broad set of steps leading to an oversized set of entry doors. The sheriff's department and jail were on the first floor. The other two floors housed the county commission, a courtroom, and various other legal, administrative, and bureaucratic offices.

"Order up," said the woman at the counter.

The sheriff thanked her, took the warm brown bag, and walked outside. Sometimes, on nice days in the fall and spring, he would settle onto a wrought-iron bench to eat lunch in the shade of one of the two old live oaks on either end of the park. The trees had grown so large; the canopies created by the wandering moss-covered limbs had grown together and shaded most of the square. The sheriff would watch cardinals and blue jays fly among the branches while he ate and would hold back bits of bread from his burger bun to feed the squirrels when he was finished. It was a nice place to think in peace. He supposed the square being deserted most of the time was at least one benefit of the town shrinking. Silver linings and all.

Once a year in the fall, the fourth-grade class at Cherry Hill Elementary would come to the square on a field trip as part of their Alabama History class. They would gather in the center of the square around a statue of the town founder, Adolphus Bedsole. The sheriff had seen it many times and silently relished in the lesson. The teacher would extol the virtues of the man, depicted in stone as a young, muscular fellow sitting on a horse while holding a sword aloft in one hand and pointing westward with the other. The inscription on the original copper plaque, now worn and sporting a green patina, was from John L. O'Sullivan's "The Great Nation of Futurity." It read, "All this will be our future history, to establish on earth the moral dignity and salvation of man -- the immutable truth and beneficence of God." The teacher would read the inscription aloud as the disinterested children fidgeted and yawned. She would then ask if anyone had questions. She rarely had any takers. They would move on to the government complex, and Sheriff Johnson would laugh to himself. It wasn't his job to correct the teachers, so he never did. But what the kids were not told was that Adolphus Bedsole had not resembled a chiseled warrior Adonis. In fact, he was nearly as wide as he was tall. And the other thing, left out for a much better reason, was Adolphus Bedsole had died just two weeks after founding the city. After striking out to conquer the West, most of Bedsole's body had been found washed up on the shores of Bassett Creek near Salipta, along with the bodies of his four traveling companions. The Choctaw Adolphus encountered must have had something other than being forcibly moved to Oklahoma in mind when they learned about "moral dignity" and "immutable truth" from the first-generation German immigrant.

The sheriff took his time walking through the square, taking in the few fallen branches and new litter of leaves and moss shaken loose by the hail and wind storm the night before. The town had been largely spared any catastrophic damage, but several trailers had been flipped in the north part of the county, and a young couple had died when a tree fell on the truck they had sought refuge in. It had been a busy night for the sheriff and his crew. He was nearly through the square when he saw a shiny black Lincoln Towncar pull in front of the government building. The man who got out resembled the real Adolphus Belsole far more than the statue. He wore a black suit with a red tie and matching suspenders. In his breast pocket, a white handkerchief poked out. Its bunched-up appearance and Reverend Gale's red face contrasted with his crisp sleeves and pressed pleats in his dress pants. The sheriff thought the handkerchief must have been working extra duty in the July heat. He wondered why the reverend insisted on the jacket even in the sweltering summer when most of the congregants could not even be bothered to wear ties to the services. Still, he appreciated the man's dedication to formality and could relate.

Reverend Gale spotted Sheriff Johnson and waited for him at the base of the steps. When he was within earshot, the reverend extended a hand, and the sheriff shook it.

"Has there been any word about my Amy?"

"I'm sorry to say, we don't have any new information yet, but we are still interviewing people and have a tail on the young man we believe she was seeing."

The reverend patted his face with the handkerchief and motioned up the steps without a word.

Cold air rushed out of the large doors when they entered. The deputies at the metal detectors waved the sheriff and reverend through even after they both set off the alarm. The men continued to the sheriff's office. Framed commendations and department awards from the state dating back twenty-five years, all in matching black frames, lined the walls in neat rows. A computer monitor and keyboard sat on a small desk against one wall. The sheriff's primary desk, a shiny cherry number, was bare except for a single picture of his wife and a small brass placard that read, "Maubila County Sheriff, Larry M. Johnson."

The reverend sat down and started immediately: "Have you searched for her at all? Other than asking questions and following that boy Tommy around, I mean. I know this isn't a normal thing around these parts, but if you don't think you are up for the job, I'm sure the state police or the FBI would be happy to take it over."

The sheriff sat and looked at the man for a moment before responding. It actually wasn't uncommon, not really. A lot of people go missing in the country. Most kids are found lost in the woods or hiding at a friend's house. Most adults are too, for that matter, if by "lost" you meant "hiding" and by "friend" you meant "secret lover." "We've questioned nearly all the people who attended the party where she was last seen, and no one saw anything suspicious. And no one seemed overly nervous."

"Overly?"

"People tend to get nervous around police, the innocent and the guilty. What's important is that everyone has cooperated with us so far."

"The man who threw the party? I understand he's not a Godly person."

"I spoke with him myself along with..."

"Did you search his house?"

"Yes, personally. A deputy and I looked through every room of the property. It's a small single-wide trailer. The search was thorough..."

"My congregation is very concerned this may be connected to those missing fishermen. There are rumors we may have an active serial killer in our town."

"There is no evidence of that. There isn't even evidence of foul play in Amy's disappearance. The odds are we'll find her safe and sound. That's usually true, despite what you see on the news, even when they have been abducted by strangers. Most are runaways..."

"Amy is no runaway," Reverend Gale said. He stood up and patted his forehead with his embroidered handkerchief. "What about her phone? You can track it. Can't you?"

"There was no tracking app on the phone, so we had to look at where her calls came from. The towers used can tell the location. Her last call was made about 8:00 PM the night before you reported her missing. She was somewhere in town.

"She wouldn't be without her phone if it were her choice. Have you seen any teenagers without phones stuck to their faces recently? No. Someone took her. You have to bring people into the station and interrogate them harder. Put the fear of God in them."

"I know you are upset..."

"You haven't seen upset yet. I'll have my people in the street in front of this place today with bullhorns and signs if you don't tell me what you are doing other than talking to people to find my daughter.

"We are putting together a search party to check out the woods over at the hunting camp where she was last seen. If your people are free today, you might urge some of them to volunteer. We can cover more ground with more people."

The reverend shot a purse-lipped glance at the sheriff and walked to the door. He turned around and said, "I'll have a group of people together in an hour.".

The sheriff nodded at the slamming door, opened the greasy brown bag on his desk, and popped a limp French fry into his mouth.

14

Throbbing pain in the back of her head and near-total darkness confused Marion when she opened her eyes. Panic set in. A shifting red glow from an unseen fire shone on a far wall, and a single thin line of sunlight extending from the roof to the surface of a puddle cast a shifting prism against another. Marion lost her balance trying to stand and reached out to brace herself. Both hands found the support of rough wooden poles. Upright she felt around the area and tried to push past one of the poles but found there were horizontally oriented ones too, and they were lashed to the upright ones. It took her a few moments of touching her surroundings for her foggy brain to understand she was trapped in a primitive cage in the sinkhole cave.

She felt at her body and the familiar silk nightgown. Reaching into the pockets, moving her hands absently, she hoped to find a nail file, pin knife, or any cutting tool but was not surprised to find both were empty. Marion knelt and felt at the floor, head swimming, but found nothing there either. Finally, putting a hand through a square of the cage and reaching out into the darkness for anything. One after the other, she searched, running her hands over the ground and finding only cold, wet stone. Halfway around, her hand bumped into something heavy, and she ran her fingers over the object like a blind person feeling someone's face. It was a gallon milk jug. And it was too large to fit through the gaps. She unscrewed the top and leaned close to the opening, smelling a subtle chlorine scent. Then she tipped the jug and drank three large gulps through the wooden bars before setting it upright and replacing the cap.

Through the next square, she found a large Ziplock bag, which just did fit, and she withdrew the contents after shifting to a more comfortable seated position on the hard stone ground. Two of them were Hershey's candy bars with almonds. She kept a few at her house and could feel the lumps in the chocolate through the wrapper. The other item was a bag of chips of some kind. She assumed her captors had grabbed these from her house as well. And if that was the case, they could be just about anything. Chuck went through chips as fast as he went through beer during baseball and football seasons and was undiscriminating about the brand or flavor. Whatever was on sale was what ended up in their pantry.

Marion scarfed down one of the candy bars and took another long draw of water. Back in a seated position, the foggy sensation lifted. Her head still hurt, and there was a lump there the size of an orange, but she was thinking more clearly. Standing no longer caused light-headedness. She felt at one of the lashings on the cave and began tracing the loops searching for an end. Finding one, working only by touch, she began to untie the thick twine. Broken fingernails twice caused her to stop working knots free, and both times she was able to muffle her cries. A third stoppage was not due to the pain but the faint echo of voices.

She struggled to make out the words from at least two of the voices, a man and a woman, deciphering an occasional "the" or "he" but no more. As the voices moved closer, shadows formed in the glow at the far end of the cave. Marion still could not make out the words but could tell from the rhythm and unison they had started to chant.

Marion went back to work on the lashing, tearing with her hands and scraping with her fingernails.

Her thoughts turned to the last time Evalyn had come after her. It had been after their fight over the direction of the coven. After most of the women had sided with Marion, Evalyn had seemed to go away for a while, but she had simply been waiting. Marion and her group had started meeting at another woman's house and on her land. Marion had assumed the woman was the owner of the property. But Evalyn had known she was renting. And so, about a month later, knowing it was a full moon and knowing the coven would be using the land for their circle, she had called the sheriff and reported a satanic cult was trespassing in the woods. The owner of the land had turned out to be a deacon at Cherry Hill Baptist and hadn't taken kindly to witches practicing on his property. He had pressed charges.

The sheriff had taken mugshots and fingerprinted all the women. None of them had had priors, and all of them had been bailed out by family that night. But it had left them mortified. What had happened the next day was much worse. They had all awoken to see the headline of their daily paper. *The Cherry Hill Register* had been in its last year of operation and desperate for a sensational story. Thanks to a certain unnamed source, who had claimed to have been a former member but left when she had found Jesus, the story had been filled with wild details of naked dancing in the moonlight, blood, and chants. According to the story, the sheriff had made it just in time to free the animals they had been preparing to sacrifice to finish summoning the devil. All of the women in the coven had been listed by name, and their mugshots had lined the front page over a graphic of an upside-down pentagram.

The embarrassment had been total. Two of the women had been fired from their jobs, and some of the others had moved away. Marion had found growing numbers of protesters crowding the entrance to her store. "Witches not Welcome," "Witches Go Home," and Marion's favorite because the misspelling seemed appropriately ignorant, "Satin Worshipers." *If one's entire life is ruled by a God with one adversary, you would think one would give enough thought and study to that scary entity to spell his name properly,* Marion thought. But it had not been about right and wrong. It had been about feeling self-righteous and stepping on other people to raise yourself up. That was what the church was mostly about in Marion's experience.

One day Marion had seen Evalyn with the church group holding a sign. Her's read, "Not In My Town." That had been the day Marion knew it was over. Not just the coven but her business too. She had folded a month later and was forced to go exclusively online. That had been bad, but now, finding herself in a cage in a dark cave, struggling to free herself, she wondered how much worse it would get.

A large knot came free, and a foot of twine unwove from one corner of the cage. She threw it aside, grabbed the horizontal pole in one hand and the vertical one in the other, and began pulling them apart. Both poles bent a few inches, but neither would give any further nor did her force generate a single crack. Out of energy, she let go. They made a loud clacking sound which echoed in the cave. The chanting stopped.

Marion knelt to the ground and felt for the twine while watching the glow. Shadows grew, then developed smaller forms. They moved closer as she brushed her hands frantically over the floor. Her left hand found the twine, and she wrapped it back around the poles and tucked the end into itself. It would be easy to pull it all back out later with little effort. She stepped back in the cage and waited for the shadows to move closer but noticed they had stopped. *They can't see me. I'm not backlit like they are. The noise could have been from a tree falling from the woods above. If I stay quiet, they will go back to the chanting.* She fixated on the shadows, and they waited for a long time, not moving. When they did start again, it was back to the glow.

When Marion heard the chanting start again, she moved to the next lashing and began to work on the net set of knots. Singularly focused on the task, through three of the lashings, she froze, noticing the chanting had stopped. The glow was still. No shadows moved in the spot of red. She let out a deep breath and saw something moving from the other side.

The object was the faint green color of glow-in-the-dark stars some children have on their ceilings or the bioluminescent algae that light up when you drag a toe in the sand at the beach at night. It drifted closer. And it was floating, not walking, even as Marion could start to make out a human shape. Closer still, she could see it was a woman's shape. Her long hair was weightless around her head, moving slowly as if submerged. But it was the feet that first made Marion scream. The woman's feet were half a foot off the ground, and her toes were pointed severely down. Her entire body leaned forward, naked and shimmering. Ten feet away, under her translucent green skin, Marion could see strings of multicolored lights running through her like blood through veins. She thought of Casey's jellyfish and shuttered.

The woman floated to the cage until her forehead struck one of the poles, and she bounced back a few inches before coming to rest at a stationary albeit bobbing position. She raised an arm and pulled back the hair that had been covering her face. Every feature except the eyes shifted shape, a slow but impossible chameleon of a face that couldn't settle on a disguise. The eyes shone goldish-green and fixed on Marion.

It spoke to Marion then, but only to her mind. The mouth, ever-shifting, did not open.

Why are you trying to kill me?

Marion pushed herself hard against the back wall of the cage, speechless.

The green woman tilted her head. No emotion showed on her face or could be detected in her voice.

Who else knows I'm here? she said into Marion's head.

Marion tried to look away from the eyes, but they held her somehow, even when she turned her head away. Somehow they held her.

"I don't know who you are. No one knows you are here. Please let me go," Marion said, looking away, but somehow not. The face had shifted, and masculine features came through. The body remained female, but the faces were male.

Marion felt a cold ooze seep through the nightgown on her shoulder, and she snapped her head back at the green thing and screamed.

It was inside the cage with her with an arm on her shoulder. Its mouth was open and growing. Marion could see rows of pointed, shark-like teeth erupting from bleeding gums. And she heard the question again: Who else knows I'm here?

This time there was anger in the voice, and Marion wanted to answer the question. A part of her had to. And she would have had the creature been patient. But when it yelled again and violently gnashed its teeth together inches from Marion's face, Marion lost consciousness instead.

15

Casey pulled through the open sliding gate next to the Red Lion Lounge, and Nina pushed it back into place. She snapped the Master Lock on the chain and watched for traffic until he had pulled all the way around back. There was none. They went inside through the back door, and without turning on the lights, Nina waved Casey past the bar to the front. These must be the new safety protocols, Casey thought.

"Where are we going?" he said.

"Upstairs."

Just inside the front entrance, Nina moved a tall potted plant away from the wall and pushed against a section of the wood paneling. It gave way an inch or two, clicked, and swung open. Casey smiled. He had been looking for a button or lever. But it was simpler. Sometimes simple was better.

Inside, Casey could just make out a narrow spiral staircase. Nina put out an arm like a server seating guests at a restaurant, and Casey started up the stairs. When the wall shut, the darkness was total. He could hear Nina moving behind him, and even though he knew it was her, being stuck in a tight dark place again made sweat bead on his face. He walked faster up and put one hand out to feel for an inevitable door. When he found it, he grabbed for the knob, pushed open the door, and entered the room at a near jog.

Casey found himself in a windowless office. A large desk sat against the far wall with two chairs in front. Two filing cabinets were against another wall next to a door, and several open boxes were filled with holiday decorations.

"Almost there," Nina said. She opened the door and walked into a closet, and Casey followed.

There she moved an empty filing cabinet aside and pressed on the wall behind. When the wall opened this time, Casey expected another set of stairs. Instead, he was relieved to see a well-lit one-bedroom apartment with a small, tidy kitchen, breakfast table with two chairs, a couch, and large TV. Casey was surprised to see the single standard-sized window by the breakfast table, but after looking out, he realized it was hidden from view both by being on the forest-facing side of the building and because a large AC unit sat between the window and the edge of the roof.

"I suppose the crop duster pilots could see it if they bothered to look, but from the ground, it's hidden away," Nina said. "Now, show me your belly."

Casey did, and Nina shook her head and gave him a scolding look. "If you were a doctor, you'd be sued for malpractice."

"I only had some gauze pads at home."

"Electrical tape? Bless your heart."

Casey felt his face turning red. She put up a hand, retrieved the first-aid box from the bathroom, and then sat him down at the breakfast table.

The cut was deep but not wide. But Nina said he would have been in trouble had the cut been even a little bit deeper. She cleaned it with peroxide. And when she poured on the alcohol,

Casey gritted his teeth as the delayed, cold sting set in hard.

Once patched up, Casey brought out the box, computer, and Marion's phone. Nina knew Marion's phone passcode, and they looked for text and phone messages first. There were no unexpected texts and only a handful of voicemails. The only important one was from Chuck. They both listened in silence and looked at each other when they heard the scream but said nothing.

Next, they opened Chuck's laptop. Casey had checked it briefly the night before, and just as then, it powered on fine. And though the screen was mostly a kaleidoscope of sharp, broken colors, about a quarter of the screen was intact and clear. Casey was able to open Windows Explorer, move it to the good portion of the screen, and scroll through the desktop files and the recycle bin. He figured if the others thought breaking a screen broke the whole computer, maybe they wouldn't know how the recycle bin worked either. But there was nothing there.

"OK. So now the box.

Casey had picked the lock when he had gotten home the night before. Three scraps of paper were inside. One was a hand-drawn book cover that matched the pattern of the one burned in the fireplace. It confirmed that Evalyn's people had found the spell and destroyed it. The second scrap of paper didn't make much sense to Casey. It looked like a bunch of squiggles and a list.

He opened the box and put that piece of paper on the table facing Nina. It showed hand-drawn, geometric shapes connected by looping lines. At three points on the outside were large spirals. A number was written inside each. Underneath was a list of items that corresponded with each number.

Nina smiled at Casey. "The shape is called a sigil," Nina said. "It's probably part of either the summoning spell, banishing spell, or both. Typically, one would draw this out on paper or on the ground with colored sand or chalk. This one would go on the ground, and in each numbered spiral, you would place the item on the list. So, the first one is a coin. Marion drew it here. The second is a lit smudge stick made from equal parts sandalwood, sage, rosemary, and marijuana. It says it must be tied together with a blue string. And the third one is a statue or idol of some kind. She's drawn it here."

"What do you know about the coin?"

"Not a damn thing. And I don't know about the statue either."

"Chuck mentioned something about idols in his voicemail to Marion. Wherever they are, I think we can find the statue."

"Maybe. But you would have to see it and compare it to the drawing to know if it was a match. Let's move on. What about that last note?"

"Riddle, you mean."

Nina read aloud the message from the third scrap of paper: "A great king here once ruled. He conquered not the jungle or mountain or river but over the plains; he held dominion. A crown of black and white he wore, and a horn of shining silver he carried. You will find what you seek when you tell the keeper of secrets when the king's reign began."

"Any ideas?" Casey asked, shifting in his chair and rubbing at his bandaged stomach.

Nina sat in thought before pulling out her phone and saying, "Let's Google it."

Casey found a brand of silver horns made by a company called King and references to a "King of the Plains" quest from some video game. Nina found more video game references when she searched for "keeper of secrets." But neither found anything related to Marion or to Evalyn.

Casey paced the room, clutching the note. He focused on the feel of the paper in his hand, hoping it would induce a psychic impression, but it did not. Meanwhile, Nina poured herself a glass of water in the kitchen and leaned on the counter.

Casey said, "So we have the sigil but not the spell. And we know what we need but not where to find two of the things."

"Three, really. Unless you know where to find marijuana."

Casey smirked at her. "I'm a twenty-five-year-old gay country boy. I can get pot."

"Oh, well, Marion didn't tell me that. Although being gay is associated with magical and psychic powers in some cultures."

"Lucky me. So we need the spell, the coin, and the statue."

"What we need is help. Dammit, I didn't want to call anyone, but I'm afraid we're at that point. And you told me you heard the others say they'd found something. It's got to be one or all of the things we still need."

"I can get some people together and go in there with guns..."

"Again with the guns," Nina said, throwing her hands in the air. "And what? Get shot up by their people with guns? Or maybe you do Rambo your way in, and you are somehow able to find where they are camping out. And if you do somehow manage to rescue Marion and Chuck, if they are even still alive, then what?"

"What do you mean?"

"What do you do about the spirit? If whatever killed Amy is part of their rituals, how do you stop that? What if there are a bunch of those things?"

Casey was silent.

"We do it the right way. Marion left us the clue. Us. That means she knew we could figure it out. You are a magic guy, right? You don't just go sawing at a box with some lady in it without preparing the box first, right?"

"I don't saw people in half."

"You know what I mean. We have a game plan. And we need to follow it until we have no other choice. Do you agree?"

"What about the guy with the beard?"

"No."

"He helped you the other night. He ran interference when the cop showed up."

"He is tricky. It's hard to tell whose side he's on. It would be to his advantage for us to think he's on our side. But he has a history with Evalyn. Marion wouldn't want you mixed up with him."

"I'll let her tell me that when I get her back from these cult assholes. If you aren't going to help me, at least stay out of my way. Give me his number."

Nina sighed and said, "Text me the picture you took of the book first."

Casey did, and she texted it to the man with the beard. "OK. Let's see what he has to say."

"Just give me the number. I'll call..." But before she could finish dialing, her phone began to ring, and she answered.

"So, you know?" she said. After a pause, she said, "Yes. I saw him do it. It's real." Then, "He's not experienced..."

Nina held the phone away from her mouth and asked Casey a question.

After thinking about it, Casey answered, "Yes. For Marion and Chuck. If it gets us the spell, I'll do it."

16

Reverend Gale had sent out a text blast to his congregants looking for search party volunteers. Thirty minutes later, the parking lot of Cherry Hill Baptist Church was half full. Many of the vehicles were accessorized with metal fish decals and various bumper stickers. Messages like, "Abortion is murder," "Make America Great Again," and "National Rifle Association Member." Jake's truck had a small NRA sticker, but none of the others. He parked across two spots at the far end of the lot to prevent anyone from scratching the paint job of his black Ford F-150. A pop-up storm had quickly turned the baby-blue sky dark gray, and the rain was coming down in sheets. He would have to run to avoid being soaked through by the time he made it inside to get more details about the search from the reverend.

He didn't care much about the rain, though. He was still fuming from his most recent fight with Lisa. Going to church, even just for a few minutes to stage a search party, made him feel better. Reverend Gale was sure to find a way to work in talk about sinners paying for their misdeeds. And that put him in a good mood. *Lisa will pay one day too*, he thought. *She'll push me too far, and by God, she will pay.*

Jake was soaked on his run to the door. He wiped his wet shoes on a black plastic mat under the two tall wooden doors at the front of the church and ran a hand over his damp head to push off the rainwater. A pile of "missing" posters was piled on a table to his left. A photo of Amy took up the top half. The picture had been a yearbook photo from before she had started coloring her hair in two tones and looking like a "regular street hussy"- her father's words. The posters included her description, information about her last whereabouts, clothing, and where she might have been going after. After drying his hands on his shirt, he took one and made his way into the sanctuary. He took a seat in the back pew and read the poster from top to bottom.

The stained-glass windows on the right wall were backlit by what was left of the sunlight and the light-activated parking lot lights. They cast their many colors into the dark wood interior of the church, painting the church in rich reds, greens, and blues. The windows were spaced evenly between thick oak arches, which met at the center of the ceiling. Most of the windows depicted scenes from the Bible: the baptism of Jesus by John the Baptist, Jesus raising Lazarus from the dead, and the conversion of Paul on the road to Damascus. A few others were simple crosses and doves with red and purple patterns behind them. The windows on the left side were darker. Still, they featured similar works, including Jake's favorite, a recreation of the bottom half of Michelangelo's *Last Judgment*, the massive painting in the Sistine Chapel at the Vatican depicting demons dragging the damned to hell.

Reverend Gale came up from behind and put a hand on Jake's shoulder.

"I'm so glad you could make it, Jake," he said

"Of course, Reverend."

Reverend Gale worked himself into the pews, and Jake slid down a few feet to allow room for him to sit. When the reverend was situated, he said, "I understand she disappeared from a party at a trailer where you stay. Is that right?"

"I keep a room there, but I rarely spend the night. It's more of a launchpad close to work and all." Jake stopped short of admitting that when he wasn't at hunting camps, he spent the night at the homes of various girlfriends more often than at the trailer, but the reverend didn't ask. Jake added, "I wasn't at the party. I wish I had been. Someone had to see something."

Reverend Gale nodded. "That roommate. He must be a friend of yours?"

"No. Our parents were friends, so we got to know each other. But we aren't friends. Let's just say we don't share the same interests."

"Not a churchgoer, I assume?"

"No, sir. He is not."

"Do you think he might be responsible for Amy's disappearance?"

The thought had not occurred to Jake that Casey might arouse suspicion. What would a gay man want with a teenage girl after all? But processing this, Jake had to keep himself from smiling when he responded, "I guess anything is possible. As you say, sin is sin."

The reverend patted Jake on the shoulder and stood up. Before he walked away, he said, "Good thing you know the lay of the land. We are going to be searching at your trailer and those woods. You'll be a great asset today."

Jake smiled at the reverend, and the grin lasted a long time. *How could Casey fit into this?* he thought.

On the way to the search, Jake obsessed over the question.

Before the night a few weeks ago, he wouldn't have cared about Casey. Their history had been insignificant. They met when Jake was thirteen or fourteen when their dads had become friends. Over the next few years, the men got together regularly for fishing trips, barbecues, and the like, and they often dragged their sons along. Jake was two years older, and he thought Casey, who was always trying to do magic tricks and didn't really care about fishing or hunting, was boring and nerdy. But he was easy to control. If Jake needed something from inside the house, Casey would fetch it for him. If he needed something hidden from his dad, Casey would hide it. And years later, when Jake needed a place to stay, Casey agreed to rent him a room. Still a pushover, a boring, controllable rube, Casey, like most people, was inconsequential to Jake except when he had something Jake wanted. In fact, he rarely even thought about Casey until one night a few weeks before.

That night, Jake was supposed to have been gone for a long weekend with Lisa. They had gotten back together and had big plans to party, but when he had a little too much to drink after dinner and had accidentally called her a cunt, an epic fight had ensued. She had run him out of her house. Drunk and closer to the trailer than anywhere else, he had decided to go there and crash for the night and try and patch things up the next morning.

But when Jake had gotten to the trailer, he had seen an unfamiliar car in the driveway next to Casey's. The lights had all been out, so he had thought Casey must have brought a girl home. Casey had never brought a girl home before, as far as Jake had known. But it hadn't been strange. Not really. Casey was a squirrelly, nice guy, and girls don't usually respond to weak men. But every dog has his day, Jake had thought, and so he had snuck into the house, careful not to make any noise. He had wanted to fuck with Casey.

Making his way down the hallway, the sounds of people in the throes of lovemaking had spilled from Casey's room. When Jake could tell for sure what it was, he had grown hard. He had thought that if he had played his cards right, he might get to see some titties. So, when he got to the door, he had shouldered hard into Casey's bedroom door, easily pushing through the flimsy lock. His momentum had carried him to the floor. When he had looked up, laughing, Casey was staring back, lying naked on his bed with another naked man standing behind him. The standing man had grabbed a pillow and covered himself while Casey slid under the sheet and shrieked at Jake to "Get the Fuck out!"

Confused and sprawled on the floor, Jake had muttered, "What the...fuck? Faggots?!" He had made it to his feet, staggered backward into the door jam, fallen again, and then crawled out of the bedroom. When he had managed to get and stay upright, he had turned and ran the length of the short hall and out the front door in a flash.

He had never met a real gay person before, but he knew all about them from church. Jake had felt betrayed and disgusted. He couldn't let that kind of thing happen under his roof, but the arrangement was too good for him. So Jake had stayed away for several days. But when he had come back, Jake couldn't keep his nature under control and found that bullying Casey and calling him names was the only way he could communicate. Still, he wasn't comfortable living with such a despicable sinner. But now the thought was interesting; The thought he might frame Casey for Amy's disappearance. It might not stick, sure, but it would be horrible for him. And that's what really mattered. Casey had to pay for his sins.

Half an hour after Jake had made it to the church, and after a healthy dose of Reverend Gale talking about sinners and damnation, the group drove to Rabbit Run Road and parked along the shoulder. The line of cars and trucks stretched from the intersection of Highway 12 almost to Marion and Chuck's house. The sheriff and several deputies were gathered at the front door of the trailer. Jake parked his truck in the driveway and walked up to the group.

"I don't see my roommate's car. Do you need his permission to search?" he said.

Sheriff Johnson turned and said, "You Jake?"

"Yes, sir. If you need permission, you have it."

"I don't believe we've talked yet. Were you here at the Fourth of July party?"

"No, sir."

"Do you know Amy?"

"Seen her at church."

The sheriff asked him a few more standard questions. After a few minutes, their chat was over, and the deputies split off to organize the volunteers into groups.

Jake walked back to where Reverend Gale was holding court and watched the sheriff return to his car and drive away.

* * *

Sheriff Johnson sat in his car and watched the goings-on until the lines of volunteers began moving towards the woods. The rains had stopped, but the ground was slick with mud, and he saw several of the searchers slip and fall on their way into the woods. He drove further down the road to see how far the lines stretched and found the end of the line was 100 yards from the home of the caretaker of the hunting camp, Chuck Spivey, and his wife, Marion. The sheriff had called earlier to let them know about the search party but received no answer over several attempts. He decided to go ahead anyway since there was no active hunting season underway and because every man and woman in the line was wearing bright orange vests and making a ton of racket. Still, he decided to drop by and see if anyone was home.

He parked in front of the garage and noticed a bit of curtain hanging out a window but filed it away. Before heading to the front, he peeked into the garage and saw two vehicles. He tried the door and found it unlocked. Pushing it open, he announced himself to the dark space. Hearing nothing, he closed the door without going in.

When he reached the front door, he saw a hole in the top right section. He studied it as he knocked. There was no response or sound from the house, so he slid around the side and saw a broken pane in a kitchen window. He drew his weapon and used his shoulder radio to call the dispatcher.

"Sheriff here. If you can spare a couple guys from the search and have them head to the next house down the road instead, I'd appreciate it. No code. It may be nothing, and I don't want to excite any of the volunteers. Just need a couple officers."

"Will do," the dispatcher replied.

Sheriff Johnson held his position, and when the deputies arrived a few minutes later, he waved at them and showed them his gun. One deputy stayed with the car and watched the front of the house as the others entered through the unlocked kitchen door.

The burnt paper was the first thing Sheriff Johnson smelled, and a bloody handprint on the refrigerator just below a bullet hole was the first thing he saw. The deputies cleared the house room by room. They had to use a ladder from the garage to access the attic. The sheriff went behind them, examining the scene. He spotted more blood on the refrigerator near the bottom and could see the entire house had been ransacked. In his years of police work, he knew, as a rule, there were no such things as coincidences. Still, the connection between Amy and the Spiveys was not clear. His deputies had called and spoken with Chuck Spivey the morning before. He answered their questions but didn't add anything new to the investigation. The couple had lived in the house for twenty years and never had any legal trouble other than one simple trespassing charge for Marion way back. All and all, they were quiet and minded their own business.

The deputies secured the house, and when crime scene investigators were on the way to take samples of the blood and look for fingerprints, Sheriff Johnson returned to his car and called Reverend Gale.

* * *

Jake was two men down from Reverend Gale in the search line and heard the reverend's side of the conversation with the sheriff. Whatever they had found had not been good. He watched as the reverend stormed off back towards the road, and he ran to catch up.

"Do you need a guide back?" he said.

The reverend looked at Jake with eyes showing both anger and concern and seemed to consider the question and answered, "Do you know the way to the Spivey house?"

Jake nodded and motioned for the reverend to follow him.

After a minute, Jake took the chance to ask a question he did not think the reverend would answer: "What's at the Spivey place?"

Reverend Gale surprised him by telling him everything the sheriff had related, though it was not much. The Spiveys were missing, foul play was suspected, and there was no preliminary indication of any connection with Amy. The reverend then added, "I know about the Spivey woman. She is a witch and used to run a store downtown. She sold satanic books and candles and things. My congregation picketed outside her store, and we ran her out of business. Praise Jesus. I should have thought about how close their house was. No connection, my foot."

Jake thought this over for another minute before saying, "You know, my roommate Casey is good friends with the Spiveys. Maybe he's the connection."

17

The Catfish Shack was packed. Casey was dropping another batch of hush puppies in a fryer when he saw the hostess rush into the back and whisper something to Dwayne. They both stared at Casey. The hostess broke eye contact and bowed back to the dining area the minute Casey looked up. Dwayne met his eyes and had a look of genuine concern Casey had never seen that face make before. Dwayne made a nearly imperceptible head tilt and carried a stack of plates to the line before walking out the back door. After Casey had pulled out the basket of hush puppies and hung them to drain, he made a smoking gesture to the other cook and went to talk with Dwayne.

Dwayne motioned him behind the dumpster out of eyeshot of anyone in the parking lot or dining area.

"She said a whole bunch of people just came in from a search party for Amy, and they started at your trailer. While they were there, they found the couple next door, old Chuck and Marion, missing. Blood was on the walls, and they found bullet holes. Your name is coming up a lot," Dwayne said.

Casey froze. The search party was to be expected, he supposed.

The sheriff finding out Chuck and Marion were gone was too. But blood? True, it had been dark when he had been inside, but he had used his phone light to navigate every room and hadn't seen any blood on the walls or anywhere else. He wondered how we could have missed it. His thoughts darkened, and he concentrated on remembering each room, thinking if he had missed any evidence of violence against Marion other than the ransacked house. And then it struck him all at once. How could he have been so stupid? He looked up at Dwayne in a panic and said, "It was mine."

"Your what?" Dwayne said.

"The blood. I barely made it out of there. I was stabbed and had to rest before I could leave. I didn't even think about cleaning up..."

"Whoa. Okay." Dwayne said, holding up his hands. "Slow down. Start at the beginning."

Casey took a breath and told Dwayne everything he knew. The details spilled out of him like a purging; the impression from the shoe, Evalyn, talking to Nina and searching Marion's house. He tried not to leave anything out, and when he was finished, he leaned against the dumpster, hands on his knees as if he were preparing to vomit for real.

Dwayne had listened without any questions, and when Casey was done, he said, "Show me the scar."

Casey straightened up and lifted his shirt with one hand. With the other, he peeled a side of the taped bandage off. He pulled it back almost all the way, revealing the inside of the bloody bandage and a thin, bruised wound on his stomach, tiny spots of wetness still gleaming between the broken line of the scab over the cut.

Dwayne studied the injury and said, "Looks like it hurts. Okay.

The blood is from when you got stabbed after you broke in to get a magic spell." Dwayne rubbed his face with one long hand and looked at Casey sideways. "You know that sounds bat-shit crazy, right?"

Casey nodded.

Dwayne nodded back. "I know we've talked about your psychic powers before. Can you tell me what I'm thinking of now?"

Casey sighed. "Women, weed, guns, baseball, snakes... I don't know. It isn't a power. It's not how it works."

"Okay, but you said you saw from Amy's perspective how she died? That's not a power?"

"I don't know what that was. I usually see a vision or a quick scene. Same as it always has been."

"Maybe it was her showing you because she wanted you to see."

"Maybe. That feels right. But honestly, I don't know how it works any better today than when we were kids and I was scaring my parents. All I know is that if I wasn't already the chief suspect, I will be now."

Dwayne looked up as if to think and said, "Unless you've been hiding more than this from me, I know you've never been arrested before. They don't have your blood in any of their computers. You aren't the chief suspect until they get the results back, and they have samples from you to test against what they find."

"What are you getting at?"

"Unless they have something solid on you, you've probably got a couple days at least until they find out you were there. I mean, naturally, once they have a match, they'll think you killed all those people and will arrest you for murder. And then they'll send you to the nuthouse in Montgomery in a straight jacket. You know. When you tell them about witches and jellyfish monsters and all. But you might have some time left to do whatever it is you are trying to do to solve this thing on your own before they swoop in."

"Well, that's reassuring," Casey said. His head was racing with thoughts of the police, Marion, and Chuck. And the damn riddle was still processing somewhere, too among all the noise, stubborn in its resistance to logic.

Dwayne smiled. "I do think it is reassuring. And I'll help you."

"Why? I wouldn't expect anyone to believe this story, much less offer to help. And to be honest, I don't think I would believe you if the shoe were on the other foot."

"First, I wouldn't believe me either. I've met me. Second, if I can make life harder for the cops, I'm all in."

"You still holding grudges?"

"Having fun while not hurting anybody shouldn't be illegal. Anyway. I digress. Let me help you. We've been best friends since we were little kids, and if you are in trouble, I want to help you out."

"It's asking too much. I don't think you understand," Casey said.

"Who fed my boa constrictors and rattlesnakes for the three months while I was in the county lockup?"

"That's different."

"No, it ain't. I know you must have been shittin' bricks with those rattlesnakes. Feeding those fuckers is dangerous as hell. So, answer me: Who fed 'em?"

"I did."

"And who yelled, 'Run, The cops are coming!' super loud in the parking lot and sent that crowd running up at Vestavia Hills after the baseball game when I was about to get jumped by their whole damn team?"

"I did. But it's not the same thing."

"To me, it is. Those assholes were all wearing spikes and holding baseball bats. They had Curtis Jackson and me on the ground. I'd be droolin' in a wheelchair with a shitty diaper in some home if you hadn't thought fast and done something."

"I can't ask you…"

"I'll decide that for myself. Plus, if you haven't noticed, this place is boring as fuck, and I could use a little adventure."

"OK. But if things get crazy…"

"Great! If things get crazy, all the better. So, you said you needed weed. I got you covered there. What else?"

"I have to meet with a guy tonight after work. I'll be getting back late, but why don't you meet Nina and me tomorrow at the Red Lion to talk about whatever I find out. If I get any info we can act on sooner; I'll call you tonight."

Dwayne clapped his hands. "Awesome! Sounds like a plan."

Casey texted him Nina's contact information and the time to meet.

As they both walked to the back door of the kitchen, Dwayne said, "Oh, and if you need a place to stay, let me know."

"Thanks, but I think if the sheriff comes looking for me, they'll check your place too."

"I'm not talking about my apartment."

"Finally got the camp house fixed up?"

"Maybe. You aren't the only one with secrets, Mr. Sparks."

During the rest of his shift, Casey noticed several servers flash him sideways glances. They all looked away when he tried to make eye contact, and no one made small talk with him while waiting for their orders at the line. He wanted to shout out to the whole restaurant. To command them all to "Stop looking at me!" and tell them, "I didn't do anything!" But it would have only made matters worse. Once the small-town gossip machine got going, it tended to work with brilliant efficiency and speed. And that night, it was in rare form. To their credit, they seemed to have gotten most of the facts correct, at least the little bits he had heard before blushing servers noticed him listening and shut their mouths. But the conclusions had all been wrong. Under the circumstances, he couldn't blame them for not realizing he was trying to help. How could they have known? And he couldn't blame them for simple gossip. It was a small town, and to be expected. But he could and did blame them for their cruelty. The thing that hurt him the most was people he had known his entire life, people he had grown up with, went to school with, and were in boy scouts with, could convict him with such speed in their minds as a cold-blooded kidnapper and possible murderer without even asking to hear his side of the story.

It was like how he was silently judged by some of the same people for being gay. Times had changed, and it was no longer acceptable to call a gay person a "faggot" to their face, even in rural Alabama, but Casey knew what went on. He had been in the closet long enough before he was forced out to have experienced a few years as an adult and an assumed straight guy. Most people were nice to your face, but behind closed doors, they showed their true colors.

When it was time to leave, Casey tore out of the restaurant without a word. As he pulled out, he looked back at the restaurant and imagined as soon as the door had shut behind him, the chirping had exploded into loud conversations and conspiracy theories. Of course, it had. Maybe Dwayne could tell him later, he thought. But by the time he saw Dwayne again, the rumors would be the last thing on his mind.

18

The directions on Casey's phone led him southwest out of town, first on four-lane highways, then two-lane roads. When he passed the sign that read, "Conecuh National Forest," thick stands of pine trees crowded the shoulder of the road like overprotective sentinels. They blocked out most of the moonlight and gave Casey a hypnotic sensation, like driving through a dark tunnel. When the phone said to turn right, Casey slowed almost to a stop, flipped his headlights to bright, and watched for a break in the trees. Finding it and easing onto the road, he had only a foot of clearance on either side. Not much but enough. He pressed on, going no more than ten miles per hour down the suffocating little lane, errant branches scratching his car as he went. A mile further, the road expanded just before taking a 90-degree turn to the left. What Casey saw when rounding it took his breath away.

The road was triple the width it had been and was lined, 100 yards or more, with pairs of massive live oak trees, each set well off the road on either side and planted precisely across from one another. Their limbs stretched high over the road, and Spanish Moss hung from each like living tinsel. A vast green lawn replaced the forest, which before had been within reaching distance. And at the end of the drive stood a huge plantation house lit up by several small lamps on the wrap-around porch and one large wrought-iron lantern suspended by chains over the front entryway.

Casey had been expecting his destination would be a shack on a river or a dilapidated camper half-covered in poison ivy; more *Grizzly Adams* than *Gone with the Wind.* As he pulled in front of the mansion, he saw the man had shaved off his beard and was left with only a thin mustache. From a distance he did bear some resemblance to Rhett Butler standing by the front door smoking a bent Sherlock Holmes-type pipe and wearing black suit pants, a white dress shirt, and a buttoned maroon vest.

"Welcome, Casey," the man said, taking a puff from the pipe.

Casey approached, and as he got closer, he could see the man was younger than he had looked at the Red Lion. *He couldn't be more than thirty-five,* Casey thought.

"Hello again," Casey said. And not knowing what to say next but feeling like it was still his turn in the conversation, he added, "Your house is beautiful."

"Yes. It is, isn't it?" the man said, looking back over his shoulder and at the porch. "You think you wouldn't forget, but when you stay in one place for a while, it's easy. It does look lovely at night," he said with a wink. "Come on in, and let's have us a chat."

To the left of the open main entryway was a large sitting room lit with candelabras. The man led Casey there and pointed to a floral printed couch with rich red-wooden trim. Casey sat. His host settled into a chair next to a small table. The man poked at the bowl of his pipe for a moment before springing up. Holding his hands together in front of him, he said, "Where are my manners? May I get you a drink?"

Casey was afraid he would be having cognac for the first time but was surprised again when the contents of the presented selection were modern staples. Casey held up a finger when the man said, "Beer." The man spun around, walked out of the room, and came back moments later with two frigid sixteen-ounce bottles of Budweiser and no glasses. Casey felt the first bit of ease then. He took a long draw of the beer and felt more.

The man sat back in his chair, took a drink of his own, and said, "It's a shame about Marion. She doesn't deserve this. None of us knew for sure what Evalyn was capable of. Had we known..."-he lifted his hands in a "what are you going to do?" gesture. "Marion is like a mother to you, am I right?"

Casey sat up on the couch and said, "You know a lot about me, and I don't even know your name. Not to be rude, but could we back up a little?"

"Ha," the man said, "Of course. My apologies. I have known Marion for a long time too. Not as long as you have, but for more than fifteen years."

"You must have been very young when you met her?"

"Indeed. Eighteen, I think it was. Maybe nineteen. Either way. I met her in her shop when I was down from Boston visiting with my parents one fall. And while they were out land grabbing, I spent an inordinate amount of time bothering Marion at her shop, asking questions about hoodoo and folk magic. You see, both my mother and father are first-generation Americans. We have a long witchy history in Scotland and France, and we still follow the old ways. But I had never been around someone like Marion, who has such vast knowledge of a branch of the craft I had not been exposed to before. I was over the moon when I found her, and I swear I followed that poor woman around like a puppy for all of those two weeks. And I won't bore you with details or describe the apoplexy I nearly gave my mother when I told her, but because of the trip, because of Marion, really, I decided to attend college here in the state, up in Auburn. Do you know it?"

"Of course."

"War Eagle."

Casey smiled and, per custom, returned the "War Eagle." "But you still haven't gotten around to your name yet."

"Getting there…" the man said, raising a finger. "Once I moved to the state, I fell in love with everything about it, especially the magic. After graduation I scouted far and wide for a place like this. Although it was in some disrepair when I found it, I restored it to its former glory. Oh, and for the record, this was never a working plantation. I mean, it was, but there were never any enslaved people working this land. The owner back then was an abolitionist, and this was a stop on the underground railroad. Energetically, that is important when you are doing spellwork here." He looked at Casey and saw him smiling and continued: "It turns out I'm not regularly needed in Boston, so I spend most of my time right here. And I love the place."

Casey still looked at him, grinning and with an eyebrow raised.

"What? Would you like another beer?"

"I would, yes. Also, you say a lot but still haven't gotten around to your name just yet."

The man returned the smile.

"Marion said I would like you if we ever properly met. Be right back."

His fitted suit showed off the muscles in his thighs when he stood up and his ass when he walked out of the room. Casey had never seen anyone in person wearing a suit from anywhere fancier than Men's Warehouse. He guessed the vest alone was probably worth more than his car. The pants, at least, were worth it, Casey thought. He also thought about what a pair they made. One looked like a men's model from the 1800s with a small, neat mustache and friendly eyes, and the other looked like a wind-blown, twink hobo in a stained-white chef's shirt, black pants, and shoes from Wal-Mart.

The man walked back in with two beers and handed one to Casey.

Before sitting back down, he said, "My name is Balthazar."

"A most common name in Massachusetts," Casey said in his best clenched-jawed Yankee voice.

Balthazar spat out his beer, laughing, and Casey could not stop himself from joining in.

"No. It's not very common," Balthazar said, coughing a little and patting down the foam bubbles on his vest.

"And not real," Casey said.

"No. It is not. But it's a name I go by in magic circles-pardon the pun-and it's what I would like to go by tonight if you'd indulge me. Tonight shouldn't be about my name. It's irrelevant to the magic we are going to be doing."

"Fine by me. But you know I don't know the first thing about magic. I mean, I've read a lot about it, but it's never been my thing."

"Think of it like tandem skydiving. As long as one of us knows when to pull the ripcord, we'll both be fine."

"But I have to trust you with the ripcord, and you won't even give me your real name."

Balthazar stood up, said, "That's fair. Be right back, " and left the room again. Casey enjoyed the view again.

Casey had been nervous about the meeting and still was, but

something about Balthazar had put him at ease. He couldn't tell if it was because of his strange mannerisms and dress or his kind face. But it was something more. And even as the conversation had taken a more serious turn, they were both keeping things light. Casey realized it was the first time he had flirted with someone since he had been with Kyle. And it was real flirting. It had been going on since he had arrived. He felt sadness thinking about Kyle. He missed him terribly, but Casey smiled to himself all the same. Despite all the rejections and horrors back in Cherry Hill, he felt like he was in a dream, having fun with this pretty stranger in the middle of nowhere in some timeless happy, safe place. Even if only for a while, it was keeping him away from what waited for him back home.

Balthazar returned, holding a book. Casey recognized the markings from across the room, and he stood up.

"Regarding trust. My intention was to hold this back until after our spell, but you make a reasonable point. So you see, I have the book. And after our spellwork, I'll tell you which one it is."

Casey took the book when it was handed to him and flipped through the pages. When he was a third of the way through, his body tensed and stopped. "The passage with the spell and story starts here."

Balthazar clapped his hands and hooted. "Why on earth wouldn't you let her train you?"

Casey marked the page with a piece of paper from his pocket and set the book on the couch. "It's one thing to see things. It's another to make things happen with potions, chanting, or whatever. I've just never believed in her sort of magic. Not until the last few days, anyway. I'm still not sure exactly what is going on."

"Are you kidding me? That worked, didn't it?"

Casey shrugged.

"Oh, come on. You wanted to know the page, and you were able to see it."

"It doesn't always work."

"What do you expect? You are not a god. Listen, have you heard of the monks who can heat up their bodies and dry water-soaked sheets in the cold just by meditating and focusing their intention? You can see the steam coming off them. Scientists have studied them and can find no explanation. Magic is essentially the same thing. It's focused intention with some power behind it."

"But what power? For the monks, it's the power of their minds, right? Some ability inherent to us all? They just know how to use it. It's not magic. It's some technique they've learned."

"But it works. You have to admit that. Some people, like you and the monks, can self-power. But most of us have to turn outward. We harness natural energy, the four elements: earth, wind, fire, and water. Some practitioners believe you can get power with the help of spirits. If so inclined, ancestors or other friendly spirits can influence things from the other side which we can't. And some believe there is power in deities, even ancient ones few people have worshiped for centuries. That's why you see people using statues of Greek and Roman gods and goddesses in their practice. Around here, a lot of practitioners, especially the old hoodoo folks, go to church on Sundays and always have. You'll find crosses, palm leaves, and all sorts of Christian symbolism in their homes.

"I thought you couldn't practice magic if you were a Christian?"

"You have to separate the religion from the practice. They aren't the same thing."

"But the church..."

"The church says a lot. Before the church was around, people were practicing their own folk traditions; ritual work, worship of gods, goddesses, ancestors-you name it. The church wanted power. And the only way to get it was to convert everyone. So, *viola,* everything people used to do got the label of evil and was forbidden. Nothing about magic is against the teachings of Jesus. He performed miracles, for crying out loud. What are those, if not feats of great magic? The church is not against magic. It's against anyone other than themselves having the power to use it."

"So, you think I can power spells?"

Balthazar put both hands on Casey's shoulders and said, "Why don't we give it a try and find out?"

19

Two men, both of whom had swapped robes and masks for dark green camouflage pants and jackets, rowed the black zodiac under a cloudy night sky. To stay unnoticed, they killed the engine when they passed from the creek into the Alabama River. Stealth was key. The plan was the same as last time.

Just over three weeks ago, the men and the Ruiner had attacked a boat full of fishermen. They had lured their victims first with sounds, then by the mesmerizing lights of the levitating jellyfish. The Ruiner had drawn all three onto the bank where it settled over one of them, killing him instantly. The remaining two fishermen had screamed and scrambled back into the water, trying for the boat. But the men in camouflage had moved it while they were distracted. And while the fishermen had tried to swim to it, the Ruiner in her crocodile form had hunted one of them down easily before he could reach safety. The other fisherman had managed to shimmy into the boat but had been unable to get it started. The men in the camouflage had taken the keys when they had moved it. The crocodile had slammed into the boat like a torpedo. Over and over again, it had struck from different angles until the piece of the craft the fisherman had been clinging to began to sink. And when it had, she surfaced and stayed motionless in the water just beyond his arm's length.

Over several brutal minutes, the last of the fishermen had stared into those emotionless, predator eyes, sobbing and screaming for help as the water overtook the boat. When the boat had disappeared under the water, and he had found himself among the only items still afloat, she had swum the short distance to him very slowly. His body had shaken like a bobber on a line getting a bite. When she had opened her jaws, he had tried to swim away, but she had taken his head in her mouth and had sunk with it. The men in camouflage never saw the man come back up again. They never saw her come back up either but went ahead and set fire to the remaining wreck as per the plan. When the fire reached the gas tank and the explosion had sent a dark red fireball over the river, they had sped away into the night.

Three weeks later and the plan was the same. Under a bridge less than a quarter-mile ahead, three fishermen in an anchored bass boat held fishing poles under bright lights they had brought with them to night fish. The light rigs worked well to attract baitfish and the much larger and delicious crappie. But the lights made seeing other boaters on the river almost impossible.

That was part of the plan. Like the last time, if everything went by the book, the fishermen would never even see the two men in camouflage. But as they neared the bass boat, the faint whooshing of the crocodile's tail joined the sound of the rowing. The men in camouflage looked at each other, puzzled.

"You are supposed to be on shore in the jellyfish form," one of the men whispered.

The plan had worked flawlessly the first time. And they had talked about using the same plan again. Indeed, they had prepared for the same. Although the Ruiner rarely spoke, she was capable of speech, even in her forms. But over the past few days, she had become restless. The closer she came to true liberation, the more unpredictable she became. It seemed to scare one of the men in camouflage, but it excited the other. The one who seemed scared had whispered to her, and her response was to disappear beneath the water.

When that happened, the men in camouflage stopped rowing and unholstered their guns. They were close to the fishermen and had no choice but to improvise. All was quiet for about a minute, then the bass boat started moving. The fishermen clamored and fought to point their lights in the water in hopes they could find the cause of their movement. The excited man in the camouflage wondered what the fishermen were thinking. Perhaps they reckoned a submerged tree or stump had dislodged their anchor, or a manatee, far north of its usual range, had done the same. He watched the boat move away, and the other man punched him in the shoulder.

"Help me row."

He picked up his paddle, and the two men struggled to keep up with the bass boat. He wanted to start the motor but didn't want to give up their position. The men in the fishing boat had not used theirs. He reckoned that would be changing soon enough and wondered what the Ruiner was thinking. She was ignorant of many modern technologies but understood motors well enough. She had, after all, traveled with them until they had shut theirs off.

The fishermen trained their lights on the water, following the direction of the anchor-turned-tow line. And the bass boat kept moving until it reached the center of the wide river. The men in camouflage rowed further to position themselves perpendicular to the fishing boat. If they needed to start shooting, this gave them the best chance to hit. Just after they stopped, the scared man in camouflage touched the other man on the shoulder and pointed at the back of the bass boat.

"Don't look at her eyes if she turns this way."

The fishermen were grouped at the front, peering into the water. The Ruiner had dropped the line, swam under the boat, and changed. In her human form, she glowed faintly green, the water giving her skin an iridescent glean when she moved. She reached the hull and pulled herself onboard. The act was quick but quiet, like a jaguar landing a long fall with padded paws on solid rock.

The fishermen did not turn around until she spoke.

"Gaze upon me."

Two of the fishermen froze when they turned around. Even from thirty feet away in the zodiac, the excited man in camouflage could tell it had happened in an instant. The expressions on their faces were vacant and confused but with a hint of lust. The remaining fisherman went for his holstered weapon before looking up. His eyes were faster than his hands. The gun stopped moving for a moment, then rose. The excited man in camouflage raised his weapon as well. And from the dark would have fired if not for the Ruiner who made a subtle gesture in his direction. He holstered his gun and shivered. She had conveyed complete confidence in the gesture. A gesture he realized he could not remember, even though it had just happened seconds before.

The fisherman with the gun continued to raise the weapon until it was pointed straight ahead. The Ruiner tilted her head, and the man brought the barrel under his own chin and fired. His body dropped and wedged between the motor and the boat. His torso and what was left of his head bobbed in the water, and his legs lay splayed in the boat. The other fishermen did not move or jump when the shot was fired. Though from a distance, the excited man in camouflage would have sworn he saw tears.

The Ruiner reached for the men. Her arms became long tentacles in an instant, and she took them both by the neck. She lifted them a few feet off the deck and slammed their heads together over and over again. As she did, new tentacles formed from her side and her legs. Her torso and head fused together until she formed a great red octopus. One of the free tentacles wrapped the corpse of the third fisherman, and she slid with all three of them into the dark water.

The men in the zodiac floated silently for several minutes. The scared one finally said, "So can we..."

"Yep. Let's finish up."

They rowed up to the boat and emptied ten gallons of gasoline into it and placed three more sealed ten-gallon containers on deck. After retreating a safe distance, they tossed flares at the boat. The third one found its target, and the men retreated under engine power. Not long after and just before pulling off the main river, the woods ahead lit up as either the containers or the gas tank exploded. It did not matter which.

20

The low sound of chanting and slow drips of water greeted Marion when she woke in her cell. A new knot on the side of her head had joined the old one on her back. And they were dueling for attention. Both throbbed, and they combined to make her head feel like a rope was tied around it too tight. It was full dark. Not even a hint was left of the shaft of light from before. So she could not tell if the head injuries were affecting her vision, but they were not doing wonders for her balance. Even on hands and knees, searching for the jug of water, she felt like she was inside a dark shipping container on board a vessel in rough seas. She held herself steady with one hand on the poles. With the other hand, she patted outside the cage but found nothing. Aside from a few glugs of water, she had not taken a drink since her morning coffee back at her house. And she had no idea how long ago it had been. On one of the last pats outside the poles, her hand had splashed in a puddle. She had returned there and tried to scoop a handful of water into her mouth. Little made the journey, but new water seeped into the dip in the rock, and after a minute or so, when it was full again, she took another sip. She sat and repeated this ritual a dozen times, listening to the chanting and watching the red glow dance along the far wall, trying to count the moving shadows.

After the drink she tried to stand, but her hand slipped, and she fell against the cage and into a seated position. *At least I didn't bang my head again*, she thought. *Thank God for small favors.* Her head was spared, but the sound was enough to halt the chanting. When she realized the sound had stopped, she tried to get up again and succeeded. A single torch moved towards her, and she stepped back in the cage. When she started seeing the outline of a vaguely human shape, she stepped up.

"I want to talk to Evalyn," Marion said. The strength in her voice surprised her. Despite the lack of food and water and with a head that felt like a scraped-out pumpkin, the voice was somehow still able to pretend to be well.

"I won't get too close. You have a penchant for fainting spells, I hear," Evalyn said, stopping three feet from the cage.

The light from the torch was blinding after the days of darkness, and Marion had to put a hand over her face to block it out. All she could see of the woman in front of her was her shape.

"Let us go. We have nothing to do with this."

"You haven't lost your ego, I see. All this time, and you are still trying to tell me what to do. That time is past. Or, at least, it soon will be."

"If you let us go, we'll leave you alone. You can do whatever you want here," Marion said. They both knew she was lying.

"Your husband didn't leave us alone. We gave him a chance too. But he was just like you." Evalyn placed separate emphasis on each of the last three words. "He just had to be in control."

Marion felt her arms twitch and the muscles contract in her thighs. She had never experienced the feeling of shaking from anger before then. She had always thought it was just an expression, but now it was happening to her.

"Let me talk to him," Marion said.

"Too late."

"What have you done, you bitch?" Marion screamed and pounded against the poles with her fists. The cage shook but was far too strong to give way. *Evalyn must have known,* Marion thought, because she did not flinch or make a move of any kind.

"You know, when you tore the coven from me and ruined my name with all the witches, you took my only love away. It's only fair I returned the favor."

"You didn't deserve it," Marion shot back. "They all trusted you and took you in, and all you brought with you was evil."

"But you were the one caught dancing naked under the moonlight."

"Fuck you!"

Evalyn howled with laughter. "I thought you'd like that touch." She advanced on Marion and put the torch close to the poles. Marion moved back from the heat. At first, she was afraid the cage would catch on fire, but then she wanted it to. If the lashes burned, she would have a chance to break through and get to the bitch hiding behind the torch.

"Things will be easier on you for what's left of your life if you tell me who is out there working against us."

"God," Marion said, "He's working against you."

"Maybe. But the thing is, God doesn't leave blood inside a fancy cabinet in your study or on a refrigerator in your kitchen. That's a person's doing. And it wasn't anyone with me. Of course, we may have caused the blood. I happen to think one of us did and should have noticed we had trapped a rat. But regardless...you told someone else about me, and I want to know who it was."

"You found a thief in an open house?"

"We found the counter-spell and burned it."

Marion tried not to show her disappointment but felt the sides of her mouth twitch.

"Not what you were hoping to hear?" Evalyn said. "Better news for you is we couldn't find your phone. I do wonder who all you talked to about us. And I am so very curious about the rat."

Marion was silent.

"It's already been done. Your copy is gone, after all, so there's no use in holding out now. It would just be so much neater to have all the loose ends tied up before the transformation.

"You're going to kill me anyway. You've killed my husband. Why the hell would I help you?"

"You'll get hungry or thirsty enough to talk sooner or later."

"If I die of starvation, I can't say anything. The human body can only go so long..."

The torch slammed into the cage, peppering Marion with cinders and flame. "Long? You set me back years when you turned the coven against me. It was mine! You don't get to have your way this time, bitch. You'll tell me who knows. And if you die, you die. When the spirit is at full strength, it won't matter anyway. Spell or no spell; it will be too late. And then, if you are still alive, I'll give you to her. And she will eat you. She will take her time. She will savor every crunch of your bone, and I will laugh at every scream you bellow until you are nothing more than a mess on the floor of this cave." Evalyn calmed herself for a moment before adding, "Of course, I would love to do it myself, but she enjoyed your husband so, it would be a pity not to let her have the pair."

Marion lunged at her through the cage, knocking the torch to the ground and grabbing a handful of her robe. She pulled Evalyn against the poles and bit her somewhere on the face. It must have been the cheek or lip because it was soft, and Marion still had some of it in her mouth when powerful hands wrenched her free of Evalyn and pushed her to the ground.

Evalyn screamed and cursed Marion. And in the torchlight from the ground, Marion could see the shapes of three people standing alongside Evalyn. And just before one of them picked up the torch, she could see she had been right about it being a cheek. It was bleeding a lot. And Marion was glad.

21

"I said I'd help you with the spell, so I will," Casey said.

Balthazar took his hands from Casey's shoulders and smiled. "Excellent. But not smelling of hush puppies, you won't," he said. "Second room on the right upstairs, you'll find a bathroom stocked with towels, soap, shampoo, and an appropriate change of clothes. Take your time. I need to do some prep work myself."

Casey climbed the huge staircase and stopped to look at two large oil paintings set in gilded frames at the landing at the top. One was an untitled portrait of a woman in antebellum dress holding her clasped hands together in front of her. A hint of a smile was evident in the corners of her mouth. The house he was in now was in the background, and the lantern was burning even though it was sunny outside. The painting depicted the house in the fall. Faint trails of smoke rose from the four chimneys, and the surrounding forest was as gray as green. A handful of brilliant yellow and red trees were interspersed among the evergreens. The house looked sad to Casey in the fall. Most things in the South looked sad to him when the weather was cold. And the fall, while beautiful, always felt like a slow wake for the year. The land here was meant to be sunbaked and wet, he thought. Winter seemed a cruel price to pay for the heat the rest of the seasons brought. But balance, after all, was probably closer to the truth. Even nature has to give to get.

Casey found the bathroom easy enough, along with the soaps and towels. He laughed to himself when he saw a single claw-foot bathtub with no shower. He turned on the water and took off his clothes, kicking them all into a pile in the corner. And finding no trashcan, he tossed the bandage on the pile with the rest of his things.

The high sides of the tub made for the deepest bath Casey had ever taken, and he let himself go completely underwater. When he came up and put his arms over the sides, he felt like a sheik or some sort of steampunk baron. The soap was earthy, like rosemary and basil. Casey had a brief paranoid thought pass through his mind that Balthazar was a wicked witch out in the woods, and Casey was seasoning himself with the herbs in a cooking pot. He smiled and let the thought drift away.

But a few minutes later it came back when Casey heard the subtle sound of water flowing through other pipes in the house. Balthazar had said he had his own "prep work" to do. It occurred to Casey then that the bath was not only preparation for the ritual; it was part of it. Just like the flirting had been part of it. There was such a thing as sex magic. Casey had sneaky borrowed a book from Marion years before and read all about it. And Balthazar had said, "Think of it like tandem skydiving." So Casey was. Few activities put bodies closer than that. Sex was one of those. The bath wasn't to season him for a meal, but maybe it was preparation for another natural need. Casey smiled.

After the bath he dried off and took the folded clothes from the counter. There were two pieces, a very thin white linen pajama top and a matching pair of long drawstring pants. Casey looked for underwear and found none. He knew then what was coming.

He left his clothes in the bathroom. He did not want to get the grease smell on him. He wanted Balthazar to find him perfectly prepared now that he understood the nature of the ritual.

Balthazar stood at the foot of the stairs and had changed into the same outfit Casey wore. Casey tried to hide his smile as he walked down the stairs but could not, utterly exposed in the thin fabric and lack of underwear. And try as he might, it was impossible not to glance at what the same material was revealing on Balthazar, who stood with his arms at his side and a wry smile on his face.

"Did you find the facilities to your liking?" Balthazar asked, extending a hand to Casey as he made the last step.

Casey took it, and Balthazar did not let it go. Casey didn't want him to. He felt himself blushing again and was not sure how to respond.

Balthazar said, "This way." And they walked hand in hand past the stairs and into a huge study with dark wooden walls and several bookcases. Sandalwood incense filled the air, and despite the dozen or so candles burning in a large circle in the middle of the room, the windowless space was dim. Piles of blankets and pillows were arranged like the bedroom of a medieval sultan.

Balthazar turned to Casey and said, "Do you know what we are about to do?"

"Yes."

"You don't have to if you don't want to. I'll understand. I'll even give you the spell."

"I made a promise."

"Are you sure?" Balthazar said, squeezing Casey's hand tighter.

"I want to." And he kissed Balthazar.

They moved to the center of the circle, and Balthazar removed

Casey's shirt and then ran his hands over his arms and chest while chanting in some strange esoteric tongue. He placed two fingers gently on Casey's wound and said something else. Finally, he knelt down and untied the drawstring. Casey felt him pull the pants down, then the cool air of the room, and then the warm embrace of his mouth.

It was slow. And Casey put a hand on Balthazar's shoulder as the other man caressed the back of his legs and back. After a long time, Balthazar rose from the ground, and the roles reversed. When Casey came up they laid together on the blankets, and Balthazar worked his way behind Casey. He kissed him on the neck and whispered into his ear, "Relax now."

He did as Balthazar slowly entered. Casey felt ecstasy but also something else. It felt like strength, like a connection much more than the sum of its parts. Balthazar was a life well. He had called Casey a battery before, but it was Casey who felt charged in a powerful new way. They changed positions and kissed. Casey could see a blue glow in Balthazar's eyes and face. It felt perfectly natural, and he somehow knew he looked the same. He was as certain of that as he was of his visions. The sex lasted a long time, and when they reached simultaneous climax, Casey had a quick vision of a pattern. It burned on his vision for a moment like the aftereffect of a camera flash, and he lay back on the blankets breathing hard. Balthazar lay next to him and put a hand on his thigh, and they stayed there still for a few blissful moments.

Balthazar rolled over and pushed himself up on one elbow, and said, "Don't tell me what you saw. It's not my business. Besides, I love secrets."

Casey looked up at him and said, "How did you know?"

"I didn't know, but I hoped it would happen. It should mean the spell worked."

"How will we know?"

"A couple ways. One is by me being able to get visions from objects."

Casey rolled over. "Wait, you stole my ability?"

"I didn't steal it. We gave our abilities to each other. So the other way to tell if the spell worked is by you counting how many people are in this room."

Casey sat upright and looked around. The candles made seeing the far corners difficult, but no one was there. Not until he looked harder at the door and spotted a woman smiling at him. Casey sprung up to a standing position and gathered blankets around his exposed body. Balthazar fell back laughing. Casey looked down at him and back at the woman. He could see the door frame through her.

"A ghost?" Casey whispered, dumbfounded.

"You don't have to whisper, and you certainly don't have to cover yourself. She's seen a willie before, I assure you. Although, I'm sure she appreciates your modest instincts."

Casey stared at the smiling woman. She curtsied and walked out through the door and out of his view. Casey dropped the blankets and stood looking down at Balthazar, who shrugged and said, "I thought this might come in handy. After all, Evalyn is crafty, but the spirit is the one you really need to worry about. So now you can see her too...well...now you can see them all if you turn it on in your mind."

"I'll see ghosts all the time?"

"Spirits, technically, and no, not all the time. You will be able to learn to turn it on and off. You could see my friend, Elizabeth, just now because I asked her to attend our session and also because you've just gained the power. For lack of a better word, you can call it afterglow."

"She's the woman from the painting."

"Astute too. Yes. This is her place. She just lets me fuck cute guys in it," Balthazar said and reached up and grabbed Casey's leg." Now put on some pants quick, unless you want to go another round," he said before making a funny growling noise.

Casey smiled and slapped his hand away. Another round sounded great, but the shock of seeing the spirit had brought him back from his romantic haze. And he knew what had just happened, as amazing as it was for him, was more business than pleasure for Balthazar. He stood in place for a while, and Balthazar seemed to read his mind when he started putting on his clothes first and said, "I feel guilty about not stopping Evalyn when I had the chance. I underestimated her, and I was too much of a pompous ass to believe Marion when she told me she was dangerous. I was never in Evalyn's coven or anything, but as you see, I have a lot of resources here. And Evalyn has a voracious appetite for learning, especially dark and complicated subjects. So, I'm afraid I may have inadvertently supplied her with the knowledge to do what she is doing now. I wholeheartedly regret it, and I hope like hell I get the chance to apologize. In the meantime, I can give you all the tools I can, maybe even make you believe in magic. And if I get a little something out of it too, all the better."

"Are you even gay?"

"I don't believe in labels."

"That's convenient," Casey said, putting on his clothes and walking past Balthazar to the front room.

* * *

Casey took a picture of the appropriate spell and texted it to Nina. She responded with a thumbs-up emoji. Casey handed the book back to Balthazar and said, "Thank you."

Balthazar shook his head and said, "Now that you have the spell, you need a bit of background."

Casey said, "OK," and sat on the couch.

"This particular book is very rare. Marion got hers from me." Balthazar paused for a moment turning the book in his hand. "This book was created in 1801 and contains popular stories of the day, legends, spells, and recipes collected mainly from the Acadians and other white settlers in the US. There are a handful of native American tales as well. The entry on the Ruiner is different. There is no attribution to the story, and the tone is far more sinister than the others. Some people I know who are knowledgeable about these things say the other tales are meant to be a kind of camouflage to keep the book safe from religious authorities who might have found them good candidates for book burnings otherwise. So really, it's a grimoire or spell book in disguise with the sole subject being the Ruiner."

"Why did you have so many copies?"

Balthazar smiled. "I could say I am a collector. That would be true. Or I could say because I have an interest in general occult memorabilia. That would also be true. But the real answer is that my ancestors acquired all the copies they could find because the spirit is especially dangerous."

"They were protecting people from accidentally summoning her?"

"It would be impossible to do by accident. No. My ancestors

wanted to know they could summon her for themselves if they ever needed to. They were not all good people, Casey. But they weren't crazy either. And not being crazy kept them from performing the rituals."

"What about the coin? I have to place it in the sigil, but I don't know where it is."

Balthazar shifted in his chair and rubbed his chin. "I would be surprised if Marion had not collected all the items. She may have had them for a long time. She hoarded old books of shadows for the same reason; to keep dangerous things out of general circulation. But as far as my people, I don't know if they ever possessed the items or not. I'm afraid I cannot help with the coin."

Casey leaned forward. "But your ancestors? They must have had all the items?"

"I assume so but cannot be certain. It was a very long time ago, and over time, things tend to get lost, sold, stolen, or simply thrown away by people who don't or can't see the value of an object. Not all of my family are in touch with our past or agree on how best it should be honored".

Casey stood and paced. "Okay. I'll figure that out later. What can you tell me about the Ruiner? What is she?"

"The legend says the Ruiner was a human, but a spell from a rival transformed her into a succubus who can be controlled like a genie, but without a bottle."

"I don't understand."

"Put more plainly, she is a trapped soul with shape-shifting powers and extremely potent persuasive abilities who is supposed to do the bidding of the one who releases her from the ethereal plane. Only the one who releases her has to stay focused at all times, or the Ruiner won't follow orders. And unlike some loveable

Disney characters, the Ruiner is said to indiscriminately kill and fight anyone or anything that stands between herself and her freedom. Even if she does bend to Evalyn's will initially, the moment Evalyn tries to put her away will be the moment when the Ruiner turns on her.

And if she gets loose, it would be like freeing a giant indestructible grizzly bear that grows more powerful with every attack. The potential for damage, not just in the woods or in Cherry Hill, but everywhere on earth is very real."

"Why would Evalyn do it? And how is she controlling it now?"

"She is doing it because she overestimates her abilities. You can't boss around a tiger and command it back inside a cage whenever you feel like it just because you were the idiot who unlatched the door. It's the same with this. And it's under control now because her spell hasn't been completed yet."

"There are two parts to the summoning. The first is the main ritual that has been done. The Ruiner is here in a very basic form. She's dangerous now and can shapeshift, but her movement is limited. She can't go far from wherever she is being held. The second part requires sacrifices. A lot of them. Hence the other reason my people didn't do it. And when the sacrifices are complete. She will be fully realized and released."

"Amy. Maybe Marion and Chuck."

"Yeah. But it takes around twelve to finish the job."

Casey sat down and sighed. "Are you saying they are going to kill a dozen people?"

"They must have already murdered some before Amy if the Ruiner had enough power to shape shift into the form you saw. It gets stronger with each sacrifice until it reaches its maturity...for lack of a better word."

"The spell I have to do stops all that?"

"It should roll back any power she's gained from the sacrifices and force her into a single form. She won't be able to shapeshift. And then you can banish her if you are able to perform a certain attack."

"What do you mean, 'certain attack?'"

"That's where it gets tricky. When she was banished to the ethereal plane, her rival had to incapacitate her long enough to successfully contain her. You have to find out how this rival accomplished that feat. There are clues, but no one in my family in Europe knows for sure. Not anymore anyway. Some of the drawings contain patterns. The same pattern on the coin you need. Marion drew it on one of her notes. Remember?"

Casey nodded.

"We always assumed the pattern was akin to a Scottish tartan. You know, the patterns associated with different families or groups? The only problem is we don't know where she was from. It could have been anywhere in the Americas. But we have always thought if we could identify that pattern, we would find the people and be able to narrow it down from there."

"How in the hell am I going to find that?"

"Either luck, superior wits, or you find out from Evalyn."

"Evalyn?"

"That's right. She had to know how it was done in order to complete the first part of the ritual. Maybe that is why it's taken her so long to get it right."

"I can't go in guns blazing. I have to make her talk."

"I'm afraid so. Plus, you don't know how you will find the Ruiner. Human form, shifted into God-knows-what, or fully realized mega-monster. It wouldn't be smart to rush into a confrontation without doing some recon first. You have to be on guard for anything."

"What about the forms? I've seen a jellyfish. And you say there are others?"

"The legend says the Ruiner was once a human and was a respected healer in her youth. As she grew older, her practice grew beyond healing and into darker magic. The villagers feared her and ran her out. She settled in a cave somewhere near the ocean, and she could swim there at any time of day without being bothered by any predatory fish or reptiles. The villagers said she could control any animal and could make them friends or foes on a whim. So, if she was wronged, she might send a shark to attack your boat. If she favored you, she might send a crocodilian to protect you on a river journey. Because of this, some of the villagers worshiped her as a water goddess and protector of aquatic creatures. They made sacrifices to her at her cave..."

"I know where they are. There is a cave on the property. It's a cenote, a sinkhole with a river at the bottom. My God. I have to go."

"You have to be careful."

Casey stood up. "I will be. Thank you again for everything."

Balthazar stood. "You are welcome. I wish you the best of luck. If you see Marion, tell her, 'Better late than never.'"

Casey nodded and started for the door before he stopped.

"If you are going back for the clothes, please just let me burn them," Balthazar said.

Casey grinned, but Balthazar had a placid look on his face and said, "I'll send them to you. You should get going now."

Casey felt the shift in Balthazar's mood and sensed the house would soon witness more spellwork, and Casey was no longer invited. Casey said, "OK," and slipped out the door, but not before glancing up at the stairs and nodding softly to Elizabeth, who returned the gesture and watched him go.

22

Jake had spent much of his afternoon attached to Reverend Gale's hip. He had been there when Sheriff Johnson had told the reverend everything he had known about the crime scene. He had been there an hour and dozens of shouted questions later when Sheriff Johnson had told the reverend the only thing he could do to help was go back to the search party in the woods. And Jake had been one of the men who had stood between the reverend and the sheriff when the former charged at the latter after being told to go back in the woods. Jake had also escorted the reverend back to the church when it had become clear he would be arrested if he didn't leave immediately. Jake appreciated the reverend's anger; he could understand that emotion better than maybe any other.

A handful of church members checked in on Reverend Gale at the church. Nothing had been found in the search of the woods. And all agreed the limited number of people had not allowed much ground to be covered, and no news didn't mean bad news. Jake sat next to the reverend as he handled almost a dozen of these identical conversations and marveled at his calm demeanor and patient restraint. The man had shown more of himself to the sheriff than he had to his flock. And he had shown even more to Jake.

Between visits and on the way back to the church, they spoke of judgment and suspects. And they agreed Casey needed a closer look.

Jake decided when he left the church he would head for the trailer and take Reverend Gale's advice. He would confront Casey. And why not? If for no other reason than to take some aggression out on someone. If anyone deserved it, it was that pervert, Casey. Jake had seen it with his own eyes back in April. He still couldn't shake the image of those two men together in the bed. Jake gagged. He pushed it from his mind and instead focused on how nice it would be to punch him in the face. He had wanted to since April but had held back. It had been more fun to scare him up to this point. But now, Casey was going to serve a purpose. The disappearance happened in Casey's own backyard. Any outsider could believe he had to know something he was not telling. And it didn't matter anyway. Jake needed to let off some steam, and Casey wouldn't be able to stop him.

Jake sped down Highway 12. On the drive, he had to regulate his speed consciously. It crept higher and higher as his imagination invented increasingly violent scenarios. In one, he imagined finding Casey somehow armed with a rifle. He played out a gunfight and the ultimate blasting away of Casey's head, leaving hunks of brains sliding down the front of the refrigerator. In another, he imagined simply beating Casey to death, punching until he couldn't move his arms. He had made it up to 90 mph during that one.

He pulled in front of the trailer within ten minutes of leaving the church. He was halfway to the front door before he stopped, returned to the truck, and retrieved his Llama .380 ACP pistol and something wrapped in a cloth from the glove box. He pocketed both items and entered the trailer. Casey's car wasn't in the driveway, and the trailer was dark and still. Jake walked into Casey's room and flipped on the light. He didn't care if Casey might notice the room was lit if he pulled in. He was past caring about anything but the mission. Nothing was going to stop Jake from seeing Casey in jail. If the day had taught him anything, it was that the sheriff needed a break in the case, and without some piece of evidence, it wouldn't happen. Jake had an idea that planting a certain item might be enough. But as it turned out, he didn't even need to.

Jake scanned the room and saw the sheriff had torn it apart with as much vigor as he had Jake's. Casey hadn't cleaned up yet. Clothes, books, and boxes of various items were strewn around the room, and on top of his dresser was a line of large ornate wooden boxes. Jake recognized these, though it had been years since he had laid eyes on them. As kids, Jake had sometimes made Casey hide things for him when he was afraid his father was suspicious and was about to search him. He would pass Casey a girlie magazine or a pack of cigarettes for quick safekeeping, and Casey's go-to spots were these boxes. They were great hiding places because they had false bottoms and hidden compartments but looked like regular boxes. What Jake needed to hide this time was too big to fit in most of them, so he tried the largest one. He found the regular opening but had trouble finding the latch to open the false bottom. Finding no latch despite rotating the box and feeling for the seams over and over again, he tossed it back on the table and picked up the next largest one. This one opened up to reveal a small empty space lined in red velvet. Examining further, Jake found a tiny black plastic strap poking out from the lip between the velvet and the outside front edge. He felt a moment of triumph and pulled the strap but let out a yell and hurled the box to the ground when the space underneath was revealed. The extra compartment was only large enough to hide a ring or thimble. He kicked the box. It struck the bed and ricocheted into the wooden frame around the closet. Jake went to kick it again but stopped when he noticed the large crack and something visible inside. The busted corners revealed the secret to opening this section (from the bottom), and Jake slid open the container and pulled out a shoe wrapped in a shirt.

Burn holes dotted the shirt, but the small canvas deck shoe was clean. He took it back to his room and found the yellow "Missing" poster he had taken at the Church earlier in the day. He checked the description of Amy's dress at the time she had gone missing. It was the same brand, color, and size as the shoe he held in his hand. Jake stood staring at the shoe, his heart beating faster and faster. He dropped the shoe, took the pistol from his pocket, and checked to make sure it was fully loaded. It was. Seven rounds in the magazine.

He went back to Casey's room and pushed the container closed before situating the box back on the dresser with the others, careful to angle it so the worst of the damage was facing the wall. He turned off the lights and then left the trailer. He had to think about some things before he could face Casey.

* * *

When he got back home very late, Casey's car was in the driveway, and the only light he could see from Casey's window was the transient dim blue of a television. He walked to Casey's door and put an ear against the thin wood and could just make out the infomercial. He pulled back and found the emergency key on his keyring and pushed it into the small hole in the knob to unlock the door. He opened the door slowly and saw Casey lying in bed, asleep on his right side. Jake pulled out the gun and stood over him, lifting the shaking gun to within inches of Casey's temple. He thumbed the safety off and placed his index finger on the trigger. *I could end this right now and be a hero,* he thought, *but where's the fun in that? The cops will want him alive. And if I just beat him, I can't get in too much trouble. But God, how good it would feel to pop this pathetic fuck.* Jake thumbed the safety back on and raised the gun over his head. With all the force he could muster, he slammed the gun, barrel first, into Casey's sleeping face.

* * *

Casey woke to sudden, bright pain and pawed at his shredded cheek. The long gash ran from his ear across to his nose, and blood flowed out over his fingers like rainwater overflowing the grates of a storm drain. He could taste blood and nearly choked on two molars floating freely in his mouth. Casey spat them out in separate bloody efforts as he tried to sit upright in the bed.

That's when he first saw Jake pointing the gun at him from the foot of the bed. Casey held out his left hand and said something. It could have been "what" or "huh." Jake wasted no time. He slapped away the hand and fell on Casey, grabbing him by the throat and jabbing the gun into his open gash. Casey screamed in pain and horror.

"What did you do to Amy?" Jake screamed, working the muzzle of the gun harder into the wound.

Casey's left arm was pinned behind him, and his right was trying to free the grip around his neck. But Jake was much bigger and stronger, and it was a useless struggle. He was gagging and struggling for air. Darkness was boxing in his blurred vision.

"What did you do to her?" Jake snarled again.

When Casey didn't respond again, Jake must have realized he was choking him too hard and let go. He stepped back, and Casey inhaled desperately and slumped back on the bed.

"Tell me!" Jake yelled.

Between deep inhalations, Casey said, "Why...are you...doing..."

Jake put the gun on the dresser and, with both hands, grabbed Casey's left ankle through the blankets and dragged him off the bed and out the door into the kitchen. The wind was knocked out of Casey again. And he lay bleeding on the cold tile floor, struggling for breath.

Jake kicked him hard in the stomach and stepped over him to retrieve the gun. Casey was in the fetal position holding his stomach when Jake entered the kitchen again. He knelt and slammed Casey's head into the floor by his hair and pushed the gun against his eye socket.

"When you can breathe again, faggot, you are going to tell me everything."

Jake released him and sat at the kitchen table with the gun in front of him staring at Casey, who was writhing in pain, half-wrapped in bed sheets at the end of a smear of blood leading back to his bedroom.

Casey was finally able to catch his breath, but with each one came a sharp pain in his side. At least one rib felt broken, and the blood still pushed out of the wound in his face. He tried to wipe it out of his burning eye but only managed to smear more of it in.

Still lying on the ground, he said, "Jake. I don't know why you are doing this to me, but I was here at the party all night. There are two dozen people who would vouch for me."

Jake bolted from the table, and Casey balled up, bracing for another blow. But instead of attacking again, Jake ran to his room and came back with something in his hand. Jake placed the shoe on the floor inches away from Casey's face.

"This is hers, Casey. It was in your secret box underneath a shirt covered in cigarette holes," Jake said. He paused for a moment before saying, "You tortured her, and God knows what else. Tell me where she is, and I'll end this quickly. Otherwise, I'll get you to confess. We're just getting started here."

"Look at the shirt. It's an adult man's shirt. Dwayne Benoit was shooting Roman candles at people..."

Jake interrupted Casey by stepping on his throat. Casey grabbed his ankle with both hands and was able to lift it enough to unbalance Jake, roll out from under the foot, and scoot back against the wall. Casey's ribs screamed again, and stars filled his vision.

"Call the cops, you fucking psycho. I didn't do anything. I have witnesses."

"You have the shoe," Jake said. "How would you have the shoe if you didn't have anything to do with it?"

"I found it in the woods when I was picking up trash after the party."

"Ahhh. Of course, you did. I mean, you are always walking all the way out to the woods..."

"I was cleaning up from the party! Call Dwayne. Call the fucking sheriff. They've already been out here, goddammit!" The yelling sent fresh stabs of pain to Casey's side, and he doubled over.

Jake fished in his pocket and pulled out an ornate knife wrapped in a rag. He moved it around in his hand to show Casey.

"I figured you would lie. Reverend Gale says you people are excellent liars. But I know what you are. And I know what kinds of fucked up things you do. You have her shoe. You can't deny it. I know you killed her. Were you fucking her when you burned her with the cigarettes? Ohhh, I bet you did. Were you pretending she was a boy when you did it, you worthless piece of shit? I'm going to ask you one more time before I stop playing around with you." Jake paused between each word. "Where is her body?"

Casey sat back upright, jaw clenched, and said, "Fuck you."

Jake flashed a sinister grin and said, "I gave you a chance to come clean. This isn't going to be pretty."

As Jake approached, Casey braced against the wall and waited until he was standing over him. When he was, Casey brought up both feet and tried to kick Jake, but Jake moved away at the last moment, and Casey's momentum took him flat on the floor. Jake fell on him and put the knife against his neck.

Casey looked up at Jake and was fixated on his eyes. There was color there, but something was wrong. It was like he was both looking at and through Casey at the same time. Like a blackout drunk with eyes failing to keep up with the spins. Casey tried to talk, but Jake pushed the knife harder against his throat when he did. Jake began to smile and pulled the knife almost imperceptibly slowly across Casey's neck. Casey felt the blood before he felt the pain. And just after the pain, he had a vision.

No longer on the floor of his kitchen but standing on the shoulder of a country road. It was full dark, and Jake's truck was parked in front of him in the grass. Casey could see Jake in the headlights, stumbling down the embankment and holding the same knife he was cutting Casey with back at the house. Casey walked to the front of the truck and could see another vehicle had crashed and a person was inside, but they were too covered with blood to be able to identify. Casey snapped back to the present when Jake pulled the knife away from his neck.

"I'll go deeper next time. It won't take much more to hit an artery."

Casey knew he was telling the truth. And he knew he had to get into another position if he had any chance to survive. "What good will it do to kill me? I can't tell you anything then?"

Jake brought the knife back to his throat, and Casey said. "OK! OK! I'll tell you everything I know. You won't believe it, but I'll tell you. Let me up. I can't breathe. Let me up, and I'll tell you everything."

Jake didn't move. He said, "Where is her body?"

"In the woods somewhere."

"Where?"

"I don't know. The woods is where I saw it drag her."

Jake stood up and stared at Casey. He didn't stop Casey from scooting back up into a seated position, and he even let Casey work himself back into the corner.

"What did you see exactly?"

"A monster. A jellyfish or something."

Jake said, "Wrong answer," and raised the knife. He ran at Casey, and when he was over him, Casey braced against the corner and kicked both feet up. This time he struck his target, launching both feet into Jake's crotch. The force drove Jake off the ground. He stumbled back, slamming his head against the kitchen counter as he fell to the floor. Casey got to his feet and stumbled against the kitchen table. He saw Jake lying on the ground, eyes wide in surprise and shock. He was neither holding his head nor his balls. He was dazed, breathing hard. Casey took the .380 and spun around. Jake was stirring.

"Don't fucking move!" Casey grunted. But Jake did move. Shaking, he managed to stand and hold himself up in the corner of the counter, slumped over slightly, still out of breath.

"You gonna shoot me? You fucking pansy. You don't have the balls. You aren't even a real man. You are lower than shit. You are a coward who preys on little girls. And now you have the gun, and you think that gives you power. Go on. Shoot me where I stand."

"Sit down and shut the fuck up, Jake," Casey said. The weight of the gun and holding it outright amplified the already excruciating pain from the ribs.

"You ever even shot a gun?" Jake laughed. "And you think I would risk shooting you before I could get your confession? It's not even loaded, you idiot!"

Casey took a step closer, and Jake shrank back against the counter.

"Not loaded, huh?" Casey said. He motioned with the gun for Jake to move back in the hallway, and Jake followed the order. "Go back to my bedroom and stand in the far corner with your face against the wall."

Jake turned and walked down the hall and into the bedroom. Casey followed five feet behind with the gun pointed at the back of Jake's head. When they had both entered the room, Casey watched Jake walk to the opposite corner of the room and stand there facing him.

"Turn around!" Casey commanded.

Jake didn't move.

"Fine. You can stand there and watch me call the cops."

Casey reached for his phone, and Jake leaped at him. Casey stepped back and pulled the trigger, but the gun didn't fire. Before he could release the safety, Jake had his hands on the gun, and they both fell to the floor. Jake put his right hand around Casey's and punched the safety out with his thumb, and forced Casey's index finger down on the trigger.

The close range muffled the first blast. Jake pushed Casey back, angled the gun away from himself, and pulled the trigger again. Casey stopped moving.

* * *

Jake let go of Casey's hand and stood for a second before narrowing vision and wobbling knees sent him down into a seated position on the bed. He could see the blood pooling underneath Casey and allowed himself to lay back and relax for the first time since initiating the assault. But when he heard Casey moan, Jake scrambled to his feet, kicked the gun out of Casey's limp hand, and stumbled to his bathroom.

He splashed cold water on his face and pulled his razor sideways across his cheek. He howled as the thin red line formed and pinpricks of blood began to run down his face. He punched himself in the cut to open it wider and looked in the mirror. It wasn't enough yet. He did it again three more times until the skin was puffy and red.

He walked back to Casey's room and smeared some of his blood on the end of the gun and Casey's knuckles. Casey was motionless but still moaning quietly. Jake brought the sheets and blanket back into the room and threw them in the corner before cleaning the blood off the floor with several fist-fulls of paper towels and hot water. The paper towels went in the trash, and Jake walked one more lap around the trailer before dialing 9-1-1.

23

When Jake heard the first sirens approaching, he pushed his fingers into the cut on his cheek to start the bleeding again and stepped out onto the rain-slick landing at the front door. A light drizzle had started to fall, and a lone sheriff's deputy, Mark Wallace, who Jake knew, was the first on the scene. The deputy drew his service weapon on Jake, who raised his hands and said, "Really? Casey is inside. I don't think he's going to make it."

The deputy cuffed Jake, escorted him to the car, and entered the trailer, gun drawn. Jake sat watching the raindrops merge into each other and slide down the side back window. Red and blue strobes of color danced sharply in each drop, but the lights painted more dull colors on the dirty tan exterior of the trailer. He was annoyed at having been put in the car but felt proud of the work he had done. He had found the killer, and with any luck, had taken him out.

Jake daydreamed about the mayor giving him the key to the city. He could get any girl he wanted. That would show Lisa. He hoped the cut on his cheek wouldn't scar too much, but maybe it would be better if it did. The mark would be a constant reminder to everyone in town of his heroic status. His balls still ached, but it had been worth it. Casey got the worst of the fight and deserved it after what he did. And it was nothing compared to what he'll get in jail if he survives. Jake smiled.

Sheriff Johnson pulled up beside the first unit. Jake made eye contact and watched him rush inside. A few minutes later, EMS arrived. Jake was disappointed when the paramedics carried Casey out of the trailer, uncovered on a stretcher. He had been hoping for a lumpy black bag. At least he couldn't see any movement. Glass half full.

Not long after, Sheriff Johnson approached the car, opened the door, and leaned his massive head inside. "Fancy meeting you again so soon. Come on inside. I've got some questions for you."

The sheriff removed the cuffs when they entered the trailer and motioned for Jake to sit on the couch. When he had, the sheriff pulled a small digital recorder from his pocket and began, "Deputy Wallace over there will get your details. But first, I want to hear your side of the story. You aren't under arrest, but you do have the right to remain silent..."

"Wait, wait. I didn't do anything wrong. Why are you reading me my rights?" Jake said, sitting up tall on the edge of the couch.

"We need to question you about what happened. It's standard procedure. We need to get your side of the story."

"My side?"

The sheriff's eyes narrowed. "Yes. Your side. I suppose the man we just wheeled out of here with two bullets inside him might have a different version of events to tell than you...That's how these things typically go."

Jake hadn't thought they'd care how Casey had been brought to justice, only that he had. And had the sheriff implied Casey was going to live? Jake subconsciously balled his hands into fists.

"OK. I'll tell you what happened. Casey would tell you anything to save himself from the electric chair after what he did. You need to hear the truth."

Sheriff Johnson raised an eyebrow at Jake and finished reading the Miranda warning. "You can start from the beginning."

"Alright. I'd gotten back home from church, and I saw a red shoe under some other clothes in the laundry room. It was the same size and brand as the one Amy was wearing when she disappeared. I knew because they had fliers at the church with her description and all. Anyway. I walked into Casey's room and asked him about the shoe. He got all pissed off and defensive. He told me it was none of my business and that I should keep my mouth shut if I knew what was good for me. It scared me. I mean, he's not a big guy, but...well, I don't know if you knew, but he is a queer. I caught him a few weeks ago with a guy in his room, and ever since, he's been real aggressive and violent towards me."

"OK. So how did he come to be shot?"

"Like I said, I was scared, but there was evidence of the kidnapping right in front of me, and I couldn't in good conscious not call y'all to come out. So I came back out here to the living room to dial 9-1-1. Then when Casey came out of his room in a rage. He grabbed my phone and flung it at the wall. It went through his speaker instead. You can see the damage right there." Jake pointed to the damaged speaker.

"Then things got really crazy. He punched me in the face, kicked me in the balls, and took my gun off the side table. He pistol-whipped me in the face and tried to kill me. Thank God the safety was on. When I saw he was trying to pull the trigger, I knew if I didn't go for it, he'd figure out quick why it wasn't firing, you know. So I tried to grab the gun. I fell on top of him, and we wrestled on the ground for a little while, but he wouldn't let go. I grabbed the gun in one hand and punched him in the ribs with the other. When he still wouldn't let go, I grabbed it with both hands and hit him with the gun. He managed to pull it down. And I guess in the struggle, the safety unlocked, and there were two shots. I didn't know if it was him or me who took the bullets at first, but then he stopped moving, and I saw the blood. That's when I got up and ran to get the phone and call 9-1-1."

"What did he say about the shoe when you asked him about it?" Sheriff Johnson said.

"He told me to mind my own business."

"He didn't deny knowledge of it?"

"No. He just got mad."

"I suppose you have an alibi for the night Amy disappeared?"

Jake's face flushed, and his stomach dropped. How dare they accuse him. "Well yeah. I was in Evergreen with Daryl Slocum, Ricky Taylor, and Donny Jenkins up at Daryl's hunting camp. We didn't leave 'til the next morning. Call any of them right now, and they'll tell you. Casey did it. The goddamn shoe is right there."

"Sit tight," Sheriff Johnson said and walked into the kitchen.

* * *

Daryl was a retired sheriff's deputy who Sheriff Johnson had worked with for years. He called his cell phone, and Daryl answered with a groggy, "Hello."

"Hey, buddy. Real sorry to call so late, but I need to verify a story here. Did you go out of town for the fourth? And if so, can you tell me who all was with you?"

"Yeah. I went hunting over near Evergreen. I was with Don,

Ricky, and this young fella, Jake something. He works with Don at the mill."

"Did any of them leave while you were up there...to get supplies or anything the night of the fourth?"

He laughed. "Hell no. We only took the one truck into the camp, and that night we broke out some watermelon moonshine Ricky had left over from a batch he made last year. We were all pretty well hammered by early evening and passed out not long after."

"Jake too?"

"Jake especially," he laughed again. "He's a big guy but can't hold his liquor for shit. He was sleeping like a baby before any of us and was still on the couch in the same spot when I got up and made coffee for everyone the next morning. He didn't go nowhere. I had the keys in my pocket all night too. Slept on the damn things and still have an ugly bruise on my hip".

"Alright. Thanks, buddy. Sorry to wake you."

"Any time, boss."

Sheriff Johnson squeezed small plastic gloves over his thick hands and picked up the shoe. He pulled the tongue out as far as he could and held it to the kitchen light. Inside, in black sharpie, he could see the "A.G." Amy had written there only a few weeks before when she had attended a church summer camp trip. He flipped the shoe over and saw the "A.G." written on the bottom too. Other girls had the same shoes, and the group leaders had asked the parents to mark them in case there were any mix-ups. The initials were not mentioned on the flier.

He turned back to Jake, who was tapping his foot and wringing his hands. "Your alibi checks out. Now, look. I'll be frank with you. I have a hard time believing Casey instigated the attack on you. The guy can't be more than 5'7" and 140 pounds soaking wet. You must go what? 6'3", 230? And we both remember Reverend Gale coming after me this afternoon. You held him back, but you've been with him all day listening to him talk about witches and evildoers. And all the sudden, you just happen to find evidence. Maybe the reverend gave you the shoe to plant. Maybe she had more than one pair. And maybe you questioned Casey a little too rough? What would you say about that?"

"He attacked me. And I questioned him about it because I found the shoe, not because he's a pervert."

"Here's the deal, Jake. I don't believe you. But I do believe you didn't have anything to do with Amy's disappearance. Still, we're going to have to take you in on this shooting."

"But I caught the kidnapper. How is it a crime to catch a criminal?" Jake protested and started to get off the couch.

The sheriff moved closer, forcing Jake back down. "You said you shot him."

"I didn't. The gun went off during the struggle. If anything, it was self-defense."

"Either way, we've got to take you in. If your story checks out, you'll be fine. But for now, you've got to come with us."

"Wallace!" Sheriff Johnson shouted, not breaking eye contact with Jake. "Get over here and take Mr. Douglas back to the station." The sheriff backed away. He glared at Wallace and tapped his watch as the deputy struggled to walk and wind excess tape at the same time.

Back to Jake he said, "Of course, I know who your hot-shot lawyer daddy is, and I'm sure he'll bail you out real quick, but don't even think about leaving town. If we have to come looking for you to ask more questions, it won't be good."

Jake rose from the couch, and Sheriff Johnson stepped forward again. This time Jake held his ground; his breath fogged the golden star on Sheriff Johnson's chest. The sheriff looked down at him with cold eyes. "Don't leave town."

24

Casey sat on a porch swing on his back deck, holding hands with someone. He was happy. The cool evening breeze blew his hair, and the familiar person he sat with looked him in the eyes, and they were both smiling. Something moved in the woods. Casey could feel the subtle drift of the swing, like the rocking of a boat. And then it wasn't just like water. It was water. He and the familiar person were underwater on his porch. The wind wasn't wind; it was a current. Something moved in the woods again, but it wasn't woods anymore. It was a patch of seaweed. The squirrels and rabbits became shrimp and crabs. Shrubs were coral. And a jellyfish hung in the center of the yard, bobbing gently. The familiar person kissed Casey, and he kissed him back and squeezed his thigh.

When Casey drew back, he could see the outline of the person's face but not the details. Lines of shimmering light kept those covered. And the jellyfish was still there. It was far out in the yard, but something else felt closer. Something else worse, maybe. Casey took the hand of the familiar person, and they swam together into the trailer, past the living room into the bedroom. Casey looked out the window. The jellyfish was closer, but something else was bumping against the trailer. A series of low thumps, not quite rhythmic but regular enough, distracted Casey, and he swam to another window and saw someone glowing white. Casey swam back to the familiar person and almost remembered who he was when the thumps became louder. Then other noises interrupted everything, like a large handful of pebbles thrown hard into still waters. The moment was over, and Casey felt a deep and lonely sadness along with confusion as he woke from the dream.

He became aware of a top-heavy woman nearly busting out of a red leather bodysuit. She was standing over a younger woman wearing a mini skirt and a blouse that barely covered her small breasts. The older woman was pointing a finger with a comically long fingernail at the other. She yelled something about "her man." An audience was jeering at the two, and a skeletal young man with stringy, unwashed hair sitting in a chair between the two women. He was wearing overalls and was yelling back at the crowd. The younger women grabbed the other by the hair, who charged, driving them both back over the chair and onto the cheap carpet of the stage. The man did not attempt to break up the fight, but two security guards were slowly making their way to the women when a commercial for a local check-cashing business came on the screen. Casey watched all of this in a numb daze and didn't at first respond to the nurse who arrived in the room.

"Do you know where you are?" she asked for the third time.

Casey turned his head and squinted at the figure in light blue scrubs next to his bed. "A nurse?"

"Yes, Mr. Sparks. I am nurse Daisy, and you are at Our Lady of Providence. They brought you in after you were shot last night."

Casey stared at her for a moment, past some white material on his face that ran from his nose to his ear, then looked back at the screen. Zero down and twenty-four months interest-free financing on a...

"Do you remember being shot?" the nurse interrupted loudly.

"I don't know. Can I have some water, please?"

"Not until the doctor checks you out."

He grabbed the metal rails on the bed and tried to push himself up higher, but sharp pains in his shoulder, arm, and ribs blasted through him, and he screamed. He tried to grab his side with his good arm, but it was met with cold resistance. Lifting his hand and craning his neck, he could see the handcuff fixed to his wrist. A wave of panic overcame him, and he frantically tried to jerk his arm free.

Nurse Daisy ran out of the room and came back seconds later with Deputy Wallace, who walked around to the right side of the bed.

"I don't understand," Casey said frantically, eyes darting between the nurse and the deputy. "Can you please let my hand go?"

"You aren't going to go running off, are you?" Wallace said.

"What? No. Run away?"

"If you try to get out of bed, this is going right back on. Understand?"

Casey mumbled an "uh-huh." He couldn't have gotten out of bed then, even if he had tried. The terrible soreness and barely subsiding sharp pain from his earlier attempt to reposition overpowered any sensation of the cuffs, which were still secured on his injured side. When the deputy freed his right wrist, Casey reached to his face and ran two fingers over the length of the bandage. It covered the slash underneath in a line from his nose back to his ear. Casey felt the ridge of the stitches and the dull ache underneath each one, but the sensations were borrowed. Like a dream, the idea of pain existed, but not the ownership of injury or any sense of permanence.

Deputy Wallace moved to a green, plastic chair by the window and looked at the parking lot three floors below, bustling with protesters from the church. They carried roughly made signs with messages like "Fry the Child Killer" and "Beware the Wrath of God." Revered Gale stood in the middle of the circling mob with a bullhorn reciting verses from Leviticus.

Sheriff Johnson would be arriving soon, and Deputy Wallace wanted to get the confession before he could, to throw some red meat to the circling sharks.

Nurse Daisy jotted notes in Casey's chart, placed the folder back on the wall-mounted holder, and walked out of the room.

Deputy Wallace stood up and leaned over Casey and said, "If you cooperate and answer our questions, there's a chance you can get out of here. If you decide to lawyer up, we'll place you under arrest right now, and we'll ask the judge to deny bail. And they will. So, it's up to you, but I'd suggest you start talking. Casey, where did you get the shoe?"

Casey looked back at Deputy Wallace with genuine confusion.

"Shoe...I...I'm not wearing any shoes."

"Mr. Sparks," Dr. Bernice Jackson boomed as she entered the room. She walked to the side of his bed, and Casey followed her with his eyes and smiled. More softly, she said, "You are one lucky young man. Both gunshots were through and through. And the bullets didn't change directions in your body. So you have no damage to critical structures and only minor vascular damage. You'll need to be here for at least a few days to receive IV antibiotics for the wounds and for the slash on your face we stitched up".

Casey mumbled, "Hi, Dr. Jackson...Who got shot?"

"Hi, Casey. I didn't know if you would recognize me. Honey, it was you, last night. Do you remember?

"Jake woke me up. He was hitting me...with a gun. Did he shoot me? Can I have some water, please?

Dr. Jackson glanced at Deputy Wallace, raised an eyebrow, and continued. "Casey, you are going to need an oral surgeon to work on the broken teeth once we can get a good head start on any infection from the gunshot wounds and the cuts. Also, you have three broken ribs; well, cracked, really. I don't think they will require surgery, but we need to keep you on pain meds while they heal. I know it hurts, but you must breathe as normally as you can, or you could develop pneumonia. And we want to avoid that, Okay. And don't worry if you continue to feel overly groggy. It's a normal reaction to the pain meds and your body healing from all of these injuries."

"Why was I handcuffed?"

"The deputy should probably answer those sorts of questions. Whatever did or didn't happen isn't my concern. I'm here to make sure we get you better."

"What did happen is my concern, Mr. Sparks," said Deputy Wallace. Turning to the doctor, he asked, "Is he able to take questions now?"

"He's on heavy pain medication and needs to rest a while."

"Right. But he's awake now, so..."

Dr. Jackson glared at the officer. "By law, I have discretion over whether or not your department has access to him at all right now. And I've granted it only because of the seriousness of the allegations and because Sheriff Johnson asked me for special consideration. I'm not a lawyer, but any attorney worth their salt could get a judge to throw out anything Mr. Sparks says while he's laid up on a morphine drip less than twenty-four hours after being shot twice and severely beaten. If you can get information that helps you find the girl, by all means, ask your questions. But he's not thinking clearly right now, and none of what he says would be admissible in court. And for what it's worth, I knew his parents well. They were good, decent people. And Casey has been friends with my son since they were both little. They played baseball together at Cherry Hill High for three years. He was always a good friend to Curtis, even when a lot of other folks weren't. Some of those folks are sheriff's deputies now and have no right to wear a badge if you ask me. The young man right here is 10 times the man those people are, and I, for one, find it impossible to believe he had anything to do with that girl's disappearance."

"I have a job to do; same as you, ma'am..."

"I am a trained trauma surgeon. I run this ER, and you will refer to me as 'doctor' or 'Dr. Jackson.' I've had more years of specialized education than you've been alive. I've earned my title, and I will not be disrespected by a junior officer in my own hospital again. Do you understand me?"

"I meant no disrespect, Doctor."

She looked at him hard and said, "I respect Sheriff Johnson, but I don't know you. So understand that I am keeping both eyes open. If I see you've done anything to worsen my patient's condition, I'll have you out of here and brought up on charges faster than shit through a goose."

Dr. Jackson turned back to Casey and put her hand on his right wrist. The darkness of her skin made his already pale arm look ghostly white in comparison. Her smile was tender. "You can ring us using this buzzer if you need anything. This other button is for pain. It releases morphine when you need it, but it won't give you too much. I want you to rest as much as you can. Okay? And I'll have someone bring you some water."

"OK. Thank you, Doctor Jackson," Casey said. Her touch and smile were so much like those of his own mother that, for a few seconds, he saw his mother's face smiling at him and felt her hand gently squeezing his arm. When she let go, Casey missed her more than he had in years. He pressed the morphine button and held it down.

Dr. Jackson smiled at Casey and flashed Deputy Wallace a stern look before walking out of the room.

When she left, Deputy Wallace stood over Casey again, and in the hardest voice he could muster, he said slowly, "I am done messing around, Casey. I wouldn't give a damn if you played baseball with Billy Graham and Jackie fucking Robinson. You tell me what happened to Amy right now, or I swear I'll see you fry in the chair down in Atmore." The deputy's mouth twisted into a sinister grin. "That is unless Reverend Gale's flock don't break in here and take you out before we can even bring you to trial."

Casey strained to look up at the young officer. And right before closing his eyes and falling asleep, he whispered, "Jackie fucking Robinson."

25

The sheriff was right about Jake's dad getting him out in almost no time, but even the reverend beat Jake's dad, having placed nearly twenty people at the hospital even before Jake made bail. The crowd had grown to fifty by the time Jake drove onto the hospital's campus. The crowd cheered and swarmed his truck as he made his way to the center of the parking lot and where Reverend Gale was holding court.

Jake was new to adulation. He knew he had to play things cool because Reverend Gale had gained nothing from Casey's arrest. Still, the feeling of hands patting his back and the righteous anger from the crowd felt good. In fact, it felt fucking amazing, and Jake could barely contain himself. Knowing what was to come didn't help things either. When Casey did finally talk, he would tell stories about monsters. The authorities would think he was angling for an insanity plea, and the investigation would be done. Jake knew enough about law enforcement from his dad to understand making a case was often more important than catching the right person. This was especially true when the victim was an important person in town, and the suspect was not.

The mob's latest chant was "Make him talk, Make him talk,"

and Reverend Gale watched his flock walk in circles with their signs as he sat on the tailgate of Jake's truck and mopped sweat off his face with his handkerchief.

"I think 'Fry the Child Killer' is my favorite one," Jake said.

"It doesn't really matter what the signs say. It's what the sheriff sees that matters. It's what all the people who can put pressure on him see that matters. He needs to know we are going to make his life a living hell until he finds my daughter."

Jake nodded.

"Do you think Casey really knows anything?"

Jake was shocked. He thought the reverend was eating out of his hand this whole time. Thought he had total command. "Sure. I mean, he had her shoe."

"The sheriff told me they found the shoe there. But it was on the floor. It wasn't hidden."

"It was when I found it."

"What did Casey say when you asked him about it? He didn't tell you to mind your own business. I know what you told the sheriff, but we both know that's a load of shit. It's your business if you are hiding something from the police. I could care less about a witch and her husband, but I want my daughter back, so I need you to tell me the truth."

Jake stared at the reverend and then looked around to make sure the coast was clear. "He said he saw a monster take her into the woods. That's what he told me."

"While you were beating him up?"

"He started it."

"Yet you are here without even stitches, and he is up there on enough pain medicine to knock out a horse."

"I did exactly what our people are chanting now. I made him

talk. And the cops have him now, thanks to me. And yes, I lied to them about what he told me. I don't know why, but it doesn't matter because he's in custody now."

"I appreciate your exuberance. But don't fuck up the investigation by lying to the cops again." Reverend Gale said the last bit louder than he meant to and had to look around to see if anyone was looking at him. He turned down his volume and continued, "And he said a monster took my daughter into the woods. Was it because you were beating the shit out of him, and he wanted you to stop, or because he wants an insanity plea?"

Jake took a moment before he answered. "I think he told me what he saw."

The reverend looked down and sighed.

Jake responded, "What is a monster anyway? People call kidnappers and murderers monsters, don't they?"

"You don't really think he was speaking in metaphor, do you?"

"It's possible. And if the neighbor couple was in on it, weren't they witches. Maybe they did it, and he wasn't supposed to see it. If it was some ritual, they could have been dressed up like beasts or something."

The reverend considered this possibility longer than the first one and spoke: "You know those woods, right?"

"I know them better than most."

"How far back have the searches gone so far? A mile?"

"As the crow flies, maybe. Less in some places".

"What else is back there?"

"Nothing. It's just woods and a few hunting cabins on the property until you hit Northbound Highway 12, where it loops back west; three to five miles deep depending on how far north of west you go."

"I still want you in charge of our search. Are you up for it?"

"Yes. I am." Jake said. Jake was not up for it. But if Reverend Gale intended to flood the woods with people, he might as well be the one in charge.

"First thing tomorrow morning, I want you out there. The rest of the night, we need to organize. I don't want there to be a single minute when someone isn't calling Amy's name."

Jake nodded, and when the reverend got up and started reading chapters from Leviticus through his bullhorn again, Jake scowled and went for a walk around the hospital to think.

* * *

It was vital Jake keep his cool. But it was also supremely challenging. At least he would not have to keep the act up for too long, he thought. And really, this was good. The disrespectful way the reverend was acting reinforced Jake's belief that he had joined the right team in all this. The reverend had been a stabilizing influence, but Jake came to realize the man was all talk. Evalyn, on the other hand, was a woman of action. Sure, it had taken him a while to see past the witchcraft, but his old hunting buddy, Daryl Slocum, and his supply of cocaine, had convinced him to have patience. It paid to be understanding when your dealer was a retired cop who still had a key to the evidence locker. It made one willing to look past things like cults of black magic practitioners.

But the real convincing was seeing the magic work. Evalyn's hexes had wreaked havoc on a host of people in Cherry Hill. One, a former friend of hers, a beloved teacher at Cherry Hill High School, was decapitated in a freak tractor accident after Evalyn had performed a spell. To this day, no one knew how or why the teacher had taken her son's tractor out during a storm and flipped it in a ditch, but that's what had happened. The teacher had spoken out against Evalyn's proposal to the school board to ban prayers before football games. Most of Evalyn's victim's transgressions were minor in comparison. It mainly had been people who had cut her off in traffic or who she thought were gossiping about her. But they had gotten similar treatment. Though most of the time, those people merely had taken ill or had been involved in more minor accidents.

And almost every time, the suffering of her targets had been brought up in church services. The good reverend had led the congregation in prayer for them. It almost never helped. Prayer, in general, almost never helped, Jake found. But taking action did. And Evalyn's most recent project was far too exciting to ignore.

Not only was the magic working, it was unstoppable. Being on the water with the Ruiner, hunting with it, was like being part of a pack of wolves or killer whales. It was beyond exhilarating. The taking of life was more empowering than anything else he could imagine. He understood now why sacrifices made the Ruiner grow. The victims had no chance, and all the energy they expended through fear, resistance, and fight, she absorbed. And for the rest of the pack, there was residual energy left over that he and the other followers fed upon like remoras riding on a shark and cleaning up the scraps. Nothing like that ever happened in church.

The only reasons to go there anymore were to keep the act alive until the Ruiner was fully realized and to sit in the pew on Sunday mornings listening to the prayers being offered up for the ones who were missing because of him, Evalyn, and the Ruiner. It provided even more energy to take into himself.

Reverend Gale was finishing up another bullhorn reading of an especially graphic bit of torture from the Old Testament when the crowd began to murmur and then shout. Sheriff Johnson was attempting to walk toward Reverend Gale and was being blocked by the church members. Twenty feet separated the men.

The sheriff, seeing no way to make further progress, shouted over the human shield, "You don't have to go, but you do have to stop shouting through the bullhorn. We've let it slide for hours now, but the sun has gone down, and you need to respect the other patients and the staff. Some very sick people need rest. This is not helping anything."

"We know our rights, and you can't make us stop," Reverend Gale said, using the bullhorn.

The sheriff shook his head. "The First Amendment to the Constitution of the United States does not give you the right to engage in free-speech activities on someone else's private property. So, yes. I absolutely can remove each and every one of you from this area and will do so if you do not cease the use of the bullhorn right away. The hospital is allowing this protest as long as you comply with their request. It is their private property, not yours."

"We ain't leaving until you give us Casey Sparks," someone hollered from the crowd.

Several other voices agreed, and soon the crowd chanted, "We want Casey. We want Casey."

The sheriff turned and walked away to cheers from the crowd.

Five minutes later, though, a bitter Reverend Gale handed over the bullhorn after receiving three texts from the sheriff. The first was a picture of the county SWAT team in full uniform. The second was detailed instructions for how to perform first aid on pepper ball and tear gas injuries. And the third simply said, "In route. ETA 10 minutes."

Most of the church group stayed, and they continued to sporadically chant, but no one had a bullhorn. Although, if they had, things would have turned out very different that night.

26

Marion was sipping a beer on the shore of a mountain lake watching Chuck try to thread a hot dog onto a straightened wire coat hanger. The sun was setting behind the tallest peak of the snowcapped mountain range, and the carpet of purple flowers they had hiked through earlier in the afternoon to their camping spot was disappearing under the shadows cast by the steep ledges above. Their sweet scent drifted down in waves that even the smoke of the campfire couldn't conceal.

Chuck managed to skew the wire through the middle of the frankfurter and positioned it over the flame. He reached for a beer of his own, and the wire hanger bent down slightly. Before he could recover it, the hot dog slid off the wire and into the coals with an ashy plop.

He looked up right as Marion, laughing, spat out a mouthful of beer all over him. Covering her mouth but still laughing hard, she watched him wipe his face, hold the wire up to her, shrug, and smile. The crow's feet around his eyes had begun to show in this past year. Those and the first specs of gray in his hair had come together like they had received invitations to the same party, but when he smiled, those wrinkles pointed to his bright-blue eyes and made them look more wise and loving than ever. He sidestepped the fire, took her hand from her still-laughing mouth, and kissed her.

As he did, the sound of the crackling fire grew louder and louder until it consumed her senses. She pulled away to see Chuck's much younger face. He was in his twenties and looked every bit the wiry rascal she remembered the first time she laid eyes on him. His smile still held some youthful innocence but also a slightly unhinged look. It was something with how the angle of his mouth played with the angle of his eyes. He only had that look for a couple years before age flattened his features and, she supposed, tamed his attitude.

He said, "Stay strong, sweetie," and began to pull away.

She held his arms tighter and said, "Don't go."

He smiled and drifted away. Marion's hands closed on themselves as he disappeared. She watched him as the image faded, and all she could focus on was his smile. It was brilliant, and it filled her with a peace she had never experienced before. She knew he was okay then. And when she woke up on the dirty stone floor of the cave, the feeling was still with her. At least for a while.

She cried as she sipped water from her hands. The little pool was taking longer to fill up now. She needed it to rain, or better yet, to find a way to escape.

She worked on the lashings again and managed to untie two sets. They had not noticed the first one she had freed. She thought the progress was good. It wasn't close to enough to allow her to slip out, but if she untied another three or four lashings, she would have a chance.

As she was starting work on another set, she saw the torch moving her way, and she stepped back further into the cage.

"Are you ready to talk now?"

Marion was silent.

"I thought you should know the police have arrested a friend of yours. His blood was on the walls at your house, and he had kept poor Amy's shoe as a trophy at his trailer. Serial killers do that sometimes, you know."

Marion looked into the darkness to one side of the torch, hoping her eyes were staring into the hole in Evalyn's cheek she had bitten into the day before.

"The silent treatment is no fun for anyone. I'm telling you the truth. The police have caught the killer and have proof he was at your house too. He'll be lucky to make it out of the hospital the way the church folks are behaving. And you know all of this will get pinned on him now. So what do you say? I've got more food and a whole lot of fresh water if you tell me who you told about us? Did Casey know, or was he just using you as cover for his killings?"

"Casey didn't kill Amy. We both know who did."

"Who else did you tell?" It won't be long now, anyway. A few more feeds and the transformation will be complete."

"If I die here, so be it. But if I helped you at all, I could never be at peace. By the way, how is your face?"

Evalyn spun around and walked back towards the red glow without saying a word.

Marion watched the torch move away and disappear back and to the right. With that small amount of light gone, Marion could see a glowing green shape far back and to the left. It was much larger than the Ruiner had been before and seemed to pulse faint lights inside itself as it floated in the air and slowly grew.

Marion kept an eye on the corner as she started working on another lashing.

27

The parking lot arc sodium lights threw a glare on the glass front door of the Red Lion Lounge, which hid the dark interior of the bar from people coming in from the outside. And Dwayne swung open the door and ducked as he was greeted by a full suit of armor looming inside the entrance with a raised ax.

"First time, huh?" a woman said with a laugh as she squeezed past him out the door he was still holding open.

"Startled me is all," Dwayne said to himself.

It was his first time inside. He had known of the Red Lion since he was a kid, but it had always been a place for older folks and the people from the neighboring dry counties. He had neither been expecting the armor nor the expansive bar to be so active early in the evening, and both threw him off his stride a bit. He was very stoned, after all, and was hoping for a dark, quiet hole in the wall. The dark part was right on, but there was far too much activity for his liking. The pool tables were occupied, and the sudden loud clacking of balls was a frequent, nerve-racking punctuation to the barely tolerable clinking of glasses, thumping of darts, and bursts of laughter layered over a base of indecipherable talking. It was a lot. Dwayne found a spot at the end of the bar and stood there for a minute, looking around, trying to identify Nina. While he scanned, he saw three more suits of armor.

He studied one of these, which was inset into a wall across the bar from him. He imagined the weight of it and the restriction of movement and sight. The massive battle-ax leaning against it had to weigh forty pounds on its own, at least. Dwayne had been to war. And maybe modern weapons could kill more people faster, but swinging an ax in close combat while burning inside a sweat-slicked metal suit must have been one of the most singular hells of human history. He thought they might think the same about modern warfare. They had catapults, sure, but the knight didn't have to worry about mortars falling from the sky. No. The fire-breathing dragons in Iraq were real; the ones in Medieval France were only fairy tales. But preparing for battle had been the same since the first two groups of assholes fought over whatever it was they fought over thousands of years ago. It must have been land, God, or women, Dwayne thought. The feeling of not knowing if you will live through the fight, of knowing what you may have to do to survive. That's always been the same. He pitied the knights because he was once one too, and there would have to be knights as long as there were men on the earth and land and gods and women.

Dwayne put up a hand when the only female bartender looked in his direction. On her way to him, he heard one of the other patrons say, "Another beer when you get a chance, Darla."

When she made it to Dwayne, he said, "I'll have a Bud. And I thought Nina was working tonight? Is she going to be in later?"

The woman took two steps back, and in a series of moves she must have done a thousand times, swiped a Budweiser from a cooler, wrapped a napkin around it, spun off the top, and threw the discarded top into a trashcan at the other end of the bar. All without looking. Dwayne smiled and took the beer when she slid it to him. "Where have you been all my life?" he said.

"Right here, probably. And Nina is right over there, setting up karaoke."

Dwayne followed her glance and saw a thin woman messing with wires behind a set of speakers and blowing hair out of her eyes. "Much obliged," Dwayne said and sat a $5 bill on the bar before walking to the karaoke stage.

Nina was pushing buttons and unplugging and re-plugging wires and cords on the machine and the speakers.

"Hi there. I'm Dwayne Beniot reporting for duty."

She looked up at him, shook her head, and said, "What?"

"I thought he told you about me. I'm Casey's friend. I want to help."

She looked at him hard and waved over a big man who was standing at the bar.

"Everything OK?" Dwayne said, watching the man walk over. Dwayne was tall, but this guy was wide as a bull and was looking at him like he had just slapped his mamma.

"If you want to help, I'll need to ask you some questions first. Let's go outside." She started to walk with the large man falling in behind her. Dwayne went to follow but noticed the power strip had come unplugged from the extension cord. He knelt down and plugged it in. All the lights blinked on the karaoke rig. A few people cheered, and Dwayne bowed to them before Nina shot him a look, and he followed her and her bodyguard outside.

Just beyond the door, the big man stepped to one side and didn't move when Dwayne walked past him to continue following Nina. She walked straight out to a fence and waved Dwayne over.

"If you are really here to help, I hope you'd understand why I have to be careful?"

"I do."

"The big guy by the door. Name's Mike. He's a regular. He doesn't know anything about this, but if you make a move towards me, he'll be over here in a flash. Got it?"

"I do."

"Good."

Nina stood staring at him for a moment and crossed her arms.

When she had not said anything, Dwayne finally started instead. He said, "Casey didn't give me a password or anything, so I'm not sure what you need. I have a text from him from last night with your name and the time he was going to meet you tonight. It's now, which is why I came up here now." Nina didn't answer. "So...um...I brought weed. He said y'all needed some for the spell."

"How well do you know him?"

"He's been my best friend since we were little. I probably know him better than anyone else."

She didn't respond. She looked scared.

Dwayne continued, "If you don't believe me, that's fine. I'll find a way myself. I don't know shit about magic or whatever crazy shit all y'all got yourselves into, but I'm going to do whatever I can to help him. I told him I would, and that's what I'm going to do. But it sure would be a whole lot easier if you helped me out, though."

She remained silent.

"You know, y'all probably shoulda had a password or something."

Nina dropped her head, shook it, and laughed. When she brought it back up, she had a smile on her face. "Yeah. Probably so. We weren't expecting to need one."

Dwayne smiled back. "That is understandable."

She waved at Mike and gave him a thumbs up. Mike waved back and went inside.

Nina said, "With Casey caught, I'm not sure what we can do. We don't even know where they are being held."

"Don't you still need some stuff? I mean, you got some riddle to figure out and some weed thing to make, right?"

Nina nodded. "I guess so."

"Well, let's get to it. If nothing else, it'll give us time to think about how to bust Casey out too."

"Bust him out?"

"I'm tryin' to think positive. Our baseball coach in high school always said success is just opportunity meeting preparation. If we get everything ready, then we've done all we can do to prepare. If we don't, it won't matter. Let's go make some weed sticks or whatever and then go from there."

"They are called smudge sticks."

"Cool. Let's get to smudging! You can smoke 'em, right?"

Nina laughed. "It's the end of the world, and you're making me laugh." She threw her hands up in the air. "OK. Fuck it. Meet me just inside the front door in ten minutes. I've got a place we can do this."

28

The hospital room was lit only by the glowing green readouts of the machines by the bed and the light poles in the parking lot below. He could see the clock on the far wall read 2:27. His thoughts were foggy, but he remembered enough to know he had to escape.

The sheriff would probably never believe the truth, and Reverend Gale would certainly not. Casey had no love for the man, but hearing his voice from the bullhorn earlier had made him want to give him a hug instead of punch him. He wanted to mourn his friend with someone else who missed her. And as flawed as he had been as a father and as misguided as he was now, Casey knew deep down the reverend had tried. And he had loved his daughter in his way. He was a victim in all of this too.

Casey's right wrist was still free from earlier in the day, and he reached over to the table beside the bed to feel for anything he could find to try to pick the other cuff. But the table was bare. He considered the IV but knew it wouldn't bend the right way. His trick cuffs were so much easier to escape from than the real thing. But there was another way he knew, and it was the only chance he had.

Casey pulled the plastic hospital wristband from his left arm. His ribs screamed with the motion, but with one excruciating tug, the wristband came free.

He chewed a straight line through one end to work with the widest part of the plastic; the thin pieces with holes would not work for this trick. He wrapped the band over the teeth of the ratchet part of the cuffs. And worked it into the space between the teeth and the locking bar. Once the plastic had been pushed in about an inch and he felt resistance, he kept the pressure on the plastic and tightened the cuff another few clicks. If it worked like it was supposed to, the wristband would cover the locking bar, and the cuffs would pull open.

He tried first on the cuff attached to the railing, but the plastic bunched up and did not go in far enough. And when he tightened the cuff, the locking bar held firm.

He only had one chance, and he wouldn't get another. If he failed again with the cuff around his own wrist, the cuff couldn't close any tighter. And it would cut off the circulation to his hand. He would need a deputy to release the cuff. He'd be fully shackled in no time. So Casey took a deep breath and pushed in on the plastic with his thumb and index fingers. He felt it moving slowly and tried wiggling the plastic to lessen the resistance. When it had gone in all the way, all he could do was hope it had been inserted far and straight enough. He took a deep breath, then pushed the plastic while also closing the cuff. When it was as tight as it would go, he jerked the ratchet. The cuff flung open, and he was free.

He fought his way off the bed and had to hold on to the railing until the vertigo passed, both from the sudden rush of blood and from the pain. He unplugged the machines from the wall and removed the IVs and the various wires, suckers, and catheters from himself. He searched the room for his phone and clothes. He found neither. Opening the room door slowly, he expected Deputy Wallace to spring up and tackle him. That or the deputy would be asleep outside the room, sitting in a folding chair like you see in the movies. But outside the door, Casey found only a deserted hallway with green linoleum floors and off-white walls lined with brown numbered doors. Casey sneaked out, letting the door close behind him, and tried the knob for the first room he reached.

A young boy slept in the bed, and his mother was asleep in a green chair by the window; a paperback copy of *Skeleton Crew* sat face-down and open on her lap. Casey closed the door gently. Halfway between their room and the next, the elevator binged. Casey couldn't make the next door on his side of the hall in time, so he hurried straight across and fully entered the room. He shut the door behind him as the elevator opened.

Casey found himself locking eyes with a girl in her twenties. One of her legs was in a cast suspended above the bed by some contraption that seemed too old-fashioned to be in a modern hospital. Thick bandages around her head made her look like a mummy.

"Just checking your vitals. You can go back to sleep," Casey said too fast before he could think of something better to say.

"Someone should check yours," she said dreamily. "You look like shit, doctor." She closed her eyes and fell back into a morphine-induced slumber.

Casey searched the room and found a suitcase in the dresser under the TV. He pulled out the only two articles of clothing with any chance of fitting him; a pair of pink sweatpants with "Big Juicy" written on the back with graffiti script and a black BTS t-shirt depicting seven, mostly blond, Korean boys standing around a table looking somehow bored, happy, tired and stupid all at the same time. One of them was holding out a rose. Casey pulled on the sweatpants. They were long enough but were too tight in the waist and hips. His smooshed package protruded indecently from the front in a series of vulgar lumps. The t-shirt was better. It was an extra-large she had brought to sleep in. It was too big for Casey but mostly covered his crotch and the "Big Juicy" stamp on his ass. He promised himself he'd find a way to pay her back when everything was over.

Once dressed, he peeked out the door. He was almost caught then, but the deputy made the turn into the hallway just after Casey pulled his head back into the room. He waited with his ear against the door and heard the clicking of the deputy's shoes get closer then pass and fade away. Casey counted to thirty and peeked again. When the hallway was clear, he crept to the next room. It was empty, but the one after was occupied by an older man hooked up to a breathing machine. Casey opened the closet and found a duffel bag with an Auburn zippered hoodie and a set of BMW car keys. He took both of them and gently closed the closet door.

Casey froze when he saw the two people sitting at the end of the man's bed. He did not know how he missed them when he first entered the room, yet there they sat. They both looked at Casey and then at each other. Casey put up his hands and was about to say something like, "wrong room, sorry," when he noticed both of the people were translucent. So, Casey instead said, "I'm sorry to bother you. I'm not a thief. I just need to escape. It's a long story."

One of the spirits smiled at him, and Casey heard its voice in his mind say, "You can have the car. He doesn't need it anymore. Good luck."

Casey smiled and left the room quietly. He straightened up as best he could and walked to the stairwell as if he had every right in the world to be there.

The stairs were a different story. Every step hurt, and every step down hurt worse. His ribs and shoulder were beyond sore on their own, and the weight of landing each consecutive step down the stairs put him on the verge of passing out. He had to stop and regain strength at each landing. He couldn't hold the railing since it was only on the left, but he eventually gutted his way to the first floor. As he reached for the door, it swung open, and two orderlies came through. Casey said, "Excuse me." And they both saw his shirt and laughed as they walked past him and up the stairs. Casey zipped up the hoodie all the way to his neck. The lobby was to his left, and a hallway to an exit was to his right.

He slid out through the hallway and walked into the parking lot. At first, he could not work out why there were so many people standing around at nearly 3:00 in the morning. Then he started reading the signs they were carrying; "Fry Casey," "Make him Talk," and "Where is Amy?" The panic began to set in. It got worse when he realized several sheriff's deputies were sitting in cars at both of the near corners of the lot. One car sat idling just twenty feet away, and Casey could see the deputy inside looking at him.

Casey looked away, pulled out the key fob, spun it on his finger, and stepped into the parking lot. To evade the police, he had to find the car, which meant walking among the protesters. Casey repeatedly hit the unlock button on the fob as he neared the crowd but saw no flashing lights and heard no horn. Closer still, he heard the conversations and saw people he vaguely recognized. He held his head down as much as he could, in part to keep from being recognized himself and also to cover his face. Walking upright and at a normal speed was torture on his ribs, and there was no way to hide the expression of pain on his face. And the bandage covering so much of his face might tempt an interested person to strike up a conversation.

When he neared the middle of the lot, most protesters were gathered to his left, around a truck there. Casey gave the truck a wide berth and, as he passed, noticed Jake sitting on the tailgate. He was looking at Jake's back when he ran straight into another man and nearly fell to the ground. Reverend Gale was knocked off balance into the side of a small Toyota but stayed upright."

"Watch where you are going."

Casey put up a hand and kept walking.

The reverend watched him limp past. Casey could no longer fake the walk, and the reverend said, "Wait a minute. You look familiar."

Casey kept walking and kept hitting the unlock button on the key fob.

"Hold it," the reverend said.

It was louder this time, and Casey saw some of the crowd had heard it and looked at him. Some of them started walking in his direction. He neared the last few rows of cars and was hitting the fob repeatedly when he heard the reverend yell, "Jake!"

Casey looked back then and saw Reverend Gale pointing at him and Jake standing up in the back of the truck and looking directly at him. Jake jumped down and started jogging in his direction. Casey moved faster. He was falling against cars, trying to stay up. The pain was searing. And just as he passed the second to last row, he saw headlights flash on a black BMW sedan twenty feet away. He sprinted with all he had to the car, and just as he put his hand on the car handle, Jake yelled Casey's name. Casey looked up and saw him close enough to make a positive ID. Jake's face went pale. Casey flipped him off and lowered himself into the driver's seat of the BMW. He hit a large round button near the steering wheel, and the engine rumbled to life. Jake had halved the distance to the car, but it didn't matter. Casey could hear him yelling for the sheriff's deputies then. If only they had a bullhorn. But they didn't. And Casey rolled out of the parking lot in a very fast jet-black car in the dead of night with a great head start on the police. But it was not quite as good for the church folks. In fact, Jake had made it back to his truck, and Casey saw him, at least he assumed it was him, coming up fast moments later.

Aside from the pursuing truck, there was virtually no traffic on Highway 12 in the early morning, and Casey fought to keep the BMW between the lines. The morphine wasn't doing much for the pain, but it had numbed his mind and reflexes more than he had realized before he got behind the wheel. The constant pain in his ribs wasn't helping, nor was the fact he had to drive with only his right arm. Casey let the truck behind him get closer. He figured it was safer than to try and lose him. At least in the short term. Long straightaways were coming up, and he was sure the BMW could smoke the truck when it came to it.

The truck followed at a distance for a while. Casey started to wonder if it was someone from the church or not. He even tried to turn on the cruise control, but the cryptic symbols on the buttons made no sense. *Why the fuck did the Germans use hieroglyphics instead of words?* Casey thought. "I bet people who own these don't have a clue what half of these buttons do." The more he pressed buttons, the more he swerved. Frustrated, he punched the dashboard. He hadn't gone through the hell and risk of escaping the hospital just to wipe out in a stolen car. He had to focus on the highway and the speedometer. It was the only thing that mattered. And just after he regained control, he saw the police lights in the distance ahead and understood. He was being corralled.

Casey slowed and took the first left he found off the highway. And he had some luck then; it was the street he grew up on. He rocketed up the two-lane and found the BMW was as fast as he hoped it would be. The truck behind fell back a good way, and Casey kept accelerating. He knew there was a bend in the road ahead and people not from the area frequently ended up in the cow pasture when they came to it with too much speed. He thought Jake would know the turn and would slow down for it. It might give Casey enough time.

Jake's headlights were no longer visible, and Casey was careening at a dangerous speed, even for someone not on pain meds. He only had a little farther to go when the first of the yellow left-turn signs reflected back at him. Not wanting to skid but needing to make the maneuver fast if it was going to work, Casey applied the brake and hit the gap at fifteen instead of fifty miles per hour. Steering the car into the existing ruts and through the fence, he immediately took a hard right away from the bend in the street, drove another fifty feet, turned around, and turned off the car. He had some cover from trees and an old barn, but if it were daylight, he would have been seen. His hope was that navigating the bend would take enough concentration from Jake, and whoever else may be following, to distract them from looking the opposite way.

Casey's only problem now was the damn lights. For some reason, even with the car off, a set of lights was still on. Casey tried again to understand the damn indecipherable buttons and pushed at them, and waited, a series of nervous experiments. At last, all of the lights were out moments before he saw the trees at the bend light up. The truck took the turn fast and fishtailed slightly before righting itself and speeding away.

Casey put his head back on the headrest and closed his eyes for a moment. The radio had come on when he was hitting the buttons trying to turn off the lights. And while one might not likely describe the voice of Paul Finebaum, the state's leading sports DJ and Alabama football apologist, as soothing, for Casey, it was. It was something normal and grounding in what had been a chaotic and horrific past few days. Casey sat in the dark, waiting for more lights to color the trees, and listened to the hours-old replay of the earlier program. People called in one after the other, telling Paul he was an Alabama hack or an Auburn hack. Casey wondered how many of these people knew the intrepid host was actually a Tennessee graduate. Not many, he thought.

Once he had grounded himself a bit, he decided to look around the car for something to drink. He knew it would hurt. He knew it would hurt a lot, but he needed water. If he was lucky, he'd find something with caffeine, except he wasn't lucky. And he found nothing. The search had been worse than fruitless. He wept in the car, mostly from physical pain. What made him stop was a light in the trees. It was from a vehicle that came slower than Jake's. Casey was sure the sheriff's deputy would do the same thing he did and slip right on in the pasture. It did not. But did shine a q-beam out into the pasture in a wide arc. And had the arc been a fraction wider, Casey would have been caught. But it wasn't. And Casey watched as they sped away.

His thirst struck again, and he realized he hadn't checked the glove box. He bent and, with much pain, opened the box and dragged everything out onto the passenger seat in two handfuls. Inside was the usual car paperwork, including a slick owner's manual. Casey thought if he ever made it out of all this, he'd want a few minutes with the Rosetta Stone of German hieroglyphics. Also inside was a clipboard with what looked to be a baseball lineup and a whistle on a cord. Casey slipped the whistle around his neck and flipped through the rest of the papers. There was nothing of value.

Casey waited another several minutes, and another sheriff's deputy passed. This time no light was shined in the pasture, and Casey thought he might have an opportunity to get back on the road without a tail. The Red Lion was the goal. If he could make it there, he might still have a chance to rescue Marion and Chuck. He pulled the car up to the road, hit some buttons to turn on the lights, and was back in business. Paul Finebaum was talking to someone about Nick Saban, and the man said, "He may get more championships before all is said and done, but 'The Bear' had better style." Casey snickered and thought, *I guess houndstooth is technically a style.* Then he said out loud, "Holy Shit!" and grabbed the whistle around his neck. "Holy Shit!" he said again and started laughing. He'd still aim for the Red Lion, but there was one other stop to make first.

* * *

Yellow police tape hung across the doors at Marion's house. Casey was far more nervous than on his previous visit. No one was expecting him the first time, but now? It was not smart. He knew it, but he also thought it was his only chance. He parked in front of the house and ran around to the back. The woods were quiet. He tried the kitchen door, but it was locked. He didn't have the energy to break the door, and the broken window on the side was too high to reach into, so he found a sharp rock and used it to cut the screen back from the patio. It took longer than Casey thought it would. Each passing minute he felt more exposed. *Of course, they would look for me here.* Only a fucking moron would return to the scene of the crime immediately upon escape. But he had to. He knew he was right about the riddle, and he remembered in the destroyed house, it was one thing they had left untouched.

Once the hole was large enough, Casey pushed himself inside. The tiny metal screen ripped his clothing and left rows of scrapes on his exposed skin. But he could not feel any pain. The ribs and shoulder reserved it all for themselves. He got to his feet, and in the living room, he looked up at the Bear Bryant painting and took a deep breath.

Bear Bryant was the "great king" who held dominion over the plains (Auburn). His black and white crown was his trademark houndstooth hat, and his horn of silver was his whistle. And to get in the keeper of secrets (a safe), you had to know the first year he was a coach at Alabama (the combination).

"Here goes nothing," he said and took the painting off the wall. Behind it was a safe with a built-in combination lock. Casey gave out a small cheer and then realized he had no idea what the combination was. He knew he was a coach in the 70s and had been for a long time, so Casey dialed in 1960. The lock didn't open. He dialed up to 1961, and the lock did not open. He made his way all the way to 1970 before he saw two sets of lights spill across the front window. He dialed the combination back to 1959 and tried again. Nothing. Two car doors slammed outside, and Casey heard people talking and walking to the front door. He dialed to 1958. If this wasn't it, he would have to run. But it was. The safe opened, and Casey pulled out a small but heavy orange velvet bag. He heard beating at the front door. He crept to the kitchen and slipped out the door into the backyard. He had gone three steps when he saw the jellyfish floating out of the woodline at him. It wasn't slow this time. Casey reversed course and dove back through the threshold into the house and kicked the door shut just as the jellyfish slammed into it, shattering the glass. Casey ran to the front and saw the front door explode in and Jake's leg coming down from the kick.

Casey ran down the hallway, past the still lowered and partially destroyed attic stairs into Marion and Chuck's bedroom. He remembered the window. It was unlocked still, and Casey pulled it up and leaped out. He landed on his bad shoulder and ribs. The world was a blast of brightness like he had never experienced before. It was a pain so intense it was spiritual. It was a feeling so real it was too real, like nothing he had ever experienced before had existed. This feeling at this moment broke the illusion of existence. Everything had a starkness and color he wasn't supposed to see. The experience lasted for a few seconds. Long enough for him to never forget it, but short enough for him to regain his composure fast enough to scramble to the car and take off just before his pursuers could snatch him.

He didn't get there fast enough for them not to catch him, though. Because as soon as he took off, he had to weave around a deputy who had tried to block him in with his cruiser. It slowed him down enough for Jake to pull his truck in behind him and slam it into the back of the car. Casey barely kept control and accelerated towards Highway 12. He was about to pass his trailer when Jake tried to hit him again. Casey turned hard right to avoid the truck, but it turned too and sped into his path. Jake was yelling from the open driver's side window for him to get out. Casey instead put the car into reverse and drove it parallel with the trailer. When Jake pulled back, Casey bolted forward and past him. He was crossing over onto the street when the truck struck the BMW in the back-left quarter panel and spun Casey around.

With only one arm to steer, Casey could not keep the car on the street, so when he pulled out of the spin, he found himself back in his front yard. He jerked the car to the right to avoid crashing into the trailer before taking a hard left to get behind it into the backyard. With more room to operate, Casey thought he had a chance to slip past Jake and get to the highway, where the BMW could easily out-pace Jake's F-150. Casey drove in a wide circle along the tree line, but Jake didn't follow. Instead, he parked his truck next to the trailer and opened fire.

The back driver's side window was the first to burst inward. In a blink, two bullet holes appeared in the windshield. Casey could hear more hitting the car's doors. The only way out was to charge Jake. Casey took a sharp angle from the tree line and sped towards him. Jake ran to his truck and turned into the path, accelerating. They were playing some insane mash-up of chicken and joust now. Casey had no intention of crashing into the truck. He was already damaged enough. There was no way he could walk away from a head-on collision.

Casey peeled off back towards the yard, and Jake followed for a moment, then fell back. More shots rang out. Casey could see the sheriff's deputy had joined Jake and was firing at him too. He was trapped. He would have to do something drastic. Casey picked up speed and made another loop around the yard. His head was down, and he could hear the car continuously bombarded by bullets. When he got to the far side of the yard, he slammed on the brakes and let the car slowly creep forward. Jake and the deputy both took the bait. Casey slumped over motionless in the driver's seat and waited for his moment. When the deputy was nearly on him, he stepped on the gas. The deputy had a fraction of a second to correct, but it wasn't enough. He clipped the back-right quarter panel of the BMW before slamming into the tree line. Low oak branches shattered the windshield and struck the deputy in the face. He had managed to stop the car before hitting any large trees, but in a daze, he fell out of the door unarmed, staggering and bleeding heavily from his head.

Jake seemed to have the same plan, but he broke away before the deputy and ended up rolling over two saplings and partially up a fallen oak tree, which pinned his front wheel just off the ground. The back wheels spun forwards, then backwards, but only tore deeper divots in the ground. Jake hopped out with his rifle.

Casey had spun the BMW around and ended up pointing directly at Jake and the deputy. The headlights lit up the woods.

"Go ahead, pussy!" Jake yelled. "You gonna run me over?"

Casey wanted to answer by flipping on the brights. And in a stroke of dumb luck, he picked the right hieroglyphic to turn. The woods, lit in two shadowy-yellow patches before, now revealed a vast area, bright as day and clear many yards past the tree line. Jake held his arm over his eyes to block the light, and Casey threw his right hand over his mouth and screamed.

The crocodile was at least twenty feet long. It moved its massive greenish-tan body slowly towards Jake from the left side of the bright square of the forest. The awkward side-to-side gait belied the explosive speed and power of its attack. It moved past Jake to the deputy, and instead of striking from behind, it slammed its snout into the deputy's back, knocking him to the ground. Jake ducked instinctively and looked over to see what was happening. Jake and Casey both watched as the deputy's shoulders slumped, and he took one step backward before the crocodile struck again. It bit him at the waist and shook. The force sent the man's legs to the ground and his severed torso tumbling to the left. Blood and entrails exploded out in an arc, thick at ground level and ending with an arterial spray reaching well beyond the top of the patrol car. Long bands of his intestines draped, dripping over the snout of the crocodile. The deputy let out a short, weak scream and fell silent as the rest of the blood drained from his top half.

Casey put the BMW in reverse and floored the gas pedal. The crocodile flipped the intestines up and off its snout and caught them in its mouth. When Casey had backed far enough away to turn around, he put the car in drive and sped past the trailer into the front yard. He didn't see if Jake had made it out.

The shattered windows of the car saved Casey. Approaching Rabbit Run Road, he heard the sirens before he saw the lights. Forced to abandon his planned route to the Red Lion, Casey turned the opposite direction on Rabbit Run Road. The blue and red flashers of the sheriff's deputies danced in the trees lining the roadway. Casey watched the colors grow brighter in his rearview mirror before fading away when the road dipped down with a hill. If they had seen his taillights speeding away, at least one car would have peeled off to chase him. But by seconds, he managed to slip down the old two-lane road under cover of the thick stands of oak and pine trees which lined the country road as it approached Highway 12.

The pain in his shoulder and ribs crept back to the top of his mind. Whether it was the adrenaline wearing off or the morphine he hadn't had in at least an hour, Casey struggled to keep the car in the right lane. As he approached the T-intersection, he was met once again with police lights blocking his planned route. A roadblock was set up 100 yards away at Highway 12 and Buck Hollow Road.

A new jolt of adrenaline filled Casey. If they were blocking off Highway 12, surely they would do the same to Highway 83. He had no choice. His only option was to quickly turn the opposite direction and hope he could get off the main roads before more backup arrived. The new route was taking him away from town. He passed two police units, sirens blaring, two miles past his last turn, but they continued straight. Aside from the leap from the window, Casey couldn't remember ever being in so much pain. Every bump in the road brought with it a jab of fresh agony. And each time he had to bear one way or another, his ribs felt crushed by his own muscles working to keep himself upright. He had to get off the road.

With every direction blocked to the camp, Casey continued on another few miles and took a dirt road he knew eventually crossed Hwy 83.

There was no roadblock this far from Marion's house at the intersection. He continued past and eventually turned back towards town, lacing through the forest on a deserted two-lane. Seeing no lights, he turned right and pulled into a parking lot past two familiar concrete lions after a minute more of driving. At 3:50 A.M., it was common for a dozen or more people to still be playing pool, telling stories, and trying to pick up a lay. The closing time was 4:00 A.M. There were only three cars in the parking lot, and Casey recognized one as Nina's.

Instead of parking in the lot, he pushed the fence as gently as he could with the car, and it swung open. He continued past the fence through the alley. He turned off the car behind the building before wrenching himself out and stumbling to a picnic table. Somehow managing to climb on top, Casey flipped over with a brutal flop and lay on his back.

A lone skinny cloud drifted across the sharp crescent moon, and crickets and cicadas made their racket in the muggy July night. The tears that escaped his right eye were absorbed by the bloody gauze bandage which covered the deep slash on his face. The adrenaline was gone. He had made it this far. It would have to be enough because he had nothing left. He watched the stars through tear-blurred eyes until they faded, and he fell asleep.

29

When Casey regained consciousness, he first noticed the sharp pain in his ribs and profound soreness in his shoulder, and the second thing was that he was inside. He opened his eyes and saw a ceiling fan above him and an empty coat rack in the corner. *Why is there a coat rack in the hospital room?* In a moment of panic, he felt he was losing the ability to distinguish between the waking and dream world. But when he saw the Schlitz Malt Liquor bullhead on the wall with glowing red eyes mounted above a flat-screen TV and the little window with the view of the AC unit, he knew where he was.

Casey stood and took a couple steps, but the pain and grogginess forced him down. He angled for the Lazy Boy recliner and just did make it, plopping down hard onto the cracked brown leather. The base lifted on one side, and the springs jerked hard, but Casey's weight was centered enough to force both sides to settle back flat. He grunted, and the chair made a loud banging sound. He looked up to see Dwayne rushing out of the single bedroom. He was standing there in only his boxer shorts. Nina poked her head out of the door and let out a deep breath when she saw Casey.

"We thought you might be them?" Dwayne said. He was out of breath, and he moved to the couch and sat down in a huff. "After we hauled you up here early this morning, there were some visitors. We're not sure who they were, but they didn't look like the police. We need to get out of here when you are ready. You look like shit. How are you feelin'?"

"Same as I look, I guess. What do you mean visitors?"

Nina walked in wearing a yellow robe. She sat on the couch next to Dwayne, and they shared a quick knowing glance.

"We saw two sets of people. One around 5:00 and another around 9:00. The first group just looked around outside, but the second group broke in and rooted around downstairs. We watched them on the security monitor in the office."

"How many people?" Casey asked, and then he sat up and made a pained moaning sound. "What about the car? Did they find the Beamer?"

"Three people each time," Nina said. "And Dwayne drove the car behind the fence in the woods."

"It was pretty fucked up. You're lucky you made it here in one piece," Dwayne said.

"You should see the other vehicles," Casey said. He shook then, remembering for the first time how the crocodile had been lying in wait and indiscriminately attacked and killed the deputy.

Nina said, "It's obvious they are on to us. The cops or the others. Either way, we aren't safe here and need to get out."

Casey looked at Dwayne. "What about your place in the woods?"

Dwayne frowned but nodded.

Casey nodded back. "Good. Because on my way back here, I got the coin." Casey fished the bag out of his pants and plucked the coin out. It was the first time any of them had seen it. The front featured the bust of a woman and a few animal-like shapes. On the back was a series of small symbols etched along the circumference and a strange geometric pattern. He held it out with "heads" facing Nina and Dwayne. In unison, they asked, "How?"

"I'll tell you on the way. And I know where they are. Dwayne, do you remember the sinkhole we used to play at when we were kids? That cave with the two big chambers and the river?" Casey said, putting the coin back in the bag and jamming it back into his too-tight pants.

"Yeah. I remember. Are you sure?"

"I think so. It's the only spot that makes sense." Casey shifted in the Lazy Boy and looked around the room. "Did y'all make the smudge stick?"

Dwayne and Nina both started laughing and failed when they tried to stop.

Casey smiled and shook his head. "Breeders."

Dwayne ceased snickering long enough to answer in the affirmative.

"The only thing left is the statue. We have to get it from Evalyn," Nina said.

Casey nodded. "Almost. We have to find out one more thing too. Balthazar said we need to know what was used to weaken the spirit when it was trapped in the first place?"

"What does that mean?" Nina said

"Who the fuck is Balthazar?" Dwayne said. Nina punched his leg.

"It's a long story too. I'll fill you in on everything on the way to Dwayne's place," Casey said.

Nina and Dwayne packed up Chuck's computer, all the

elements needed for the spell, along with all the first-aid supplies and food left in the apartment. Once they had Nina's Jeep loaded- they thought her vehicle would be less suspicious than Dwayne's- the trio set out from the Red Lion to Dwayne's fixer-upper.

* * *

Casey did not tell them about his visit with Balthazar or the previous night's events on the ride to Dwayne's place. It was partially because all three were too busy being on high alert to have a conversation and also because the bouncing of the Jeep was playing hell on Casey's battered body. Casey did manage one question to Dwayne about pain meds, and Dwayne smiled at him through the rearview mirror. Casey had that to look forward to, if nothing else. As they approached the turnoff to Dwayne's house on Highway 12, fat drops of rain splatted on the windshield: one or two at a time with a pause between them.

Dwayne pointed out the turn and told Nina to take it very slow. And then he turned to Casey and said, "OK. Hold on, man. This is going to hurt." And it did hurt. A lot. The shoulder where the highway met the dirt road was large enough to bottom out any car and most trucks. The Jeep cleared it by half a foot, but it bounced the occupants violently. It would have been country boy fun under most circumstances, but it was agonizing for Casey.

Nina stopped short of a gate set about thirty feet back in the woods, and Dwayne hopped out of the bed and ran to open it. A quick lurch later and a re-lock was all it took for them to disappear in the woods. The rain would wash the tracks away soon enough, and no one was going to look for them at the old Terry place anyway. Dwayne was leasing it from his family out of state on a strictly off-the-books arrangement. As far as anyone in Cherry Hill knew, it was just another tree farm in a sea of them owned by the family of a man long ago departed. They passed an old moonshine still, and Dwayne let Casey and Nina know it had supplied the hooch for the Sheriff's Department Christmas party for forty years up until 2004, but unless it was operated by ghosts these days, there was no reason for any cops to visit.

Another couple hundred yards in, the house appeared. It looked like the typical dilapidated shotgun house you might pass on a lonely country road with kudzu growing out of the windows or the top of a tree poking out from the roof. The kind you wonder how long it would be until a storm finished knocking it down.

"You've been working on this house for how long?" Casey asked.

"You have no idea how hard it was to make it look like this," Dwayne said. "You'll see."

The rain had started falling with more frequency. And when Casey got out of the Jeep, he could see the sky above was blue and clear, but to the west, a wall of bruised thunderclouds sailed in his direction. Those first drops of rain on the burning rocks and shells produced a steam of dirt and ozone. The petrichor smell reminded Casey of his younger years and trips to Mobile with his parents in the summers. Every afternoon, storms worked themselves up and poured themselves out in a few violent minutes, leaving the city blanketed in a thick hot fog. Casey had always thought the smell came from the rain on the asphalt roads, but it was more organic. It was a natural smell, pre-electric. It overpowered the tar and signaled an imminent change in conditions. It was like the smell of salt in the air that hits you as you approach the shores of the Gulf of Mexico, where the continent and the ocean meet.

Dwayne pulled out a key and, before letting the others inside, said, "The only reason y'all are here is because it's an emergency. You are trusting me to help you, so I need to be able to trust y'all too. Do I have your words you won't tell anyone about this place?"

They both said yes, and Dwayne unlocked the deadbolt and pushed open the rotten door.

Holy Shit!" said Nina, walking on Spanish tiles past the foyer into an open living room with a huge flat-screen TV and leather wrap-around couch.

Casey inspected the front door once it was open. It was real rotten wood on the outside, but it was a false face fixed to a perfectly normal heavy wood door. The windows had light boxes behind them, so when you looked in from the outside, it gave the appearance of looking down a dank hallway. But it was just a painting. A very convincing painting.

Casey looked at Dwayne, who was smiling. "I can do a little misdirection too. Come on. Let's close the door. Don't want anyone else knowing my secret."

They walked past a door fastened shut with two master locks. Casey looked at Dwayne, who shook his head and kept walking. They joined Nina in the living room. She was looking out a large window onto the backyard. There was a covered parking area with two four-wheelers parked underneath and a shed. Casey couldn't tell if it was pretending to be ram shackled or if it was the genuine article. A tall, wooded hill further back extended up in a rough horseshoe shape, hugging the backyard.

"There's nothing over there but forest for several miles," Dwayne said. "It's very unlikely anyone would come from that direction. The solar panels are on the roof on this side too. If you were to trek up, you could see them. But if you drive up the way we did." He didn't have to finish.

"Why haven't you brought me up here before?" Casey asked.

"I don't know. Plausible deniability, maybe. If you don't know about the place, you can't tell anyone about it."

"How can you afford this?" Nina asked. "Don't you wash dishes for a living?"

"I do what you do," he said to Nina. "But the drugs I sell aren't legal around here yet."

"You make enough selling weed to afford this?"

"The answer is yes, but the how is for another day. Suffice to say, I've got us a place to stage and go get Marion and Chuck. If they are in the sinkhole like you say they are, then they are about two miles over yonder," Dwayne said, pointing through the window at the hill.

Casey said, "Alright, Let's get over there and scope it out."

"We need a plan first," Nina said"

"I have an idea," Dwayne said.

30

Dwayne parked his four-wheeler half a mile from his first target, an uncapped abandoned oil well, and hung his rifle over a shoulder. The second target, another well, was further from the sinkhole, and he would be able to drive right up to it. But this one was too close. Even with the white noise buffer of the rain, which was falling steadily, Evalyn's followers would hear him if he rode any closer. The plan was simple. Create a diversion and hope it drew any guards away from the sinkhole. He would do that by setting off two explosions. One close to the hole and another further away. The first should get their attention, and the second should lure them further away. If that worked, Casey would sneak into the sinkhole to make sure they were in the right place and scope out the scene. He needed to see the Ruiner to gauge its progress. And he wanted to lay eyes on Marion and Chuck to verify they were okay. And finally, he had to locate Evalyn. It was imperative he make her tell him how to kill the Ruiner. Only she knew the secret.

Before Dwayne set off the first explosion, he called Nina using one of the walkie-talkies he kept stashed at the house.

"This is DB. Do you copy? Over."

"I copy. What's your status?" Nina said.

"About to let the first one go if y'all are in position. Over."

"We are. And you don't have to say over every time."

"10-4, over. Going to set it off in five to ten minutes. Be ready. Over."

"Be careful, and bye."

Dwayne crouched and hurried through the woods to the well. He spotted the bright orange flag first, then the thick black five-inch pipe. It stuck out of the ground two feet, and Dwayne did not know how deep it went but hoped it was like the others. On occasion, when he was a kid, he had dropped rocks down and waited for the splash. He only heard splashing three times out of roughly ten attempts and only after a long time.

The rocks of his youth had been replaced with Mason jars filled with homemade napalm. He had found the recipe online and opted for this mixture instead of gasoline because the homebrew was supposed to burn longer. It may have been unnecessary since the second thing he dropped down the pipe was a sprinkler bomb (another Internet search gem) which should have made a huge amount of racket itself, but go big or go home, he thought. Both were child's play compared to the toys he got to play with in the military, but they would do the trick.

He dropped the napalm down the shaft and immediately lit the sprinkler bomb. He waited for the exposed single sparkler to burn down a few inches before placing the bundle over the center of the pipe. He let go and turned to run at the same time. Halfway to the four-wheeler came the sharp and ungodly loud explosion. Just after, he felt like he was running on a barge, yawing on a rough river.

He knelt for a moment by a tree and radioed Nina. "Was it loud where you are? Over?"

"Very. And the guard is headed your way. Casey is about to go in. It worked."

"Good. Over."

Dwayne was about to run the last bit to the four-wheeler when he saw someone in the distance in the direction he was heading. The man, who had a strange gait Dwayne recognized from somewhere, wore a dark orange robe and milled around for a moment before waving his rifle at something out of Dwayne's view and moving in that direction.

Dwayne jogged to the man's original position, slowing only when he was close to the turn. He saw him again after peeking from behind a fallen oak. He had made it half the distance Dwayne had covered but was still a good fifty yards ahead. Careful to keep his distance, Dwayne continued tailing him and managed to get closer than ever before. The man stopped at a relatively clear area and checked his phone. Dwayne crawled under the low canopy of a nearby magnolia tree. He knelt among the limbs at the base and was raising his weapon to look through the scope when the sound of breaking sticks came from behind him.

* * *

Besides the hole itself, there was one cave entrance Casey knew. It was on the outside north-facing section of the crater-like hill which surrounded the sinkhole. An unusual tree grew there at an angle next to where the hill began to rise. Some of the branches on the south side would have been several feet in the air if the land had been flat there. One of these branches hung just above the entrance, forming a thick cover protecting it from view outside and inside the cave. Leaves, sticks, and runoff from the hill had collected on the branch over time to leave the entrance in permanent shade. Casey had found it playing capture the flag when he was eleven. He and Dwayne had been behind enemy lines hiding when Casey had spotted the branches against the hill. When the coast was clear, he had run to hide under one. When he had backed up, crouching, he had fallen, but not all the way in. It was more like sitting on a toilet with the seat up. But when he heard other kids coming, he finished lowering himself all the way in.

Casey and Nina approached the area with caution even though Casey had spotted the follower from a long distance and knew he would not see them coming in. The deer stand was a smart move, but having a guard dressed up in an orange robe, even a dark-orange one, made him stand out in the summer. And to have him facing the opposite direction meant either Casey had missed a different guard or Evalyn's crew did not know about the other entrance.

Once Casey and Nina reached it, Casey inspected the area and found the sticks and leaves were intact, but the bottom lip had been disturbed. It took Casey a moment before he realized what the markings were-the slick rubbing of a crocodile slipping silently out into the world. Casey shuttered and waved Nina back. They settled down the hill under a sassafras tree. Looking up through the branches, he could see the baby-blue sky trying to peek through the thunderclouds. And for a moment, he watched one lone puff of white cloud trying to grow, drifting slowly from north to south. From this vantage point, he could also see the bottom of the deer stand and the back of the guard. And Casey and Nina were there watching when the explosion tore through the tranquil silence of the woods.

The guard hopped to his feet and looked in the direction of the rising black smoke with his binoculars. After a short time, he turned around and climbed down the ladder. For a split second, Casey was sure he had been seen, and he froze in place. But the man kept climbing down, and Casey thought he had misinterpreted the man's slight delay. Once the man was out of sight, Casey nodded at Nina and headed to the cave entrance.

He crawled through the muddy opening like the resident crocodile and spilled into a small passage-like offshoot of the larger chamber. The walls were lit by a fire in the middle of the chamber, and four smaller fires burned elsewhere around the cave. Slipping around the corner, he saw no movement, but there were clear signs of use. There were four sleeping bags, two blue Coleman coolers, a camping stove, and several canvas chairs around the largest fire.

Past the camping setup and to the right, a natural light reflected ripples from an underground stream onto the far wall. That way led to the sinkhole. To the left was another opening. He crept with his back against the cave wall until he got closer to a set of torches. Nearly to them, he saw something on the ground. Ten human skulls sat stark white in a circle, each positioned neatly inside a rib cage. And like mulch between bushes in a garden, hundreds of small bones from hands and feet filled the spaces between the displays. In the middle sat a statue made of stone, feathers, and bone.

He started for the statue but stopped. Something told him to locate the Ruiner, Marion, Chuck, and Evalyn before he disturbed anything in the cave. He rounded the corner, still sticking to the wall for another fifteen feet, and when the new space opened up, he looked across the room and saw torches around a single cage. He could only make out the figure of one person there. But there was something like a huge octopus suspended in the air in the far corner, much larger than the jellyfish form he had seen before. It picked at a pile of bones beneath it. Casey felt drawn to the creature. Even without it knowing he was there, a kind of attraction, a natural force, glowed from it like its luminescent skin.

Casey couldn't go any further without giving away his position to the spirit. He peeled his attention from the creature and started to creep back out to the main chamber to grab the statue. But as he turned the corner back into the room, a woman with a weeping, torn cheek was standing there, holding a knife to his throat.

* * *

Dwayne closed his eyes trying to heighten his sense of hearing. Whatever was approaching was large and moving fast. It stopped close as if it was inside the canopy with him, and for a moment, Dwayne thought the cold barrel of a rifle was about to chill the skin at the back of his neck. He was sure whatever had been coming had arrived. The crunching started again and made half a circuit around the tree. Dwayne opened his eyes and saw another man in a robe with his back to him. The man further away shrugged.

"Hey," the closer man shouted.

The further man waved his arms and held a finger over his lips.

The closer man turned and fired just over Dwayne's head with a pistol. Four shots went into the canopy, including one which would have gone through Dwayne's stomach had he not been hiding behind the trunk. The man fired three more rounds into the woods to the right of the tree and the rest into the woods to the left. He started laughing. "Why be quiet? Why pretend we are alone out here?"

The shooting had happened too fast for Dwayne to get off a shot of his own. And when the man turned around and walked away toward the other follower, he eased his finger off the trigger and placed it on the guard.

The two robed men found shelter from the rain under the bows of a large pine tree and removed the robes. Dwayne recognized them both. The skinny man with the strange gait was Deputy Wallace, the undercover cop who once put Dwayne in county jail for three months for marijuana possession with intent to distribute. The other man was Casey's roommate, Jake. The men kept checking their phones, and before long, they looked at each other and took off running in the general direction of the sinkhole, not to the site of the explosion.

Dwayne abandoned the plan to set off another explosion and instead slipped through the woods back to the four-wheeler. He took a path that arced towards his house and away from the direction the two men had headed towards. After parking as close as he dared, he hiked to Nina. On the way, he came close enough to the hole to see the rim. It was bare. No sign of anyone using it. He had expected to see all sorts of witchy things. Then something drew his attention. To his right were a dozen plainclothes people, Jake and cop boy included, cresting the far hill. Some wore "Army of God" t-shirts Reverend Gale had handed out at the hospital protests. And they all had guns.

"Holy Shit," Dwayne said and snuck back down the hill to Nina's position near the cave entrance.

Dwayne slid down a hill adjacent to the sinkhole hill and hurried around until he saw Nina waving her arms from under a sassafras tree. He ran to her and grabbed her in a tight hug.

"Baby, we need to get out of here now. Church people are here with guns, and Jake is one of the guards. A sheriff's deputy is one too. The whole damn town is in on this."

"We can't leave Casey. He's still inside."

The two had agreed Dwayne would go in after Casey, but they heard voices from above. On the hillcrest, men milled around, one after the other, looking nowhere in particular but all holding rifles. One of them yelled, "Come out, come out wherever you are, Satan worshipers."

These men appeared and disappeared from their view like a lost patrol walking in circles. Had Dwayne tried a run for the entrance, he would have been seen. All he and Nina could do was hunker down and wait it out. Reverend Gale was among the group. Despite the heat and the long hike to get to the place, he wore a dress shirt under a camouflage vest, dress pants, and dress shoes. The storm was ending, and the humidity from the evaporating rain was intense. The reverend patted his face with a handkerchief. Nina's phone vibrated, and she saw a text. She held it up to Dwayne, who sighed, and she typed a reply.

31

Evalyn held the knife an inch from Casey's throat. "Well, lookie what we've got here now. You shouldn't be here, boy," she whispered.

"Give me back my friends, and I'll leave," he said, answering her in kind with the same hushed tones.

"No time for that anymore."

"Why?" Casey said louder.

His voice made her jump, and she started shaking. Casey understood. She didn't want the spirit to hear her any more than he did. It occurred to him then that he was their scapegoat. She intended to pin all the murders on him. And it wouldn't do for him to be eaten, not yet, anyway. Not until this thing was fully unleashed. Casey tilted his head forward to make the knife touch his neck. It worked to give him a vision. He thought if he saw anything it would be her terrified of getting caught by the monster, but what he saw instead filled him with horror. It was a vision in real time. He could see what was in the other chamber of the cave, and he could see it coming for him.

He jerked his head back. His fight-or-flight response took hold, and he opted for both. In one fluid move, he ducked and kicked at

Evalyn's legs as hard as he could, catching her just below the left knee. She folded to the cave floor and screeched. She kept screaming as Casey ran as fast as he could to the tiny cave entrance. He looked back halfway there and saw the octopus now morphing into a pointed squid-like thing, making up the distance in bursts and starts. He knew he was not going to make it. But then he heard the dull music of, "Come out, come out wherever you are," spoken sing-song from outside. Casey turned to look back and saw the squid had followed the noise instead of him and moved impossibly fast towards the stream and then out of the cave. Casey slithered through the cave entrance, grasping at the ground to pull himself through faster. He popped out onto the leaf clutter and looked down to see Dwayne and Nina looking up at him from the base of the sycamore tree. They held their arms out, motioning him to stay where he was. But he ran towards them instead, making his own arm motions and yelling, "Get Down!"

* * *

The timing could not have been better, Jake thought. The morons from the church had taken the bait and were in position. And a few minutes before, he had seen Casey at the bottom of the hill. Jake thought for sure he would have run away, fled to Mexico, or disappeared to some big queer city. But no. For some reason, he still thought he could win. Dealing with him would come later, though.

Jake had managed to get the reverend and the crowd to the sinkhole simply by telling them he had found Casey's hideout. Easy as pie. A tiny part of him felt something, though. It was closer to nostalgia than regret, but some core sadness was there. After all, he had loved Reverend Gale, or at least he had loved his fire and brimstone sermons and how easy he had been to manipulate. He felt nothing for the rest of them. A few had been good hunting and fishing buddies. That was true. And one of them scored him whores every now and then. But they were not good people. No, they had all preyed on Jake's weakness or tried to use him to feel better about themselves. One way or another, they all fed off him. And it was time for Jake to feed. It was time to watch the sheeple go to slaughter.

Jake had started by yelling the phrases "Where are you" and "Show yourself." He knew it would be contagious, and it was. He let it go on for another few minutes, then yelled, "Reveal yourself unholy, Leviathan!" A few of the church people looked at him sideways, but most of the others murmured approval. It was okay to go a little off book. A splash of creativity never hurt anyone, unlike what he did next.

Jake casually moved away from the rim of the sinkhole amid the yells. His yells had primed the mob, and his until-recent position had nudged the group to the edge. The last line, "Come out. Come out, wherever you are," finished his job. Immediately after yelling this, he ran to the side of the hill and knelt beside a tree. He had wanted to drop to the ground and roll down to safety. Had wanted to run as fast as he could. But he couldn't help it. He had to watch. He needed to see them all pay. It was more important to see it than to escape. Besides, the Ruiner didn't want him dead. Not really. At least, he hoped not. He was her best disciple. And even if she could get a bit carried away at times, if he stayed by himself, he'd probably be okay.

The couple of people who noticed him running forgot immediately when they heard the screams and looked back in their direction.

Jake watched most of the bloodbath from next to the tree. Tentacles with long, piercing needle-like claws at the ends impaled the faithful, and they were pulled one by one into the hole. One of the deacons ran towards Jake as if to share in what little safety a tree would provide. And he surprised Jake because the man had not been going for the tree. He had been going for Jake's gun. Not just going for it, but actually got it. Jake didn't even give up a fight. He was so enthralled by the chaos that giving away his weapon seemed consistent with the mood. He watched the man turn and indiscriminately blast away towards the center of the sinkhole. Jake found himself pulling for the man in some strange way. *Good for him*, Jake thought. *You don't have to take this shit.* The man ran towards the hole and began firing directly into it. A tentacle wrapped around his neck and toppled him inside. Jake clapped. Jake clapped like a lead-poisoned emperor watching a deer poacher pulled apart by dogs.

He saw Reverend Gale then. He had been trying to pull a man free from a tentacle when a different one pierced him through the belly. The reverend looked down and screamed. The claw protruded a foot, and Reverend Gale gripped it with both hands and was trying to push it out when he was snatched backward and pulled like a rag doll into the hole. The screams were intense, and the slaughter was almost complete.

Deputy Wallace was standing stupidly among the remaining churchgoers. At first, Jake thought Deputy Wallace was crying but then realized he was laughing. Hysterically laughing in the faces of people who were screaming. That made Jake smile. Wallace was an idiot, true, but he could be alright sometimes. Hell, he could be downright heroic, like when he hid Amy Gale's second shoe from the other sheriff's deputies the night Jake was arrested. Bringing the shoe along had been a good idea, in theory. How could he know Casey would have the other one? But leaving it in his room had been sloppy. Good old Deputy Wallace came to the rescue, though. He had been on his toes that day. And now Jake watched him and hoped the spirit would let him live, but just as he had the thought, a spike from one of the tentacle arms shot through the back of Wallace's skull; the tip came to rest on the teeth of his bottom jaw. And even as the tentacle was lifting him off the ground to pull him into the hole, the spike casually tapped single teeth in a row like a bored child pressing the keys of a piano.

Can't win 'em all, Jake thought as he sneaked further away and eventually down the hill. At the bottom and rounding it to the north, he saw Casey, Dwayne, and some lady he didn't recognize huddled together. Jake went to raise his gun but realized he didn't have it in his hands. He remembered the deacon and started laughing to himself. He didn't know if it was the shock of seeing so many die or if it was something magical the Ruiner was doing. Or maybe it was a type of ecstasy one experiences when something you dream about comes true, but the feeling was overwhelming. It had felt the same way the other times too, especially with the two groups of boaters. Watching them die felt like being charged up from the sun.

Lacking the gun, he made a move to go back, and then he reversed course to charge at Casey and his friends. Dwayne went for his gun, and Jake dove to the ground and then scampered away in the opposite direction. He ran aimlessly for half a minute until he heard the roar.

* * *

The roar shook the ground as a monster burst from the sinkhole into the sky. Casey could not make out much as he shielded himself from the leaves and small limbs raining down from the trees around them. But what he could see what huge, dark, and racing away from them at great speed.

"We're too late," said Nina.

"Let's get out of here," said Dwayne.

"No. No. This is perfect. We can get in now. Marion is in there. I saw her and Evalyn. No one else. The monster is gone. Jake is wherever. This is our chance."

They all looked at each other and started towards the entrance.

"Wait out here," Dwayne said to Nina.

"The hell you say. That crazy-ass Jake is around somewhere. I'm with y'all."

"Fine. Stick with me."

"No," Casey said. "Nina, you come with me. Dwayne, stay just inside the entrance. From there, you can see anyone coming from the hole or our way. We need you to cover our backs. And remember. We need Evalyn to talk."

The three climbed inside the cave and waited for a moment to let their eyes acclimate to the darkness. They could hear yelling from the other chamber.

Fires were still burning, and Casey whispered to Nina about the bones ahead. He didn't want her making any noises to alert Evalyn. But before they reached where the bones had been, Casey could see the stacks had all been blown down and lay strewn across the cave floor. He and Nina stepped over dozens of bones before they rounded the corner.

When they did, both the yelling and the source became clear. Evalyn held onto the cage bars screaming in at Marion. Her voice was equal parts hatred, victory, and anguish. "She is going to tear you apart, bitch. Just like your husband."

Casey and Nina crept up on her. Marion saw them, and a quick look of surprise rose on her face before she looked away. She later told Casey she thought she was dreaming.

The face alerted Evalyn, and she whirled around on the intruders. "If you come any closer, she dies."

Marion moved to the front of the cage. "Is that you, Casey?"

Evalyn followed her, holding the same knife she wielded earlier in one hand and the cage in the other. "Shut up."

"Drop the knife, Evalyn," Nina said.

Evalyn laughed. "She's going to eat you all. You know that, right?" She lurched at Marion. And with the hand which had been grasping the bars, gripped Marion's hair instead, supporting her weight against her. Marion screamed, and the two ended up face to face with the knife still at Marion's throat.

Dwayne appeared next to Casey and leveled the rifle at Evalyn. "I can take her out. It's not far," Dwayne whispered to Casey.

"What are you doing. You are supposed to be watching our backs. And we can't kill her," Casey said.

Casey whispered something else to Dwayne, and seconds later, Dwayne put down the gun and sighed.

"Finally, one of you does something smart," Evalyn said, easing her grip a little and moving the knife away from Marion's throat.

Casey held the light on his phone tight against a finger and turned on the flashlight app. Dwayne saw him do it and yelled for Marion to get down. The light must have blinded Evalyn and Marion for a few seconds. Marion did get down, but Evalyn didn't, couldn't, at least not quickly. Casey was sure he had blown out her knee, and if she fell, she wasn't getting up again.

Casey and Dwayne advanced on her. She swung the knife wildly and kept them at bay for a moment but then lost her handle. She was bound to with only the one hand keeping her up. As soon as the knife struck the floor, Marion popped up and wrenched open the corner of the cage. She had not managed to remove enough lashings to get her body out, but there was plenty of give for a head.

Evalyn could not react fast enough, and her own grip on Marion's hair helped pull her own arm and upper body into the cage with Marion. Marion let the bars go and put both hands around Evalyn's neck, and pulled hard. Casey yelled at her to stop, but Marion kept pulling long after the woman stopped moving. She did not let go until Casey had cut the lashings with the knife Evalyn had threatened both of them with.

She staggered out of the cage and hugged Nina and Casey. Casey wiped sweat from his brow and looked down at Evalyn's body. "We needed her to tell us…"

"I did it for Chuck," Marion said.

Dwayne offered her an arm and helped walk her to the exit. Casey went to the field of bones. He pocketed a few candles and other ritual objects lying among the disaster. *Any clue can break the case at this point,* he thought. He found the statue pinned under a ribcage at the far end of the cave.

He had to touch the bone to retrieve the statue, and he didn't think before he moved it out of the way. When he did, a vision came. He saw his own backyard and a shooting star. *It had to be Amy's bones,* he thought, but they looked too big to be hers. Dwayne called to Casey and tapped a non-existent watch. Casey snatched the statue and rejoined the group.

At the entrance, Casey went through first. He pull-crawled out, certain Jake would be waiting. But Jake was nowhere to be found. The others came out and piled on the four-wheeler and rode back fast to Dwayne's house in the woods.

* * *

The first call was from the Conoco station, where the manager, Ned Reiley, was talking so fast that the deputy who took the call couldn't understand a word. A minute later, the phones were covered up completely, and every caller had the same message: a dragon was destroying Cherry Hill. Sheriff Johnson was being told all of this when the building began to shake. He rushed to his office window to see what didn't look like a dragon so much as a manta ray with a giant eel head gliding twenty feet above Main Street. Mr. Pearl, the owner of the hardware store, was walking his dog. His fight or flight chose neither, and he simply stood in place as the creature glided towards him and took his whole body, sans the left arm holding the leash. The dog ran after the thing barking with a leash and the still-gripping arm trailing behind it. The sheriff turned to call the state or the marines, or whoever when the power went out in the building knocking out the internet and VOIP phones. The cell towers had already been knocked over.

32

Nina helped Marion to the only bedroom in Dwayne's house. She brought her some water, and after twenty minutes, a Salisbury Steak Hungry Man TV dinner.

Casey and Dwayne both grabbed beers and walked out onto the front porch to smoke. Neither said anything for a long time, and they both scanned the woods for Jake and the sky for the monster. They were finishing their cigarettes when a shiny Chevy truck drove up the driveway. Casey started and looked at Dwayne, who stood still.

"Your, uh, friend with the house," Dwayne said.

Balthazar stepped out of the Chevy, looking less like Rhett Butler and more like a model from the LL Bean catalog. He grabbed a bag and rushed to the door. Casey tried greeting him with a handshake, but Balthazar pulled Casey in for a hug instead and then extended a hand for Dwayne. After the obligatory handshake, Balthazar said, "Now let's please get the fuck inside. That thing flew over the highway about fifteen minutes ago, and I don't want it seeing me."

The three men took fresh beers and stood watch at separate

windows in the living room.

"I didn't expect to see you. What are you calling yourself these days?" Casey said.

"We can stick with Balthazar. I didn't expect to be here either, but Evalyn sent her goons to take me out. She must not have known I have a terrific security system and was alerted before they even made it onto my dirt road. You didn't get to meet Hansel and Gretel, my Doberman pinschers, but those poor guys did. I figured it was just a matter of time before she would bring a bigger force, or the Ruiner would come herself to tear down my house. Besides, I owe it to Marion. And to you, in a way. I should have told you..."

"It's OK. I guess we both got what we were after that night," Casey said.

Balthazar took a long pull of beer. "So what have I missed, apart from the Ruiner achieving flight?"

"A lot. We saved Marion, thank God; she is sleeping upstairs, but Chuck is dead. Evalyn is dead too."

Balthazar didn't respond for a long time. When he did, he said, "We have to get it back here."

"How do we do that?"

"Perform the ritual."

"She's fully realized. It won't work."

"Why not?"

"Well..." Casey said.

"Nobody said it couldn't work. We'd have to be crazy to try it since it will most likely swoop down and kill us. But no one said it couldn't be done. And we don't really have much of a choice anyway."

"What are we waiting for?" Dwayne said.

"How they weakened her," Casey said to Dwayne. To Balthazar, he said, "We have everything else-the statue, the coin, everything. Is there anything else about the legend that might help?"

"Let me see the statue," Balthazar said.

Casey placed it on the counter in the kitchen, and Balthazar studied it for a long time. He inspected the feathers and markings and shook his head.

"Is there anything else from the legend? Did her rival hit her with a club or shoot her with an arrow? Do you know anything else?" Casey asked.

"Nothing for sure."

"You said the pattern on the coin might be a tartan. Why did you think that? They aren't plaid."

"No. They are not, but there is some strange language about dangerous velvet. That might lend itself to clothes. And thus, the tartans. Personally, I always thought it might refer to herbs or a potion since she and her rival both practiced witchcraft. And a velvet bag of poisonous herbs might rightly be described as dangerous. But it's not spelled out that way in the legend, unfortunately."

Casey sighed and pulled out the other items he took from the sinkhole. There were two candles, some sort of hand-stitched fabric, and a coin. He picked up the coin he took from Marion's house and laid it next to the one from the sinkhole. The markings were different, but the patterns on the tails side of each matched up. Casey gasped.

"This is what I saw at your house after. After the ritual."

"So much for secrets," Balthazar said.

"These alternating pyramid shapes. The pyramids pointing down were light brown with a darker brown circle inside. Then there was another pyramid pointed up. It had a light background, a smaller dark brown pyramid at the top, and two dark circles at the bottom. When you lay the coins like this, you can see the pattern."

Balthazar moved over to see the coins at the proper angle. He looked for a moment and shook his head. "Some kind of esoteric seal or rune. I am not familiar with these markings."

Dwayne walked over and stopped.

"You got to be shittin' me." He touched the first coin and said, "Light brown and a dark spot, right?"

Casey nodded

"And this one is a white background, and these shapes are dark brown?"

Casey nodded again and raised an eyebrow.

"Hot damn, I've got one."

"Got one what?" said Balthazar.

"Dangerous velvet. A fucking Terciopelo, that's what," Dwayne said with a huge smile.

Balthazar and Casey shared a puzzled look, and Dwayne continued, "A *Bothrops asper*, a *Fer-de-lance*, Lancehead." They both shrugged.

"Jesus, don't y'all watch Discover Channel? It's a fucking fowl-tempered pit viper native to pretty much everywhere from Mexico to the top of South America. And one of its common names is Terciopelo, which is the Spanish word for velvet."

"Wait, you have one?" Casey asked.

"Yeah, I told you I had quite the collection going...on account of the, um, second job," he said as he stole a glance at Balthazar.

"You have one here? Now?" Balthazar asked.

"Hell yeah, I do."

"Let's see it."

"OK, but I'm not taking it out of its enclosure unless I have to.

You have to come down to see it."

Dwayne removed the two locks from the hallway door and stepped into another hallway. Inside this one was a door on either side, both with two locks and both with signs. The sign on the door on the right was a bumper sticker with a graphic of Bob Marley smoking a joint. The sign on the door on the left was bright yellow with the words "warning dangerous animals" written in red block letters. Casey wondered if a judge sentencing Dwayne for a marijuana-growing operation and keeping illegal venomous reptiles would give him any time off the sentence for the warning sign. He figured it might be good for a month or two. Maybe.

The piney scent of marijuana was thick in the hallway, but none of them said a word. Dwayne unlocked both the padlocks and placed them in his pocket. He turned to Casey and Balthazar and said, "Don't tap or shake any of the enclosures. And if I say to get out, don't ask questions, just do it, okay. Some of these guys are escape artists."

Casey and Balthazar shared a concerned look, but each nodded to Dwayne.

Inside the simple converted bedroom, three walls were filled with snake enclosures. On the far wall and the wall to the left, enclosures were stacked three high and five wide. Casey and Balthazar looked around, distracted from their mission by the wildlife display.

Casey could see snakes of various colors and shapes, and he recognized a few species. Rattlesnakes and copperheads (Dwayne had two of each) were easy enough to identify since they were native, but others, like the pythons and boa constrictors in the much larger enclosures on the right wall, he had only seen on television.

He inspected the cages and saw many more he had never seen before. Dwayne stood behind him calling out names when Casey would move to another enclosure. A pair, one a stunning yellow, the other turquoise, hung next to each other like tight knots in fake tree limbs. Dwayne said they were called variable bush vipers. They looked like dragons to Casey. Other snakes slithered around the edges of their enclosures.

One, a particularly thick snake with an enormous diamond head and tiny dots for eyes, crawled to the front of the enclosure like a caterpillar, keeping its body in a straight line. When it reached the glass, it raised its head and looked at Casey. Casey knelt down and studied the strange pattern of alternating rectangles and hourglass shapes laid out in a perfect line down its back and rough diamonds along its sides.

"That's a *Bitis gabonica,* a Gaboon viper," Dwayne said.

"It's the most terrifying snake I've ever seen," Casey said, "That pattern is nuts."

"It's one of my favorites. It's got the largest fangs of all venomous snakes, one of the fastest strikes, believe it or not, and it's the one I'd least like to be bitten by in this room. You don't want to know what happens when you do... It ain't pretty even if you do survive."

"Is this a cobra?" Balthazar said, watching a stunning orange and black-striped snake coming to the front of its enclosure and hooding.

"Yep. It's called a coral cobra. Beautiful snake. There's no antivenom, though, so that's one I have to be extra careful with."

"Are these all poisonous?"

"Venomous, you mean. Generally, poison is ingested, and venom is injected. But no. I keep both here. The big enclosures have non-venomous boas. And sometimes, if I want to handle a snake without getting killed by venom or crushed to death, I have a funny little corn snake over here."

Casey stepped back from the Gaboon viper and looked around the whole room, taking it all in. "I knew you had the pair of rattlesnakes. When the hell did you get all these others?"

"I've been adding to the collection slowly over time. I have clients in more lenient places, Louisiana and Texas mainly, and sometimes we arrange for trades."

"Is it legal to have these?" Balthazar said.

"Some of these are legal- the corn snake, for example. Some aren't."

"Holy Shit," Casey said, standing in front of the *Bothrops asper* enclosure. "This is exactly what I saw."

Balthazar held the coins up to the cage and nodded. "Venom would be a kind of potion, I guess." He looked at Dwayne. "Is it venomous?"

"Extremely. You really don't want to get tagged by this."

Casey looked up and said, "This has to be it."

"Yeah, but how are we going to get it to bite her?" Balthazar said.

Dwayne frowned and sighed. "We can't throw it at her; can't make it bite her. We have to get the venom under her skin. I have to milk it and find a way to inject it into her."

"Do you have tranquilizer darts?" Casey said.

"I wish."

"I have a syringe in the truck," Balthazar said. "The one time Type-1 diabetes comes in handy."

"OK then. Go grab it and meet us back in the living room," Casey said. "Time to put the plan together."

* * *

Marion slept while Nina joined the men downstairs. The plan was simple. At the sinkhole, Dwayne and Balthazar would cover the others while they performed the ritual. Casey would lead the chanting since he had proven he was a capable "battery" at Balthazar's house. Once the spirit was trapped in one form, one they all agreed shouldn't be able to fly once the ritual was over, Casey would chase it down, inject it with venom, and they would call it a day. Marion said it had to be Casey but would not reveal why.

"What about Jake?" Balthazar said.

"We all have to keep an eye out. We'll be watching for the spirit anyway."

"Do you have extra guns?" said Nina. "If you do, we all should have them."

"I have two 9-mm handguns, a 280 rifle, and a 20-gauge shotgun. Balthazar and I should have the rifle and shotgun, and if you and Marion want the 9s, I guess that's okay if Casey doesn't mind."

"Fine by me," Casey said, then added, "Do you have any more napalm or anything else we can throw? If the spell doesn't work or if she comes back before it's done, do you think a 280 and a 20 gauge will keep her at bay?"

"What do you want, a tank or a bazooka?"

"I don't know. What about the flame throwers?"

Dwayne smiled.

"Are you fucking serious?"

"Why didn't I think of that? You didn't think I had really gotten rid of those, did you? I had a client hold on to them for me for a while for an ounce of weed."

"OK. Good. Now we are onto something."

"It may not be enough to kill it, but I can't see anything trying to cross it."

"If I can get the ritual done quick enough, you can hold it off."

"I think so."

Dwayne headed for the front door and waved the others to follow. While walking around the house to the back shed, he said, "If either still works, I have a new plan for our weapons. And before you ask me, Nina, I don't think these are legal either. But they work great. Scary, but great."

Dwayne opened and entered the shed and handed Casey a strange, L-shaped metal item, and said, "It needs to be charged up." And then walked out of the shed with a tank strapped to his back connected to what looked like a pressure washer's spray nozzle. "Let's see if it works. Stand back." They all did. Nina and Balthazar had puzzled looks on their faces, but Casey was smiling and hoping there was life left in the weapon.

Dwayne pressurized the system, lit the pilot, aimed the nozzle, and pulled the trigger. A continuous stream of fire flew twenty feet into the air. Dwayne and Casey let out dual cheers.

"I think it might be better than a shotgun," Casey said.

"Yep. Just a bit."

"Bring the other one inside. I need to clean them both off and get 'em ready for combat. Balthazar, I got a YouTube video for you to watch. You will use the little one. It's easier to fire and plenty badass." Balthazar gave him a thumbs-up, and they all hurried back inside the house.

* * *

While Balthazar used Chuck's computer to watch an instructional video on flamethrower operation, Casey looked over the ritual and visualized how it would go. Nina went to the reptile room with Dwayne to assist him with the venom extraction. They set up a folding table and placed a pint glass there along with a water bottle and Balthazar's syringe.

"I've only done this a few times and never with this snake," Dwayne said. He went to a mini-fridge in the corner and pulled out a beer. "Want one?"

She shook her head.

He drank half and belched. "I don't know if this is going to work, but on the plus side, these snakes produce a lot of venom. I should only have to do this once if I do it right."

"What do you want me to do?"

"Just be here for moral support. If it gets free, get out of the room and close the door. If I get bit, call 9-1-1 and drive me to the highway. Otherwise, just wish me luck and keep back. They can freak out and move a lot faster than you think, so keep your distance at all times."

He downed the rest of his beer and grabbed his snake hook.

Nina softly chanted in the corner, and Dwayne stopped for a moment to watch her before sliding open one side of the enclosure and fishing out the four-foot snake with the large hook.

The snake had never before ridden the stick without going haywire, but this time it was calm. Dwayne placed it on the table and was able to pin the head easily. "Don't stop chanting," he said and grasped the head of the viper. With enough force to hold on yet gently enough to not hurt it, Dwayne eased open the snake's mouth and brought it to the corner of the glass. He dipped the fangs into the cup at an angle and pressed. Nothing happened at first, but when he used his other hand to put pressure on the venom glands on the snake's head, two lines of yellowish liquid flowed down to the bottom of the glass, forming a small pool. Dwayne walked the snake back to its enclosure. He placed it fully inside with the head at the far end, took a deep breath, and in one motion, let go and withdrew his arm from the enclosure. Using the snake hook in his other hand, he slid the glass door shut, then sat on the ground and let out the longest breath of his life.

"That never happens," Dwayne said. "Those are some of the most difficult snakes to work with on the planet. They are permanently pissed off, fast, and aggressive even when you aren't fucking with 'em. And she just acted like it was a day in the park. I don't get it."

"The chanting was for your protection and to calm the snake."

"Snakes can't hear."

"It doesn't matter. It didn't have to hear."

Dwayne stood and stretched his long arms to the ceiling and caught Nina glancing at his exposed, flat belly. He smiled and drew water from the bottle into the syringe before squirting it into the glass along the residue lines of venom. The water washed everything into a little pool of slightly murky-yellow liquid.

"Is it enough to stop her?" Nina asked.

"It's enough to kill someone, probably a lot of someones. But I can't say what it will do to whatever she is."

"It will have to do."

Dwayne stirred the solution and pulled it all into the syringe, and replaced the cap.

* * *

Once everyone was ready to head to the sinkhole, Casey used his phone to call the sheriff. The others gathered around to listen in the kitchen.

"Sheriff Johnson. This is Casey Sparks. (Pause) No, sir, I don't want to turn myself in, but I want to help you solve the cases. (Pause) I guess you've seen the creature flying around or heard reports? (Pause) So you know I'm not crazy now. (Pause) I'm not worried about myself anymore. If you want to stop it, help us. (Pause) It doesn't matter. It lives out behind Marion's house. She's with us. They killed Chuck, though, and Amy. (Pause) We need y'all to come down here and bring your guns. We have some too. (Pause) We think we can lure it back with a ritual. (Pause) No sir. Not about me, but they were right about some others. Some of their own, actually, including Jake. He's still unaccounted for, but some of the others are dead. A lot of them. The demon got them. (Pause) Bring your people down here. (Pause) Do what you need to do, but if you don't believe me by now, I don't know what else we can do to convince you. (Pause) Sinkhole down the hill from Cabin 3. Follow the smoke. You can't miss it."

Casey hung up the phone and looked at the group. They were looking at Chuck's laptop, and Marion was crying.

"What's wrong?" Casey asked.

"I found these pictures on Chuck's computer," Balthazar said.

"He didn't tell me he had pictures of the crocodile," Marion said. "If I had known, we would have gotten out of there. None of this would have happened."

Nina hugged Marion, and Casey moved closer and looked at the picture on the screen. Balthazar had it zoomed in, looking at the cold, yellow-gray eye of the crocodile. He zoomed out to its original size, and Casey lost his balance and had to catch himself on the counter. The rainbow stripes on the shoe.

Kyle, the man he had connected so well with, had fallen in love with, and who he thought had ghosted him after Jake walked in on them, had been wearing the same pair of shoes. And that is when the visions finally made sense. When Casey had touched Jake's knife in his trailer, he had seen Jake and a car in a ditch. He couldn't recognize the blood-covered person in the car then, but now he remembered the car with the HRC sticker on the back bumper. And the vision in the cave that very day. The ribcage was not Amy's. It was Kyle's. The man in the rainbow-striped shoes had not ghosted Casey. Jake had ghosted the man in the rainbow-striped shoes for real and given him over to the Ruiner. Casey did not feel rage then. He became rage. Feeling anything else was impossible.

33

Dwayne rode like a bull rider in the bed of the truck on the way to the sinkhole. With one hand gripping the top of the roll bar and the other holding a 9-mm, he bounced through the trail paths, which were better suited for four-wheelers than full-size trucks. Balthazar had insisted he drive. He told the group he didn't care about the paint job and it would be a safer ride in and out.

The drive over gave Casey some time to refocus on the ritual and the spirit, but he could not stop thinking about Jake. He would come for them again. And Casey wanted him to. It would be worth it for Jake to show himself. Had Casey understood the first vision, the one brought on by Jake's knife to his throat, he could have saved a lot of people. He would have shot Jake down right then and there. Casey would not waste another chance.

Because there was no longer any need for stealth, Balthazar pulled the Chevy to the edge of the hill.

The area was not only deserted but quiet. Scary quiet. It seemed even the birds and bugs could sense the wrongness and gave the area a wide berth. Like how some animals run to higher ground to avoid tsunamis long before humans are aware of the threat. The only noise was from the last drops of rain falling from the trees with gusts of wind.

The group gathered all the weapons and ritual items from the back of the truck. Dwayne strapped on the flamethrower backpack and helped Balthazar secure his. Nina and Marion got the 9-mms they wanted. Thus armed, the group hiked up the hill in a tight formation with Casey in the middle. *This must be what it's like to be famous*, Casey thought.

Near the top of the hill, the formation dissolved. Casey and Dwayne snuck to the rim and scanned the area. There was no movement from the surrounding hills or the sinkhole. Just the eerie *drip, drip, drip* with the hollow wind. The group crested the hill.

Marion and Nina scoped out the area and found a spot next to an extinguished campfire where a different sigil had been drawn before. Most of it had been washed clean by the rain, but a little chalk swirl, like a nautilus, remained on the white stone at the edge of the sinkhole.

"We should set up opposite of this," Marion said.

While Dwayne and Balthazar scanned the ridge of the encircling hills, Marion and Nina used colored chalk to draw the sigil on the ground. Casey stood off to the side, looking into the sinkhole and whispering the spell to himself over and over, trying to focus his rage and anguish into the words. He felt a vibration rising from his stomach to his chest. The smell of burning herbs was thick in his nose. He walked to the new sigil where Marion had placed the smudge stick, and Nina was preparing to place the coin and statue.

"Are you ready?" asked Nina.

"Not yet. Don't place the coin until I'm done," Marion said.

Marion, using the knife Evalyn had wielded against her, pointed in each of the cardinal directions and chanted a few lines for each. Nina lit candles around them and on the sigil.

Balthazar leaned over to Dwayne, who was watching Marion. "She is casting a circle of protection. That will help them. Maybe. But we have these." Balthazar patted his flamethrower. "Let them do the ritual. We need to keep our eyes on the ridge."

With the circle cast, Marion looked at Casey and motioned for him to proceed. The vibration in Casey's chest reached his head, and his entire body buzzed. He nodded to Nina, and she placed the statue and coin in their respective places. Casey's ears popped, and he felt a weight all around him pushing harder, as if he were sinking deeper and deeper and the water was crushing him. Marion and Nina shared a shocked look. In a panic, Casey was tempted to kick the statue into the sinkhole. Anything to have air again. But he looked at the spell instead. And at that moment, he thought of Kyle and Amy, and Chuck, and he began to recite.

With all his rage, anger, and grief directed at the Ruiner, Casey roared the words of the spell. The pressure released as the lines flowed from him. Winds picked up and blew leaves and small sticks from the trees along with the remaining rain. They formed a vortex over the sinkhole like a dirty snow globe. *It's working*, Casey thought. He recited the spell faster.

Halfway through, a high-pitched shriek rose from above. Dwayne yelled, "Flame throwers!" And Casey looked up to see the creature diving at him. The speed of its descent left Casey frozen as he watched it careen almost all the way to him before Dwayne and Balthazar let loose with the fire. Long ropes of flames came from either side of Casey and shot twenty-five feet into the sky. Some of the flame wrapped around in circles with the winds, but most of the fire found its target. The creature pulled out of its dive and banked to the right. A blast of hot air passed over Casey. It put out the candles and knocked the statue onto the rim of the sinkhole. It rolled towards the opening.

Casey leaped for it and secured it in his right hand just as it was teetering on the edge. His ribs and shoulder exploded in pain, and he stayed still, trying to catch his breath. He managed to pass the statue back to either Nina or Marion. He could not see who took it but could feel the buzzing return in his body when it was back in place.

Casey willed himself up and tried to focus on the spell but was aware Dwayne and Balthazar were talking back and forth, trying to keep their eyes on the creature. It dove again, this time from behind. Casey felt the heat on his neck and back when the creature pulled away, and for the first time, he heard gunshots.

Casey looked up to see the sheriff and ten deputies firing on the creature from the ridge across the sinkhole. They held their position as it rose into the air away from the flames and suddenly banked and barreled into them. There was no time to react. Trees snapped and slammed to the ground, and limbs exploded. Four of the officers were crushed by its weight or from the fallen trees. The creature began to change. Casey watched this in horror as the ray drew in, shrinking and changing into a burgundy color. Tentacles grew from the body, and without warning, it thrust itself towards Casey. Dwayne pulled the trigger on the flamethrower and dowsed the squid thing with burning gasoline. The squid did not turn away. Instead, it jerked forward again, all the while being dowsed with fire until it was just twenty feet from Casey. Marion and Nina opened fire then, and the creature dove into the sinkhole. Steam rose from the opening like an awakening volcano.

"Might want to hurry up," Dwayne said, "We don't have much fuel left in these things."

Casey turned his attention back to the ritual, and just as he finished the chanting, the hill began to shake. Cracks formed on the ground coming from the hole.

Marion grabbed Casey's arm and yelled, "Move back. We can finish without the sigil!"

Casey went with the others almost to the edge of the hill and continued chanting. Marion was right. He was practically high from the buzzing, which remained steady despite the sigil being wiped clean.

The shaking stopped, and for a moment, all was quiet. Then the land outside the hole gave way to create a larger opening, and a huge shape fired out. Casey's first thought was it looked like a great white shark breaching the surface of the ocean to attack a fleeing seal. But this was bigger. Much bigger. It was closer to the size of a whale than a shark, and after it breached, it crashed down. The body exploded into dozens of dark pieces, and everywhere these puddles of darkness fell, smaller creatures poured out and attacked the people closest to them.

Crocodiles like the one Chuck caught on the webcam charged at the sheriff's deputies. They opened fire and took them down. But as soon as they had killed one, another would emerge from a dark puddle to charge all over again.

Scores of crabs and flying jellyfish spawned near Casey's group. Dwayne and Balthazar held them off with fire, but the fuel was running out. Nina and Marion took out large crabs, but their handguns had no effect on the jellyfish. Like the deputies on the other side, the waves of enemies kept coming, and it was a matter of time before they would be overrun.

Casey tried to hurry. He saw a deputy taken down by a crocodile and tried to yell the spell over the man's screams. But he couldn't mute them out. Nina took a severe sting from a jellyfish before

Dwayne was able to force it back with the nozzle of his flamethrower and melt it away with what looked to be the last of its fuel.

Casey ran towards the middle of the sinkhole, ever reading the spell. The crocodile released the deputy and charged at Casey. The crabs and jellyfish, too, changed direction. Two lines to go. The crocodile had shimmied down the hill and was careening towards him, and Casey backed up as he started reading the last line. He felt a searing pain on his back and neck, which drove his head up. He forced his eyes back down to the paper and spoke the last three words. He closed his eyes as the crocodile, head turned sideways, bit down on his legs.

Casey had heard stories about how shark attack survivors sometimes claimed the bite was painless. The cut was so clean and fast that they felt nothing at first. Casey did not feel pain in his legs, but he did feel a wet heat. He was certain it was blood from a severed leg, but when he forced open his eyes, he saw he was instead covered in the black, muddy fluid from the puddles where the creatures had emerged.

Everyone was looking around, bracing for new threats. But the creatures were gone. The puddles were disappearing. Even the wetness on Casey seemed to be evaporating rapidly.

Casey called out, "I'm going after her." He took a single step and felt a hard scraping against his thigh.

Dwayne yelled out from behind him, "I'm hit," and fell to the ground holding his left leg. Another shot rang out, and Casey pointed in the general direction. Nina and Marion opened fire while Balthazar and Casey ran to Dwayne and drug him to the very edge of the hill and started to ease him down. Another loud shot and Casey saw red on Balthazar's shirt. It grew, but Balthazar kept holding his side of Dwayne. Casey looked at him, and for a second, everything seemed normal. But his face went white, and he lost his grip on Dwayne. Casey didn't let go, and he and Dwayne slid down the slick hill together. When Casey reached the bottom, he looked up and saw Balthazar sitting on the hill. His spirit was standing over his body, looking down.

Nina and Marion ran down a few yards away and yelled for Casey to move. Following orders and going through the surreal motions with a numbness he had never before experienced, Casey dragged Dwayne the rest of the way to the truck and helped him into the bed.

He took off his shirt, and Nina came from behind and snatched it from him. She stuck her gun in her belt behind her.

"You can't even put a proper bandage on yourself, Dr. Sparks. I've got this." She tied a tourniquet around Dwayne's lower leg.

Casey ran halfway back to Balthazar. Hoping he could still be saved, but the body was lying down now, and his spirit was wandering up the hill. Almost to him, Nina screamed.

He looked back and saw Jake holding Nina around the neck with one arm. He had a rifle in the other hand. Casey met his stare and charged. Weapon or not. Jake must have felt the energy. And he muscled Nina in front of him, sticking the end of the rifle under her jaw.

Casey halted. He could risk his own life, but not hers. Jake's eyes were glossy, and he looked angry and confused at the same time.

"You fuck up everything!" Jake yelled. He walked backward toward the cave, half dragging Nina along with him. "I have to do it all over again now by myself. I'm going to take you all one by one, but I'll start with her."

"I won't let you," Casey said.

Jake brought the gun down without aiming and fired in Casey's direction.

Nina squirmed madly, and Jake lost his one-armed grip on her. He kicked at her feet, and she fell to the ground. Casey ran around the truck, and Jake brought the gun down and, this time, aimed. But just before he fired, Nina kicked back at him enough to knock him off balance, sending the shot high.

Casey peeked over the truck as a translucent green arm reached from the cave entrance and grabbed Jake's ankle. Jake looked at it and then into the opening. Before Casey could cover the distance, Jake grabbed Nina and fed her into the cave entrance before disappearing himself.

34

Casey slid through the hole. He was expecting to get shot or dragged in at any second but made his way in freely. Nina's backpack and gun were next to Jake's rifle at the entrance, and Casey emptied both weapons, dropping the ammo to the cave floor. He still tingled with electricity, and something about the guns felt wrong. They felt like they would help her, not him. He picked up the backpack by the top strap to move it and received a clear vision then. He picked up the unloaded 9mm and decided to bring it after all along with the bag. This felt better. He checked his pocket for the syringe and found it there.

He let his eyes acclimate to the darkness for a moment before going any further. The fires were out. If any crocodile were to be waiting in the dark, he would be easy pickings. But if the spell had worked, she should be in her human form. The arm that had reached out for Jake seemed human, at least in shape. He hugged the wall and snuck towards the other chamber. Apart from his occasional misstep, the cave was silent. He knew it had to be the bones he could not avoid stepping on and over. And with each one, his rage at Jake, Evalyn, and the Ruiner grew.

A blue-green glowing appeared at the junction and as he looked around the corner saw Nina standing against one wall and Jake against the other. They were frozen in place. A light green version of the Ruiner was standing in front of each of them face to face. The one by Nina was a man; the one by Jake was a woman. And at least a dozen more green women stood around the room. The spell had forced the Ruiner into her human form, but she was still able to replicate herself and still able to mesmerize her victims. He could see the real Ruiner standing on the other side of Nina. She shone brighter than the rest, and looking at her, he realized he was not supposed to see the others, but the ability Balthazar had given him allowed it.

It was also the moment he understood why he was the one who had to take her out. The Ruiner surely thought she could control him with her feminine forms. That was how it had always worked before. So, Casey simply had to pretend she could control him the same way and then hope to get close enough to inject the venom. No one else in the group could trick her the same way. All of them would have been instantly mesmerized and killed. It had to be Casey, and it was all about misdirection.

The spirit women at once ordered Casey to give his weapons to Jake. He heard her, the Ruiner, the loudest, but the others chorused in his mind as well. Casey held his ears as if to struggle with the suggestion, but when they calmly ordered again, he strolled to Jake and placed the bag at his feet. Jake, in his own mesmerized state, still managed a wry smile. It took all Casey had not to show any emotion.

Instead, he held his ears again and pretended to stumble to get closer to Nina. As he did, the women surrounded him, their faces shifting in the same way as their mother. They all looked at him with the same confused expression too. When he was nearly to

Nina, the choir erupted again.

"Stop. You didn't give us all of your weapons."

Casey stopped in a panic. He assumed she knew about the venom, but then he realized the 9mm was still in his belt.

"I forgot," he said absently. He took it from his belt and held it out in front of him by the barrel. "Who should I give it to?"

"Give it to Nina," boomed in his mind.

Casey began walking toward her, and the command changed.

"Shoot Nina in the head. And then give the weapon to Jake."

Casey pretended again to resist and then muttered, "You are so beautiful. I am so sorry for hurting you." He started to cry. "I want to serve you," he said and touched the Ruiner on the arm.

In a flash, he knew her plan, but his brazen act must have removed any doubt she had that the situation was under control. She wanted either him or Jake to kill Nina so she could shift again. She thought Casey would do as he was told. He was being difficult, but men always succumb eventually. She thought he would too, until he dared touch her. Casey did not know what she thought after that, but just before his hand left her arm, he learned of her backup plan, a sheriff's deputy she had dragged down earlier in the fight. Casey had missed him earlier. He was in the other corner holding a gun to his temple. A shifting green woman stood above him.

Casey knew all the plans were off. Now he had to be faster than her.

In his right hand, he held the gun, and in his left, he gripped the syringe of venom. He began to raise the gun and heard the shot from across the cave. He spun around, and she was on him. Her face had become one of an angler fish. Huge, pointed teeth like thin daggers in the dark flew towards his face. Had he not focused his vision on Nina, Casey didn't think he could have pulled it off, but he did. He jammed the needle into the chest of the spirit and pushed the stopper as hard as he could. The daggers gnashed together in a wet snap an inch from his nose.

She lunged backward and began to morph into all manner of species, and she leaped at him again but with little power. "What are you? she said as she ripped at his arms and chest, partially in an attack and partially trying to stand. "What have you done to me?"

Casey sluffed her off and ran to Nina as she slumped to the ground. She looked past him and whispered, "Jake" in Casey's ear.

Jake was across the cave, and he hurriedly unzipped the backpack and reached in. The pain must have been grand. He jerked out his hand in a start and dropped the bag. His face contorted with rage, and he ran at Casey. Casey ran at him and braced for the impact. But before they could meet, Jake stumbled. He grabbed his throat and gasped for air. A small stream of blood flowed from two small holes in his hand. Jake twitched before losing consciousness, and he stopped breathing.

Casey walked back to Nina and helped her to her feet. He switched on his cell phone light and scanned the room. The snake was still in the bag, but he had no interest in zipping it back up. They rounded the corner and heard their names being called from outside. Casey and Nina ran to the small exit and shimmied out to the blinding light above.

35

The voice had been Sheriff Johnson's. He helped Nina out of the hole, and she ran to Dwayne and held him for a long time. She pulled away and, blushing, said, "Your snake's going to escape the backpack bag. I brought a snake hook and a grabber too. They are in the truck."

Dwayne looked at her, surprised.

"I had her so calm from the chanting I figured a little backup wouldn't hurt."

Dwayne shook his head and kissed her. She kissed him back.

Casey emerged from the hole on his own and went to Balthazar's body. Sheriff Johnson followed Casey and stood by silent while he cried. When Casey had control over himself, he stood and put his hands together for the sheriff to cuff.

Sheriff Johnson waved him off. "You'd just break out again anyway. But I do have a lot of questions that need answers. Going to lawyer up?"

"No, sir. Ask away."

The sheriff asked Casey, Nina, Marion, and Dwayne questions from the back of Balthazar's Chevy for over an hour. His remaining deputies worked on the other side of the hill giving first aid to their injured and receiving the paramedics who came to rush two of them to Our Lady of Providence. They were all under strict orders not to talk about what they had seen.

When Sheriff Johnson was done with the debrief, he had two officers escort Casey back into the cave. He was too big to fit himself, and the main entrance of the sinkhole was unsafe. New chunks of the surrounding land slid in with loud splashes every few minutes.

Casey had told the sheriff about the snake during the debrief and warned the officers before taking them into the cave. Casey took the snake hook and grabber with him in case they found it. Dwayne bet him twenty dollars that the snake was long gone, but it was still there when the officers shined a light into the backpack. It didn't move aside from a tongue flick when Casey used the hook to hold the bag down and the grabber to securely zip it up. It must really have been magic keeping the snake in before.

The deputies had bright flashlights and took several pictures with their phones. The number of bones they documented was staggering. They counted eight skulls, but Casey told them there had been ten before. He reckoned the missing ones were under some of the piles that had been pushed to the sides when the Ruiner had exploded out and then retreated back in her huge form. The deputies decided to wait for a forensic team before moving anything else.

They took special interest in the bottom of the sinkhole where the savaged remains of several bodies had fallen. They recognized Reverend Gale and one of their own, Deputy Wallace. They found more carnage in the other chamber, where the officer's body sat against a wall not far from the cage where Evalyn's corpse was wedged halfway inside. Jake's body lay inside as well. Eyes wide open. The officers shared these images and many others with Sheriff Johnson. Casey and the group fielded many more questions.

Sheriff Johnson spoke with his deputies for a while before returning to Casey's crew.

"I lost seven deputies in the last twenty-four hours. Six just now today." He paused for a while, taking off his hat and wiping sweat from his brow. "There is too much here to process, and I can't let y'all go just yet." He looked at Dwayne's tourniquet and the bloodstains on his pants. "But seeing as you could all use medical treatment, some more than others"-he looked at Nina, "it seems reasonable that you would all agree to temporary stays at Our Lady of Providence."

No one responded, but they all looked at each other.

Sheriff Johnson continued, "A lightly guarded stay at the hospital would be my preference over arrest if I were in your position. The only reason y'all aren't in cuffs now is that I saw you save lives today." He turned to Casey. "I saw Jake murder your friend in cold blood and shoot Dwayne trying to kill you. Just like how he tried to kill you before. I knew he was lying because he had a story for the broken speaker. He said you did it that night, but it was already busted when we questioned you right after Amy disappeared."

"So the deal I'm offering is that you stay where we can keep tabs on you until the investigation is done and I've satisfied myself about a few more things. If everything checks out, you will all be released from the hospital in short order."

"What do you need to check on?" Dwayne asked.

"That's my business. But it's not about the snakes or the flamethrowers or the lighting oil wells on fire. Work for you?"

Dwayne looked at the rest of the group. "I've been to county.

It's not a fun place. Trust me, the hospital is way better. Oh. Also, I got shot, so I kind of have to go there anyway."

Nina shook her head at him and smiled. The group agreed with the arrangement.

"Paramedics are on the way. You'll go with them. And there is another condition. Until the press release comes out, your only statement to reporters, your family, and your parish priest is 'No comment.' Got it? No exclusive tell-all book, no drunken YouTube videos. No deathbed confession. No comment now and no comment forever. Do you understand?"

They all did.

* * *

From the *Mobile Press Journal*, July 10th: Suspect in series of Cherry Hill murders kills himself and executes prisoners as deputies attempt raid.

CHERRY HILL, AL (Mobile Press Journal)

On Monday afternoon, a Cherry Hill man, Jake Douglas, 27, killed himself and several others, including five Maubila County Sheriff's deputies, while the deputies attempted to take him into custody, according to Maubila County Sheriff, Larry Johnson.

At a press conference yesterday, the sheriff fielded questions from reporters from around the region regarding the bizarre and tragic chain of events that rocked the small town of Cherry Hill over the last week.

"We believe the suspect, Jake Douglas, was responsible for the abduction and murder of eighteen-year-old Amy Gale on July fourth of this year and the murder of Chuck Spivey, aged sixty-nine, on July fifth. Sadly, there are other prior victims who we are working to ID based on multiple sets of additional remains we found amongst those we have already identified. We are working with state and neighboring local officials on this effort now."

"Yesterday, as our deputies closed in on the suspected retreat of Jake Douglas at a remote area within the Mitcham Breech Hunting Camp, the suspect set off a series of explosions. These tragically took the lives of several Cherry Hill Baptist Church members, including Reverend Jordan Gale, age fifty-two. Mr. Douglas triggered a final explosion once he understood he was surrounded. That one ended his life."

Several questions concerning six missing boaters were met with the same answer, "We are still working to identify all the remains and cannot rule out any possibilities at this time."

Sheriff Johnson was also questioned about a suspect they had taken into custody before this incident. "The prior person of interest was deemed to not have been involved in any of these activities. They were in the wrong place at the wrong time. He has been fully cleared, and no charges are forthcoming."

Jake Douglas was also the primary suspect in the potential tampering of the water supply in Cherry Hill yesterday as multiple reports of a dragon-like creature flooded local law enforcement offices. At this time, Sheriff Johnson believes the suspect introduced a substance such as Lysergic acid diethylamide, also known as LSD or acid, or psilocybin, which is the active compound in hallucinogenic mushrooms, to the water system in an attempt to cover up his crimes or to sew confusion in the community. The sheriff noted such a scientific explanation is more likely than group hallucination.

"This has been an extraordinarily trying week for the citizens of this town. On behalf of the victims and their families, we ask that, to the extent you can, please respect their privacy as the funeral services will likely span over a long time here given the nature of the crimes committed and the number of victims."

EPILOGUE

Casey held a smaller party the following fourth of July. Dwayne said he was crazy to host another one. And while everyone in town knew he had not been responsible for all the terrible events the previous year, most of them must have agreed with Dwayne. Barely a dozen people showed up. And nearly all of them left directly after the fireworks.

Marion had recovered from her physical wounds and moved to Montgomery to be closer to her family. She told Casey she could not stay right where everything happened. Casey understood. Who wouldn't?

Nina showed up, though. She came as Dwayne's date. They had become sort of an item, though neither of them would admit it. Casey thought it was due to the age difference, but it didn't matter to Casey or anyone else for that matter. They had been there for each other when things were at their craziest, and the bond had simply stuck.

After the other guests left, the three of them picked at ribs, coleslaw, and potato salad. They slapped at mosquitos, chatted about the weather, and overanalyzed the Atlanta Braves lineup, but they didn't talk about the previous year. They all knew Casey had thrown the party this year to honor the people they had lost. And they all knew it would be the last. Casey thought he needed to do it just this one more time.

When Dwayne and Nina were gone, Casey watched the sky and listened as the last pops of fireworks sounded in the south Alabama sky. He hadn't told anyone what he had seen after he fired the venom into the spirit or when Jake had fallen. Most of the spirits were still there. Casey tried not to see them, but clear as day, they loitered. Some were confused and stared down at their bodies. Jake was stuck in a pattern of pacing and sitting cross-legged on top of his, weeping and rocking back and forth. The ghost of the Ruiner simply floated around in a wide circle. It was crying too. And even though Jake and the Ruiner had brought so much pain, it bothered Casey that a soul would mourn its body. He had always thought nothing happened at all, or maybe when you were freed from the shell, you would feel exalted release, even victory for making it through boot camp Earth. At the very least, it didn't seem right for death to not at least be a reset.

On the hill outside, Balthazar had looked indifferent. His death had been just as violent and fast, but maybe he was ready. Maybe he knew something he shouldn't. He had taken Casey's gift after all.

The morning after the sheriff released them from the hospital, Casey hiked to the sinkhole alone. The sheriff wasn't the only one with unanswered questions.

The site was still an active crime scene. The intact bodies had been removed, but some of the bones remained. He could see that from the top of the sinkhole. More of it had collapsed, but about a quarter of the original rim was intact. He saw the ghost of a chalk circle on the white stone and wiped it away with his right hand. He considered slipping through the side entrance, planned on it even, but the possibility of seeing the spirits of the Ruiner and Jake was too much. Instead, he sat on the ground where the hill started to rise, opened a bottle of tequila, and took a drink.

He felt silly, but it was better than most of what he felt lately.

"I don't know if any of you can hear me. But I'm so sorry this happened. If anyone is here and wants to talk. I'll be here."

For the rest of the morning, Casey sat listening to the birds and the leaves moving in the wind. He had only taken two pulls from the bottle, and he left it open by the rock when he started for home.

On his way back, he took a different course. Instead of coming out on the main hunting camp road and then to Rabbit Run Road by Marion's house, he took the woods and aimed for his backyard. He knew the direction well enough. The woods were thick, and even in the noon sun, little light penetrated to the ground. As he made it closer to where he thought his backyard was located, he spotted a pathway of broken limbs and leaves. He knelt and looked in the direction of his trailer. It had been the path the jellyfish made when it took Amy. And at the tree line, there she stood, holding hands with her dad and talking to another ghost. Casey stood upright and swallowed hard.

Amy turned and winked. In Casey's head, he heard her voice say, "I brought your friend to say, Goodbye."

Amy and Reverend Gale held hands and disappeared. The remaining ghost floated towards Casey as Casey walked towards him. Kyle said, "I know it wasn't your fault."

When they reached each other, Casey tried to touch Kyle's face but felt only a dim static charge. He balled his fist in frustration, and tears came. "I'm so sorry, and I miss you so much. I finally have you back and can't even touch you."

"It's not our time anymore. It was once. It was short, but it was wonderful, and it was ours."

"Will we see each other again?"

"I think so. I'll try to visit in your dreams. I have to go."

"Hold on," Casey said.

He held his hands up in front of him, and Kyle placed his palms inside of his. Casey closed his eyes and moved in for a kiss. Kyle met his lips. Casey felt the soft buzzing in his hands and mouth. Then a total warmth enveloped him, body, mind, and soul; a sense of peace so profound he had to share it with someone else. But the only one he wanted was gone when he opened his eyes.